Dear Readers,

It's even more ... to own all four of these sizzling new romances. So stack 'em up, curl up in a comfortable chair, and indulge!

Kate Holmes, multipublished as Anne Avery, used to work for the state department in South America—hence the romantic Rio de Janiero setting for her first Bouquet romance, **Amethyst and Gold.** A shy young teacher and writer, Melisande visits Rio to do research, never dreaming that she will be swept into the sensual rhythms of Carnavale . . . and into the arms of a handsome tycoon!

Veteran author Ann Josephson (you may know her as Sara Jarrod) has created one of the most appealing romantic heroes we've ever encountered in Brand Carendon—lawyer, athlete, and father of an eleven-year-old son he never knew he had . . . until first love Dani Murdock finds her way back into his life. Brand vows to make up for lost time . . . and to find **Enduring Love.**

Newcomer Debra Dawn Thomas takes her readers into the exotic, breathtakingly exciting world of Spanish bullfighting in her debut novel, **Wrap Me In Scarlet.** Sensible Stephanie Madison, a journalist looking for a story, finds much more in the arms of "El Peligro"—"The Dangerous One"—in a world of intoxicating adventure . . . and passion!

Suzanne Barrett, herself a facility engineer, gives her exciting profession to feisty heroine Karin Williams. She's sent to England to prove her skill alongside Rowan Marsden—a man who'd vowed never to work with a woman again. But Karin's talent, wits, and beauty combine to provide success in a business partnership and, ultimately, in **Taming Rowan.**

Decorate your life with a Bouquet on every table . . . four fresh new ones every month!

The Editors

"As fresh and new as the coming millennium . . . a run-away read."

—Patricia White, *Under the Covers*

PREDATOR . . . OR PREY?

"Would you like to see an eagle's nest?"

Karin flashed him a smile. "Yes! I've never seen one before."

Fifteen minutes later they stood on an enormous granite outcropping. As he balanced on a ledge slightly above her, she stared at the ripple of muscle across his back, visible beneath the close-fitted black turtleneck. Her gaze lowered to the faded denims stretched tight across his buttocks.

"Look. There!" Rowan pointed in the direction from which they'd come.

Karin stared hard at the top of the high, rocky crag. "I don't see any—" She stopped midsentence as Rowan stepped up behind her and rotated her toward the east. He pointed again.

Aware of his long fingers curled around her shoulders, Karin felt her pulse hammer. Suddenly an eagle glided into view. The sun changed the hackles on its back into gold, silhouetted the slender, gold-tipped wings. The bird caught a surging downdraft and rode it into the valley below.

"I see it!" she cried. She turned her focus away from the warmth of his body and onto the beauty of the magnificent bird.

It reminded her of Rowan. He was an eagle—bold, predatory, elusive. What was it he hunted?

"People think you have to walk miles to see a golden eagle. But not if you know where to look." His whispered words fanned her cheek.

In spite of herself, she leaned back into the muscled hardness of his large frame and closed her eyes. . . .

TAMING ROWAN

Suzanne Barrett

Zebra Books
Kensington Publishing Corp.
http://www.zebrabooks.com

ZEBRA BOOKS are published by

Kensington Publishing Corp.
850 Third Avenue
New York, NY 10022

Zebra and the Z logo Reg. U.S. Pat. & TM Off.

First Printing: August, 1999
10 9 8 7 6 5 4 3 2 1

Printed in the United States of America

ONE

"Go to England? Now? You can't be serious!" Karin Williams sat in her boss's San Jose office, long legs crossed, hands tented over one knee. She had known something was up; Leonard Dalkey never called her out of a staff meeting. Her gaze inched upward. Lines of strain deeply etched the older man's craggy features.

Leonard shifted his body in the massive leather chair. "Karin, I know it's a bad time to pull you off those projects, but it can't be helped. You're my best engineer—my *only* structural expert with a working knowledge of telemetry." He leaned forward, eyes level with hers. "I don't have to tell you how badly we need this contract. The future of Dalkey and Williams is at stake."

Karin's breath caught. And maybe her own future? Leonard wouldn't say that, but the implication was clear in his somber expression and furrowed brow. Not a man to brood, Leonard was worried; the tension in the older man's face transmitted itself to Karin. Despite her current project responsibilities, she couldn't afford to jeopardize her chance for promotion. More important, she couldn't disappoint Leonard, who'd placed so much confidence in her ability. Working with the Pickering consortium, she conceded, would add valued status to her position at the company. The British firm topped the list of structural engineering companies.

Karin paused, the thought of working with the elite English staff suddenly daunting. Hadn't she read something about one of their engineers in *Design News* last year? Something . . . disturbing. She frowned as the memory surfaced.

"What about Marsden?" Karin said finally. "How will he react to suggestions from someone my age? Not to mention my being a woman?"

"You're as capable as anyone in the field—and that includes your father. Still . . ."

Karin uncrossed her legs and smoothed her hands over the rough slub of her linen skirt. "What's up, Leonard? You're hiding something."

The older man's face tightened as he ran a hand through his salt-and-pepper hair. "I—well, I'm not sure sending you is a good idea, Karin, Marsden being what he is. But there's no one else."

"What? Does he have two heads or something?"

Leonard stroked his chin reflectively. "Rumor has it that the man is uncommonly . . . ah . . . prepossessing." Even after thirty years in the States, the speech of the Yorkshire Dales still hung thick on Leonard's tongue.

"Doesn't his work stand up to outside scrutiny?"

Leonard laughed outright. "Don't kid yourself. Marsden's the best in the business, but"—he paused, choosing his words carefully—"his attitude toward women has alienated him from the higher echelon at Pickering. Marsden believes no female can excel as an engineer. In fact, the ones who've worked for him have been quickly dismissed for one reason or another."

That was the story about him she'd read. There'd been some charge of sexual harassment, never proven but . . .

Could she work in an environment where she constantly had to prove herself? Karin chewed on her lower lip. Leonard had thought the world of her father. The older man had stepped in as a surrogate parent, making her stay in school after her father died. It was Leonard who had urged her to go on for her advanced degree, then had challenged her with increasingly complex assignments—tasks that had propelled her into her present position as design specialist.

She stared at the pale blue eyes. Marsden or no, refusing Leonard was impossible.

Sensing his desperation, Karin looked up at him and sighed. "All right. I'll do it. I'll be on that plane Tuesday."

"Uh, before you leave . . ." He fastened his gaze upon her, a smile tugging at one corner of his mouth. "Marsden's desperate for help. If you're successful in completing the project to his specifications, not only will we gain a permanent slot on the consortium list for future contracts, but"—his smile broadened—"that vacant staff post will be yours."

Karin snapped to attention, her eyes widening. Chief engineer at twenty-six! Unheard of at Dalkey and Williams. But, she reminded herself, she'd worked hard for this chance, putting in hundreds of extra hours on her own time. She suppressed the elation that surged through her as Leonard filled her in on the task, knowing deep inside she'd have accepted the assignment for his sake with no thought of a promotion.

Marsden needed an antenna-support platform. Last spring she'd done a similar one in Nevada. This one should be a piece of cake. The only thing standing in the way was an opinionated English project officer with out-of-date notions about women engineers. Well, she'd show him.

She gave her boss a heartfelt smile. "You won't be disappointed, Leonard. I promise."

Where the hell was he, this Williams? Rowan Marsden glared once more at the monitor listing the flight arrivals, then withdrew a folded fax from his vest pocket and reread the brief message. *K. M. Williams arriving Manchester Wednesday noon, British Airways flight 4452.* This was Wednesday. He'd got that right, but flight 4452 had been canceled. He'd learned the news after arriving—a bomb scare at Heathrow. The replacement craft delivering his new structural engineer was five hours late. He shoved the fax back into his jacket pocket, then took a determined stride toward the information desk.

And stopped in his tracks.

Claudia! What the bloody hell was she doing in Manchester? He pivoted away. For that matter, what was she doing in England? He forced his gaze back to the woman emerging from the arrival pod.

Somehow, this woman looked different. The same rich, dark red hair as his ex-wife, but pulled back into a hair slide, wayward tendrils escaping at her temple. A creased, slim-cut trouser suit in a shade of soft green. The cropped, open jacket revealed her nicely rounded derriere and equally attractive long, athletic legs. Willowy. He paused in midstep. That wasn't Claudia. This woman had to be at least half a head taller.

Relief washed over him. Still, the resemblance was uncanny.

The woman looked up and met his gaze. An awareness flickered in her brown eyes, which he found disconcerting. But it was not Claudia, thank God.

Rowan tore his gaze from her, glanced at his watch and charged along the concourse. He'd have Williams paged.

Karin shifted her carryall to her other shoulder. Through the huge plate-glass window, she watched orange fingers of light fade as dusk darkened the hazy Manchester sky. Chandeliers gleamed overhead, sending reflections dancing on the glass as she propelled her travel-stiff legs along the concourse. Her eyes felt grainy, and a frontal headache pounded. As usual, sleep had eluded her on the flight. She fervently wished for a cup of tea, two double-strength aspirin, and a soft bed.

At the baggage area, she paused near a plaster column and reached into her purse for a compact. She frowned at her reflection. An oval face, accentuated by high cheekbones and a narrow, straight nose—too narrow, and a trifle long, she acknowledged. Smudges of violet shadowed her wide-set eyes. The seemingly endless hours in flight had done nothing for her appearance or her disposition.

People flowed past her, some intercepted by families or friends, all moving toward the baggage carousel. No one looked even remotely like a Pickering representative. It was hardly surprising. Her original flight from Heathrow had been canceled. Snapping the compact shut, she sagged onto a bench near the baggage area.

After what felt like an eternity, luggage spewed out of the chute. Karin elbowed her way through the throng of passengers and retrieved her brown leather duffel.

As she did so, the loudspeaker blared: *Will Mr. K. M. Williams please report to the information desk.*

Karin shrugged into her coat and shouldered her carryall. Laden with luggage, she trudged down the aisle toward the automated walkway.

By the time she reached the opposite end of the terminal, both arms ached. She stepped into line behind a middle-aged couple and let her bags slide to the floor.

With the toe of her shoe, Karin shoved her duffel another foot nearer the information desk and glanced around the terminal. A tall, dark-haired man in a tweed jacket, black sweater and jeans stood a few feet away. She'd seen him a moment ago, staring at her. He was well over six feet. Attractive, Karin thought. The British had a word for it—dishy. He was definitely dishy. She stared, aware of a tiny pulse at the base of her throat.

Cool gray eyes looked her over, then fell away. The man glanced at his watch, scowling. He then interrupted the service clerk. "Page Mr. Williams again." He spoke crisply, his voice deep and commanding, with a hint of North Country accent. Like Leonard's, she thought.

Will Mr. K. M. Williams . . . ?

The dishy man was asking for her! She stepped closer. His imposing height intimidated her, and several seconds passed before she was able to speak. "I'm Karin Williams. Are you from Pickering?"

He pinned her with silver-flecked eyes. Thick,

brown-black hair stopped just short of his jacket collar. Up close, he was extraordinarily good-looking, with sun-bronzed skin and a square jaw. As he continued his perusal, an odd flutter ping-ponged off the walls of Karin's stomach.

"If you're *Mrs.* Williams, there's been a mistake. We have no married quarters on-site. I'm afraid your coming along has been for nothing." His gaze shifted as he scanned the room.

"I am Karin Marie Williams, representing Dalkey and Williams," she asserted, her voice firm. "There's been no mistake. You're here to meet me, Mr. . . . ?"

His gaze snapped back to her face. "They sent a woman?" He clapped a hand to his forehead. "Five bloody hours I've been waiting for that damned plane, and they sent me a woman? God in heaven!"

Karin bristled. "Yes, they sent me! And it's five and a half bloody hours, to be precise." Dishy maybe, but incredibly rude. "I'm pleased to meet you, Mr. . . . But it's been a long flight, and I'm too tired for a gender argument. Could you show me where I'm to stay?"

He glowered down at her, opened his mouth and abruptly closed it. "Sorry. You're not at all what I expected." With strong, warm fingers, he slipped the duffel bag from her grasp, setting it on the tile at his feet. "I'm Rowan Marsden."

Karin watched a muscle in his jaw twitch. So this was the renowned satellite expert. Well, he certainly wasn't what *she* had expected, either! She had pictured a stoop-shouldered, elderly man, not this stern-faced giant. Surreptitiously, she studied his features. Straight dark brows. An aquiline nose that jutted in an almost predatory manner. A deeply cleft chin. Assessing eyes with a flash of something she couldn't identify. Fear?

As they boldly returned her stare, she felt herself blush.

With effort, she matched his cool tone. "I've heard a lot about you, Mr. Marsden. It will be a pleasure working with you."

"No, it won't."

Her brows lifted. "I beg your pardon?"

"You will not be working with me."

"But . . . I'm your structural engineer."

"No, you're not." Marsden exhaled. "I expected a male engineer, Miss Williams, not some . . . bit of fluff."

"I beg your pardon?"

"Fluff." He snapped the word.

Karin froze. She had expected surprise at her gender, but not contempt. She took a moment to curb the anger that boiled up inside her. "Aren't you being a little—"

"Chauvinistic?" he supplied, flashing her a heart-stopping smile. "I'm sure I am. But I don't allow women on site. However"—he ran a leisurely gaze over her—"I'll see you to a hotel, and you can schedule a return flight in the morning." He lifted her heavy bag in one hand and motioned her toward the exit.

Didn't allow women on site? And he had the nerve to call her "fluff"? Fuming, she set off after him, almost running to match his enormous stride. Her blood pressure soared as she raced past him. If he thought he could dismiss her on the basis of *her sex* alone, he could think again.

She turned in the doorway and confronted him, hands on her hips.

"Now just a minute!"

He halted before her, and his gaze held hers.

Fury surged through her. "I'm here to save your bacon, mister. I demand a better explanation than that."

A portly baggage clerk tapped her on the shoulder. "Excuse me, miss." She moved aside as he barreled through the door behind her.

Marsden grasped her shoulder, then snatched back his hand. He gestured toward a coffee shop off to one side of the main concourse. "I suggest you listen to my explanation in a less hazardous spot."

Karin shrugged off his hand. She marched ahead of him to a booth and slid onto the cushioned bench. Dropping her carryall onto the seat, she ran her fingers over the wrinkles in her linen slacks. She waited in tense silence to place her order.

Sneaking a glance at the silent man across from her, she noted that fine lines etched the space between his nose and mouth, and the dark shadow of beard stretched over a firm jaw. But rather than appearing unkempt, Marsden looked sexy, mysterious. And somehow off balance by her presence.

She sensed his perusal of her as he drank his tea. Finally he spoke, his tone weary. "You asked—demanded, rather—an explanation. Well, here it is, Miss Williams. We are located at a remote site in the mountains. There are no other females on our crew, and no amenities. We eat together, and we sleep on-site in caravans. We do not go into town except on weekends."

Karin looked straight into his eyes. "That poses no problem for me. I'm used to such facilities. I am completely adaptable."

His dark eyebrows slanted upward. "I find that hard to believe, but no matter. I am unwilling to risk my operation by having you on-site."

"Why? What risk? You don't know a thing about me." A sudden ribbon of pain knifed through her temple, stifling further retort. She squeezed her eyes shut, cupped a hand to her forehead. After a long moment, she opened her lids.

He glanced at her, then at his watch. "You're tired," he said in a softer tone. "Let's get you to a hotel."

He rose, paid the bill and shouldered both her duffel and carryall. Numb with pain, she allowed him to steer her toward the exit.

Despite the sledgehammer pounding on her forehead, heat from his hand burned through her clothing like fingers of flame. Her breath caught. She twisted to turn out of his grip, but found herself hauled against the steel of his arm.

"Stay right here," he growled. "I don't want to have to search for you in this crowd."

Too exhausted to protest, she let him guide her to his car, a lean, sleek Jaguar, brilliantly red. Oh, perfect, she thought. He hates women and loves cars.

Rowan handed her onto the padded leather seat and stuffed her luggage in the trunk. Karin watched him ease his tall, well-defined body into the driver's seat with a singular economy of motion. Then he jammed the key into the ignition and pressed the accelerator. The powerful roadster sprang to life, and they roared out of the parking lot and into the night.

He remained silent, frowning at the road before him. Karin glanced at his profile, rigid in what appeared to be concentration. She recalled her conversation last weekend with her mother. Athena was wrong. Men *did* complicate one's life, and this arrogant Englishman was no exception. He might be good-looking, but he was also demanding and bad tempered.

Despite the Englishman's mood, though, she sensed something different about him. What was it? Candor? That, at least, was refreshing. She closed her eyelids against the pain as the throaty hum of the car's engine lulled her. She needed a night's rest.

It seemed only moments later that she felt Rowan's hand touch her shoulder. She jerked awake and stared out through the window of the Jaguar into the dimly lit evening.

They had left the lights of Manchester behind and were now parked on a dark, tree-lined street next to a multistoried building. He came around to her side of the car, slipped his hands around her elbows and pulled her up, out of the seat.

Electricity leaped from his fingers to her skin as she stepped onto a cobbled walk. She swayed, and found herself righted at once against his chest. At five feet nine, she was tall enough to look directly into the eyes of most men, but not this one. Her gaze reached only to his shoulder. She stared at the crisp dark hair that peeked out from the neck of his sweater, and she breathed in his clean, woodsy scent. His chest was firm and warm against her hands. When he put her aside to get her luggage, she felt oddly bereft.

He propelled her inside the hotel and approached the desk clerk while she waited near the door. Unnerved at her body's reaction to him, she made a study of a grouping of prints on the wall. When he turned toward her, she reached for her carryall.

"I'll take it." He lifted the bag from her grasp and guided her down the corridor to the elevator.

Once in the upstairs hallway, he unlocked the door to her room and stepped inside to set her luggage on the bed, then turned to face her. "I'm in the adjoining room if you need anything." His voice flowed over her, resonant and crisp. His eyes shone with silver lights, softened by the glow of lamp light.

Not in this lifetime, she thought. Keeping her voice even, she managed a thank you.

A smile lifted one corner of his mouth as he slowly turned away. "It's the least I can do."

"Mr. Marsden . . ."

He swung back. His gaze moved deliberately over her tousled hair and the features she knew must be pale with exhaustion. She licked her lips, suddenly uncomfortable under his study. Had she sprouted horns? He seemed so . . . intent.

He's going to learn something about "fluff," she thought determinedly. If he was trying to frighten her off, it wouldn't work. She drew herself up as tall as she could. "Mr. Marsden, I've worked on all-male crews before. In the Nevada desert, I slept in a miner's trailer."

"Oh?" Dark eyebrows raised, he looked down with polite interest. He had difficulty keeping his gaze from dropping to the tautly stretched jacket of her travel suit.

She began again, swallowing as a lump lodged in her throat. "Mr. Marsden—"

"Rowan," he corrected, his voice silky.

His gaze lingered on her breasts, and she had the disconcerting conviction that her nipples were swelling in response. "Look," she began, tugging the jacket over her chest. "I don't mind hardship. I can sleep in a trailer again."

He said nothing, just stared at her with an odd, tired smile.

Karin straightened, arms crossed at her waist. She

returned his gaze. "Well," she began, "you could at least—"

"All the caravans are occupied, Miss Williams," he said at last. "The only available one is mine."

He smiled slowly, revealing straight, white teeth. He chuckled as he opened the connecting door to his room, then turned, all humor gone.

"Be ready at eight. I have to return to the installation, and I want you on the early flight out. Good night, Miss Williams. Sleep well."

Despite the weary smile he gave her, his eyes gleamed with dark light. He stepped across the threshold and pulled the door shut, the click of the lock amplified in the room's silence. Frustrated, Karin kicked off her pumps and tossed the wrinkled suit jacket across her bed. She eyed the mahogany nightstand, and in a split second closed her fingers around the heavy glass ashtray, aching to fling it at the door after him.

Wait, she reasoned. There were other ways of dealing with Marsden. She paused for a long moment, smiled, then set the ashtray carefully back on the polished wood. Still smiling, she slid the trousers down her legs. Tomorrow, when she was rested and more herself, she'd teach Mr. High and Mighty Marsden a lesson about "fluff."

TWO

The cumbersome square-rigger broached, caught the sudden force of the wind, then pitched heavily on the angry sea. Waves pounded against the black hull, saltwater sloshed over the bow and ran in torrents along the deck. Clinging precariously to a stanchion along the ship's side, Karin stretched as far forward as possible, just beyond the grasp of strong hands that reached out to push her overboard into the brackish maelstrom. Her fingers clawed desperately to reinforce her hold as the bow shot upward. She braced herself for its downward plunge into the wake. Water rolled over the gunwale, and she was again thrust forward.

"No!" she screamed. The hands moved closer. "Don't touch me."

Too late! Hands pried her fingers free. "No—" Her scream was cut off by a hand clapped over her mouth, forcing her head back.

"Come now, Miss Williams," echoed a deep voice close to her ear. "If you don't stop yelling blue murder, you'll have the concierge up here."

Her lids snapped open, and she found herself looking into the penetrating gray eyes of Rowan Marsden. What on earth was he doing in her room? And sitting on her bed!

She shot to a sitting position, and he removed his

hand from her mouth. She sucked in a lungful of air. He held up a key. "I knocked several times, but was unable to waken you," he explained, inspecting her face.

She flinched under his scrutiny. "I—I must have been dreaming." The malevolent vision was still vividly etched in her consciousness, but she hadn't a clue as to what she'd done to bring him into her room. Whatever it was, he obviously wasn't going to satisfy her curiosity with an explanation. His annoyance was gone. Written across his hard, handsome features she detected concern, and something else. A carnal awareness that, while not blatant, was not subtle, either.

Her senses registered his appraisal with a queer flutter that surged through her belly. She looked away and raked the tangle of hair away from her face with an unsteady hand. The silence lengthened.

Suddenly he rose, towering over her. "I'm afraid I can't allow you the luxury of sleeping in. I must return to the site shortly and"—his mouth firmed into a grim line—"you have a plane to catch."

She blinked, her eyes focusing on the sage-colored cords fitted over his narrow hips, then on the cream silk shirt, open at the throat. Powerful shoulders stretched the smooth fabric casually tucked in at his waist. His hair fell into loose waves, its dark length a rich umber.

When his gaze locked with hers, she turned her head away.

He reached for the silver foil packet by her bed. "Do you make a regular habit of taking sleeping tablets?" His searching eyes followed the curve of her breasts outlined beneath the rumpled sheet, then moved back to her face.

Karin felt the cold bite of his words, the colder assessment in his eyes. "Only when I've been up for thirty-six hours straight," she retorted, working to keep the sharpness out of her voice.

His expression remained impassive. "It's not a healthy pursuit."

"I know that." She pulled the sheet higher, answering a sudden and disconcerting need to increase the barrier between her flesh and his scrutiny. "I never use them except as a last resort."

Rowan's gaze flickered away, and he turned toward the door. "I'll give you a few moments to make yourself presentable."

"Thank you," she said.

"I . . ." He paused. She itched to know what was on his mind as he stood motionless, his gaze pinpointing the painted door. But she could not bring herself to ask.

"I'll meet you in the lobby," he murmured suddenly, then strode out.

As soon as the door closed, Karin tore out of bed and raced toward the shower. Under no circumstances would she give him the opportunity to accuse her of dawdling. Nor would she let him send her back. As the shower pulsed onto her shoulders, she rehearsed what she would say.

Twenty minutes later, she walked purposefully into the lobby. The room was a display of comfortable but faded elegance; overstuffed sofas and chairs in various shades of blue flanked a worn Oriental rug. Nearby, Rowan leaned against a column, studying a menu. When the staccato of her step resounded on the tiled floor, he lowered the menu and gave her a leisurely inspection.

She grew warm under his perusal, even though she knew she looked professionally correct in a navy and taupe plaid coatdress of crisp gabardine. A wide leather belt accented her waist, and small gold studs adorned her ears. Her leather attaché case, suspended from its narrow shoulder strap, slapped against her hip with each determined step.

A smile curved his mouth as he gestured toward the dining room. "Shall we?"

Seated, they gave their order. After an interminable silence, broken only by background tunes from *A Chorus Line,* their breakfast came.

Rowan expertly sliced the top off his boiled egg, then scooped out the inside with deft, swift motions. He had long, well-shaped fingers, and without wanting to, Karin found herself staring at his hands. His silence wasn't making her speech easy.

Dropping her gaze, she buttered a bite-sized chunk of toast, then another, waiting for the right moment to speak. He remained intent on his meal, sparing her only an occasional glance as he reached for the pepper. Finally, Karin took a swallow of coffee and plunged ahead.

"Mr. Marsden, I don't feel we finished our discussion last night. What, exactly, do you object to about my qualifications?"

He glanced up, spoon poised in midair. "Nothing. Your paperwork is quite in order, Miss Williams. I understand you're a specialist with a master's degree in structural design. You've been highly recommended. One could hardly find objection to qualifications such as yours." His voice remained dispassionate, his eyes cool and assessing.

She felt like a biology specimen awaiting dissection. "Then what *is* the problem?"

He pushed the eggcup aside and tented his hands on the table. "Simply put, Miss Williams, this: There are no women on-site. Nor do I want any, for reasons I don't care to discuss. Our installation is remote. The men live in caravans. *Small* caravans. A bedroom at each end with a shared bath in the center. There are no amenities, just a bed, a desk, and a chair."

He motioned for more coffee, then continued. "There's little to do besides read, and even that can become tedious after a while. Walking on the fells is out of the question." He flicked the collar of her dress with one long forefinger. "And trappings like these would be out of place."

She edged away from his touch. Did he actually think she had brought a suitcase full of business suits to work at a test site? Rowan Marsden was as antiquated in his attitude as her father had been. And as single-minded.

"I know how to dress for this job, Mr. Marsden. I would appreciate your not prejudging me. You have no basis on which to assume I don't understand the working environment at a remote installation. I know more about it than you could possibly imagine. And," she added, giving him her iciest look, "my clothes are none of your business."

He shot her a surprised smile. "Perhaps you do." His smile vanished. "But you forget, Miss Williams. I am the project engineer."

"That gives you only the right to tell me how you want the job done." How could she deal with this preposterous man? With her blood coming to a full boil, she laid her napkin beside the plate and rose to her feet.

"Sit down," he said calmly.

Karin clenched her hands until the knuckles whitened. Marsden was just like her father.

Bart Williams hadn't wanted an educated daughter, he had wanted a pretty, idle ornament. Only his business partner, Leonard, had understood her deep need to do something, to succeed on her own. If she didn't complete this assignment, Dalkey and Williams would be hurt. She would fail Leonard, and she would die before she'd do that.

"You think you have all the answers, don't you, Mr. Marsden. Well, you haven't. I'm a very good engineer," she said in a low voice taut with anger. "I have experience with antenna installations. I'm qualified in structural design and stress analysis, I have the clearance needed for the job, and all you can comment on is my 'trappings'? I would have expected better of a man in your position."

She waited in silence, her gaze met by Rowan's odd stare. Marsden had seen her résumé and references, acknowledged her experience and still refused to have her on his crew. Obviously he'd made up his mind the moment he'd seen her. Damn the man to hell! She'd like to tell him exactly what he could do with his job.

She opened her mouth and closed it abruptly. Out of regard for Leonard and by sheer will, she managed to curb her tongue. Leonard had worked for months to negotiate this contract with Pickering, and she wasn't going to dash his chances. Or hers. She wanted this assignment. She wanted it a lot. In spite of Rowan Marsden.

Another idea formed in her mind. She rose and

walked swiftly toward the elevator. She'd try a new tack on the way to the airport.

Rowan caught up to her in the foyer. "I'll meet you here in twenty minutes."

Karin strode into the elevator as soon as the doors opened. She jammed her thumb on the white button. A look of surprise shot across Marsden's face as the doors snapped shut between them. Good, she thought. She liked surprising him.

Instantly, she recalled her physical awareness of him the night before. *That* was a surprise, too. She remembered the overt appraisal in his pewter-colored eyes, the feel of his fingers on her shoulder. The musk-scented warmth of his powerful body as he had hauled her against him in the parking lot still haunted her. Blood rushed to her face. Damn it all, why couldn't she get him out of her mind?

Rowan walked to the desk to pay the bill. He'd give her full marks for spirit. Karin Williams might look like a Dresden doll, but she was a gutsy lady. Too bad he couldn't use her. Impeccable qualifications. Even he had been surprised when he'd read the report from the home office. And the résumé giving only her initials—probably old Pickering's way of getting it past him. But no matter, he'd been down that stream one time too many. He would never again trust a woman. He'd made it an ironclad rule: no women on-site. He was getting Karin Williams on that plane straightaway.

He took the exit stairs to his room, two at a time. Better ring up Pickering and insist they find him a new structural engineer. One without a delectable body and soft, brown eyes.

"Put Neville through," he told the receptionist at the other end of the line.

After a lull, a raspy voice answered.

"Hallo? Marsden here. . . . Yes, I collected Williams. . . . Yes—but there's a bit of a mistake. *K. M.* stands for Karin something. Dammit, Neville, you know my feelings on this—no females on-site."

Rowan listened for a moment, then clenched his jaw.

"I don't care if she's the Queen's own engineer, I made it clear that I don't— Oh, she does. Hmmm. Yes, of course I need . . . and the clearance, too, does she?"

He half-listened to the older man's discourse. Pickering liked to talk. Much as he admired him, Rowan knew Pickering wouldn't see a problem—he never did. But then, he'd never had to work with women on-site, watch his crew lose their focus. And, Rowan thought, more to the point, Pickering had never known betrayal at the hands of a woman.

His knuckles whitened on the receiver. Why the thought of Claudia's infidelity should still evoke that reaction, he didn't know. But it did, and he'd do everything in his power to see that he never got himself into a situation like that again. His rule stood. No women on-site. It was better that way. For the job. For the crew. And certainly for him.

He listened as Pickering droned on.

He sank onto the bed, switched the receiver to his good ear. He breathed in and out slowly.

"Say that again? . . . Christ, Neville, those rules are for the good of the crew." He gripped the instrument tighter. "No one else—are you sure? Yes, Neville. Yes. Thanks." He dropped the phone onto its cradle.

"Oh, Jesus!"

* * *

Karin sat stiffly beside Rowan as he raced the roadster through a roundabout, then angled the car north, away from the city. Half an hour had passed since he'd shoved their bags in the trunk and gunned the Jaguar out of the hotel parking lot in Grand Prix fashion. Now, puffy white clouds scudded overhead, dappling the August sky. As they hurtled through another roundabout, Karin turned a puzzled stare toward Rowan. "This isn't the way to the airport. We were supposed to turn at that sign back there."

"Very observant. Were we going to the airport, we would indeed have turned there."

"Then where—"

"We're en route to Keswick."

"But that's . . . that's where your installation is! Why the change?"

"Certainly not my doing, Miss Williams," he said, his voice noncommittal. "After breakfast, I put through a call to the home office. Apparently, you are the only licensed engineer with both the antenna expertise and the clearance required for this job. To use an Americanism, I'm stuck with you."

Karin shot him a withering glance. "I can see this is going to be an unforgettable experience."

"I'm no happier about this than you, Miss Williams, but we have much to accomplish in a very short time, and I have to move forward on it. I . . . ah . . . am prepared to forgo my personal feelings for the sake of the project." For an instant, his gaze drilled into hers. "But only to a point, mind you. I'll brief you while we drive." He glanced inquiringly at her. "You *are* cognizant of the nature of the work being performed, aren't you, Miss Williams?"

She nodded. "Since we're going to be associates, would you mind not calling me Miss Williams? It sounds like somebody's maiden aunt. My name is Karin."

A frown darkened his features. "As you wish . . . Karin."

For the next several miles, during which they skimmed the motorway north toward the M6 and Cumbria, Rowan outlined his needs for installing several antennas on the new structure she would be designing for him.

Karin glanced over at him from time to time, listening and jotting brief notes on a yellow pad. Despite his apparent disapproval of her, it did not affect his ability to communicate about the task at hand. His explanation was thorough and interesting. She found herself watching his mouth as he spoke, listening to the clipped syllables that were so much like Leonard's. Rowan's voice was deeper, more intense. If she closed her eyes, she could imagine . . .

Good grief, she'd come here to work, not daydream. Chastising herself, she focused on his words. When he paused, she spoke. "What is the soil composition on-site?"

"Primarily granite."

"Good. That will make the job much easier."

"What would you do differently had it been shale, for instance?" he challenged.

She thought for a moment, then explained, adding, "That, of course, depends on your stability requirement."

"And our Force 11 winds?" His voice was controlled.

"Seventy-five miles per hour?" She looked up through a sweep of dark lashes. "No problem. But I'll need to study your codes."

"There's a book in my office," he said, giving her a sidelong glance. "Anything else can be obtained in York." He reached for a cassette tape, his hand grazing her thigh. As if burned, he jerked it back.

Her heart slammed against her ribs. Her thigh tingled, and she took a shaky breath, directing her eyes on the road. "I have my own copy."

Eyebrows raised, he flashed her a disbelieving look. *"The British Standard Code of Practice?"*

"Trust me, Mr. Marsden. I know what standards you work to." She rattled off the numbers, making no effort to hide her amusement at his surprise. *Fluff lesson number one, Mr. Marsden.*

Toward afternoon the terrain became hilly, and she relaxed her attention occasionally, watching green fields and docile dairy herds. At Penrith, they headed west. Karin noted Rowan's adroit maneuvering of the powerful car up gradients while maintaining considerable speed. The afternoon sun peeked around cloud masses and glinted through the windscreen, warming the walnut-paneled interior. The heat radiated through her dress. Moisture trickled between her breasts.

She reviewed the information Rowan had given her. Other than describing the requirements for the platform he wanted, he'd given her no hint of the job at all. He hadn't asked if there were any supplies she might need. Nor had he told her where she was to stay, except for his absurd insinuation the night before.

Warmth surged through her at the thought of sharing a trailer with him. Or perhaps a bed . . . Her mouth went suddenly dry.

Karin shook her head to clear her thoughts. Of course, last night he had been trying to frighten her off. She took a deep breath. She had to get a grip on herself if she was to work through that layer of resistance. She would prove to him she was made of sterner stuff than he thought.

Rowan's voice broke into her reflection. "Don't delude yourself that because you've answered a few questions satisfactorily I'm ready to turn the building operation over to you *carte blanche.* I remain in charge. All designs and revisions pass my desk."

"Do you doubt my ability, Mr. Marsden?"

He glanced toward her, then focused on the road. A long moment passed before he answered. "Let's just say that I prefer to double-check your work."

"As you wish. Just don't tell me how to do my job."

Rowan gave her an odd look, then shoved the car into a lower gear. They came to a sharp descent into Cairnbeck, a slate-roofed village identified by a small white road sign. Shaggy beeches lined the road, and in the distance, rough stone walls divided the fields.

Abruptly, he broke the silence. "We'll be arriving soon. Anything you need in the village before we drive on? Speak up now if there is."

Rowan did not look like the type to enjoy browsing through shops, she thought. Nor could she imagine herself enjoying it with such a surly companion.

"No, nothing." She would explore Cairnbeck later on her own.

Forty-five minutes later they arrived at a graveled parking lot set among rows of mature, silver-barked alders. "This is it," Rowan announced, slowing the car as the tires crunched onto the rough stones.

Karin looked over the installation. It was indeed remote, set in a shallow basin surrounded by naked mountains, and at least twenty miles from the sleepy village they'd driven through at the base of the mountain. Three large diesel-powered tractor-trailers with an assortment of cables and antennas projecting from the tops squatted on concrete slabs. A wooden platform rambled around the perimeter, and a half-dozen conventional trailers jutted to one side.

Rowan braked the Jaguar to a stop as a bearded blond giant in denims and a sweater burst out of the end unit. " 'Ere, lads! Rowan's back."

The trailer door flew open and two more men jogged toward the Jaguar.

One of them, slender and dark-haired, looked no older than Karin. A middle-aged man puffed along behind him, his spattered apron proclaiming him the camp cook.

Rowan climbed out, stretched, then opened Karin's door. "Don't say anything—let me handle this," he cautioned.

Puzzled, she unsnapped her seat belt and swung her legs out of the vehicle.

"Did you bring my books?" the dark man called out as the three crewmen strode toward the roadster.

"Books, hell!" the blond exploded in a heavy regional dialect. "Did you bring the porter? We need . . ." The words died on his lips as he spotted Karin. His initial surprise faded as he flashed a broad smile at her, then turned to Rowan. "Aye, man! You've brought better than porter! But I thought you didn't—"

"Miss Williams is the structural engineer on this site," Rowan broke in.

"Did you hear that, boys?" the blond chortled, looking first at his companions, then at Karin. "Our Rowan's gone and hired himself a lady engineer."

Rowan stiffened. "Go to the devil, Raisbeck!"

Karin's face flamed. She took a step backward, her movement halted as she came up against Rowan's rock-hard chest.

He clapped a firm hand on her shoulder to steady her. Current traveled from his fingers to her flesh, and she inhaled sharply. It seemed that he held her a moment longer than necessary before he stepped aside and faced the group. He cleared his throat to get their attention. "Miss Williams will be reporting directly to me."

Did she imagine a trace of huskiness in his voice? Before she had time to ponder this, Rowan gestured toward the blond. "Cyril Raisbeck, from Liverpool. One of our lab technicians and"—he threw Cyril a menacing look—"not a man of limitless tact."

"I'm Derrick Sumner," the dark man said hesitantly.

The third crewman, gray-haired, stocky, and considerably shorter than Karin, stepped forward and thrust out a thick hand. "Clive Thornycroft." Pale blue eyes, deeply crinkled at the corners, stared at her from a leathery face.

"Thorny takes good care of us," Rowan said, his smile directed at the older man.

Thorny shook her hand warmly. "Chef extraordinaire, at your service."

Rowan addressed the three. "Back to work, lads! I'll see you after I've got Miss Williams settled in. And yes"—he looked at Derrick—"I do have your books."

"And the porter?" Cyril asked.

"And the porter."

Derrick Sumner smiled shyly. "It's nice to have you here, Miss Williams." He followed the two other men toward the motorized vans.

"This way," Rowan ordered. He lifted Karin's suitcase and shoulder carryall in one hand and headed toward a silver trailer nestled in a stand of scraggly pine trees. He pushed open the door at one end and stood aside as Karin stepped into a small bedroom.

In all, she doubted the room measured more than eight feet square. A desk with a reading lamp sat along one wall, a two-drawer file beside it. Along the opposite wall stood a narrow bed covered with a beige comforter and an olive drab woolen blanket. A topographic map had been tacked to the wall above the desk. A bookshelf containing several thick volumes rested against the other wall.

A bleak place to live, she thought. It was, as Rowan had said, spartan. But it was only for a couple of months. She'd manage.

Rowan dropped her cases on the bed. "You'll stay here," he said bluntly. "It's been my office, but there's a small closet and some shelves for your personal things in the bathroom." He jerked his head toward the center section, closed off by a narrow sliding door. "In there."

She shrugged. The layout was the same as the miner's trailer she had occupied in the Nevada desert. A center bathroom, flanked by . . . She took a deep breath. A bedroom at each end.

He hadn't been joking. She was actually going to share the trailer with him. Her heart missed a beat. "Is your—is the room at the other end yours?"

"Yes. But I have a separate entrance. I'm afraid we'll be sharing the bath. And the closet." He looked down at her, his face unreadable. "I said it was a remote installation. Don't expect favors. You're just part of the crew."

He flicked his gaze toward the bookshelf. "Some of these might be of use to you. Help yourself. Dinner's at six, in the blue caravan." He turned and descended the first step, then halted and stared back at her with deliberate coolness. "Ah, Miss Williams, it wouldn't be wise to become too friendly with the men."

Karin sucked in her breath. "What's that supposed to mean?"

"It means you're here to work, not fraternize with my crew. I expect their full concentration on the task at hand. Do I make myself clear?" He stepped onto the ground and strode off.

"Perfectly!" She shoved the door shut. The trailer shook with the force, and something shattered on the bathroom floor. "Oh, hell!"

What did he think she was going to do anyway, seduce his men? No one had ever before questioned her professional behavior. Or her values.

She'd manage her own life, thank you. But it wouldn't be easy. Not with Rowan Marsden fighting her every step of the way. He was rude, overbearing—impossible, really. And yet, he was the most magnetic man she'd ever laid eyes on.

"Just you wait, Rowan Marsden, I'll show you 'manage.' Just you wait!"

THREE

Cautiously, Karin pushed open the sliding door separating her room from the bath and peered inside. A small blue china dish lay in pieces beside the minuscule lavatory, and several large brown pellets were scattered alongside. Karin scooped one into her palm. Cat kibble! Could Rowan share his trailer with a cat? Impossible. Animals wouldn't put up with him.

She scooped the shards into a wastebasket, then gathered the kibble in a tissue and flushed it down the toilet. More blue dishes teetered on a shelf just above the lavatory. Beside them stood a large kibble-filled jar. She poured a small portion into another dish and set it on the floor. "Maybe he likes cats better than people," she muttered.

The connecting door stood ajar. Curious, Karin pushed it open just enough to look inside. A pair of spit-polished cordovan oxfords peeked from beneath a scarred but uncluttered oak desk. An open volume lay on top. A Windsor chair served as a valet, gray whipcord trousers draped over the back. His room layout was the reverse of hers but with a full-sized bed. A fringed blue woolen throw partially hid a fluffy comforter, and curled up in the center, a dark orange tabby observed her through slitted eyes.

Karin tossed a nervous glance toward the trailer door, then stole to the bed and stroked the cat's soft fur. A deep rumble stirred in its chest. "What a pretty thing you are." Karin smiled and quietly retreated toward her own room.

The open book on his desk caught her eye. Wordsworth. So Rowan Marsden read poetry! She imagined engineering journals would be more to his liking. In fact, a moment ago she'd have laid money that Pickering's project officer topped the list in insensitivity. How intriguing! Was it possible that a romantic heart beat inside that arrogant British chest?

Back in her room she unpacked and stowed her cases under the bed, then checked her watch. Five-thirty. Enough time for a quick sponge bath and a change into something more suitable. The drive up had been warm, but now the wind on the mountain rattled the windows. She remembered the sweaters worn by Rowan's crew and pulled a teal hand-knit from her half of the bathroom shelf, careful not to disturb the neat stack of masculine pullovers alongside. Gingerly, she touched one of his, a black guernsey knit, and hesitated. It smelled of pine woods and moss.

Like a thunderclap the irony of the situation hit her. Sharing a trailer with Rowan Marsden was ludicrous. He had a lot to learn about women, but she wasn't going to be the one to teach him. A tightness settled between her shoulder blades as she recalled his pigheadedness. Good looks or no, working with such a perplexing man, one who clearly did not like women, would be a trial. She preferred someone confident, yet softer around the edges. Someone willing to share, not dominate. She sighed in resignation. No wonder she was still single. A man like that was impossible to find.

Karin closed the connecting door, struck by a thought. Was she too choosy? Her mother hinted at it, but was she really? Or was she just being discriminating? After all, why let someone completely unsuitable into her life?

As she tidied her new accommodation, straightening the books on the shelf and plumping up the bed pillow, she again recalled her conversation with her mother.

She'd pulled up in front of Athena's creekside cottage, anxious to see her before leaving for England. . . .

"Karin?" Athena Williams' musical voice echoed over the intercom. "The door is unlocked."

Karin pushed open the glass-paned door and stepped into the living room. Instantly, she was enveloped in a pungent cloud of incense. She peered in, curious to see what new whim of her mother's might be reflected in the ever-changing decor. Her gaze fell on a three-foot belching gargoyle, and her smile spread.

"What do you think?" the melodic voice asked.

Karin poked her head into the small, sunlit studio at the rear of the cottage, marveling as always at the youth of her mother's face, now framed by a dramatic upsweep of silver hair. Seated in a wheelchair before a canvas, Athena Williams deftly blended pastels into a leaden sky. In the foreground, a man and a woman stood locked in each other's arms. Below them, raging water roiled against a rocky promontory.

"It's hideous," Karin commented.

Athena looked critically at the rugged seascape before turning sharp eyes on her daughter. "I *am* having difficulty with the pose," Athena reproached her, "but you needn't be so brutal."

Karin laughed. "Not the painting, Mom. I was talking about that thing on the hearth."

Athena swung her wheelchair around. "That 'thing' as you call it is over three hundred years old. It's part of the trim from a Lancashire castle." She propelled herself toward the kitchen. "That's enough painting for this morning. Come have tea and tell me about your trip."

Karin outlined everything Leonard had told her earlier in the week, watching her mother's face. In the nine years since the automobile accident, Karin had maintained close contact with her mother, particularly after she had moved out of the cottage and into her own place, closer to her office. Sometimes she worried over Athena's welfare, but she could see that her mother enjoyed being self-sufficient. Karin acknowledged that it was she herself who benefited most from the visits to her mother.

Though widowed and paralyzed from the waist down from the auto accident, Athena refused to bow to grief or disaster. She made her painting pay. Publishers scrambled to have book covers done by Athena Williams.

"Don't worry about me. I can handle things here. And if I can't," Athena added, "Leonard stops by almost every other day."

"Mom, you're the most capable person I know, but . . ."

Athena brushed a lock of hair into place with a delicate hand, giving Karin an oblique smile. "I know. If I'm not careful, I'll be smothered by unwanted male attention." She fussed with a skewed table scarf, then straightened a stack of books. "You said you're going to Manchester? For how long?"

Karin shrugged. "Don't know. Someone from Pickering is meeting me at the airport, but the installation is somewhere in the Lake District. I may have to spend time at their main plant in York. It depends on how much information is available on-site. And"—she paused, taking a slow sip of tea—"how much cooperation I get from Rowan Marsden."

"Rowan who?"

"Marsden. A project officer with Neanderthal ideas about women."

Athena smiled. "Sounds challenging. Can you talk about the task?"

Karin shook her head. "It's classified."

Athena's eyes twinkled. "Just like your father. I never knew what he did half the time."

"I may do the same type of work, but inside—"

"Inside, you're like me," Athena supplied. "I know. Sometimes I wish you were less so. You work constantly. You have virtually no social life. . . . It's not healthy. Take some time off for yourself, dear. Too much tenacity does not endear one to men."

"Huh? All the men I work with are either self-centered super studs or dull as dishwater. You don't need a man to make your life worthwhile. So why should I?"

"But I do get lonely sometimes," Athena said wistfully.

The admission drew a startled look from Karin. Athena lonely? She stared for a moment at her mother's smooth features. Only her hair had changed. Sometimes shadows passed over her mother's still-

beautiful face, but Karin attributed those to fatigue.
Surely Athena couldn't mean . . . Karin began stacking saucers and cups to carry to the sink. "Well, I don't need a man to fill *my* life, Mom. My life is plenty full, thank you."

"We'll see," Athena said, flashing a knowing smile. "Methinks you protest too much."

Karin laughed to herself. If Mr. Right had appeared, she'd have noticed. And there'd have been no protesting. But interesting men who were confident enough in their own achievements that they didn't need to dominate the women around them did not exist in her realm.

Now, looking out the trailer window at the waning sun as it passed behind a cloud, Karin cut short her thoughts of home. She glanced at her travel clock. Time for dinner.

At six o'clock sharp, Karin stepped outside and jogged toward the blue mess trailer. Her oversized sweater was tucked neatly into faded gray denims, and she had casually thrown a matching jacket over her shoulders.

Inside the trailer, seven men were gathered around a long wooden table, Rowan at the head. When the door clicked open, he looked up, then motioned her in. Inches taller than the other men, his presence dominated the space.

Karin lowered herself into the vacant chair at the opposite end from him, between Derrick and the bearded blond, Cyril. Derrick flashed her a shy smile.

"We're a bit of an odd lot," Cyril informed her, moments later, in his heavily accented speech. He made an expansive wave that took in the rugged-looking crew. "Mac here is from Scotland and is our electrical engineer." He gestured to a stocky red-bearded man on his right. "Paddy, next to him, is our test engineer. As you might well imagine, he comes from Eire. We're trying to Anglicize him, but he still spouts off in Gaelic when he's had a drop in."

"Which is more often than not," the Scotsman added, deep crinkles forming at the corners of his eyes.

Karin's smile faded when she caught Rowan's stare. He was not smiling, but rather fixing her with a curious stare.

The room hushed. Someone coughed.

Then Paddy, the ruddy-cheeked Irishman, laughed and extended a callused hand to Karin. "These lads may have brought us the language, but we're teachin' them how to speak it."

"Jack here does setups, and Robin analyzes the data," Cyril went on, introducing the two men across from Karin.

Jack, a dour, thickset man, nodded and rose.

Karin felt Rowan's eyes still on her. Her palms grew moist. Deliberately ignoring him, she turned a smiling face to Derrick. "What do you do?"

"I . . . uh . . . I . . . ." Derrick's face grew red.

"This boyo's our programmer," the man called Robin supplied. "He does a damn fine job of it, too."

"Not bloody bad, and him just a *gossoon,*" Paddy added.

"A young lad," Cyril translated, to Derrick's complete chagrin.

"Well, it sounds like he handles as much responsibility as the rest of you," she said evenly.

A grateful smile shimmered to life across Derrick's boyish features.

She looked up and met Rowan's gaze. He'd exchanged the silk shirt for one of rich, pine green wool that outlined the breadth of his shoulders. A warmth spread through her, and she flashed him a tentative smile.

His teeth on edge, Rowan settled back in his seat and turned away. Damn her! He didn't want her smiling at him, beguiling him with those big, chocolaty eyes and that bee-stung mouth that invited kisses. He didn't want to be reminded that he was a man with needs. In short, he didn't want her here on his crew— much less in his caravan.

If Neville hadn't insisted, he would have refused. But, dammit, he loved this job and he respected the old man; and by God, he'd see it through if it killed him. He'd take Karin Williams on board, treat her with the respect she deserved, for the good of the project. But he didn't have to like it.

Jack sidled up to him. "So that's your choice for structural. I say, old boy, aren't you on dangerous ground?" Jack cupped a beefy hand around a tumbler of water and took a swallow, wiping his mouth with the back of his other hand. "Thought you'd never allow a female on-site."

Rowan turned to his lead engineer. Friends since school, Jack Allsop had worked with him on the last three assignments. "Keep a button on that, Jacko," he whispered.

"Why'd you take her on?" Jack persisted, following Karin with his perceptive gaze.

"I . . ." He paused. "For the good of the project.

She was the only one available. And I'm convinced Miss Williams is capable of doing an excellent job."

Jack shrugged. "If you say so. Don't say you weren't warned."

"Point taken." Rowan unfolded his napkin and spread it on his lap. Jack seemed to have set himself up to shield Rowan from life's troubles. Rowan hadn't the heart to tell him otherwise. They all needed to look out for each other on long assignments such as these.

He stared at Karin a moment longer. Keeping a cap on his emotions might prove difficult, but he didn't see that he had a choice.

Karin dragged her gaze from Rowan. A chill settled over the room, and she dropped her gaze to the marbleized Formica tabletop. He was rude, she thought, shifting uncomfortably in her chair. And arrogant. And very sexy.

Thorny set down a steaming platter with pieces of meat, rolled and skewered, then a bowl heaped with riced potatoes. Karin tasted the meat. It was tangy and slightly sweet, unlike anything she had eaten before. "What is this?"

"Don't ask," Cyril cautioned. "One of Thorny's secret recipes."

Robin chortled. "All of Thorny's recipes are secret. Between the lot of us, we think he makes them up out of what's left from the day before."

"The week before's bloody more like it!" Paddy added with a wink.

Thorny clasped both hands over his heart. "You wound me, lads. Makin' Miss Williams think ill of my culinary prowess."

Rowan kept his gaze focused on Karin. Between

bites, she forced herself to concentrate on the banter around her instead of his assessing eyes.

After she had eaten, Thorny whisked her empty plate away and set a small dish in front of her. "Here. Perhaps you would like to try my Queen's pudding?"

Karin dipped her spoon into the creamy dessert and tasted it. "Mmmm. Delicious!"

Thorny beamed.

"Is this your first trip to England?" Derrick asked.

"Mm—hmm." Karin nodded, her mouth full of pudding.

"You've worked on antenna structures before?" Robin questioned.

Her gaze moved down the table and rested on Rowan. He held a coffee cup in one hand, the fingers of his other hand stroking the smooth, blue glaze. He had large hands, to match his frame, and long, tapering fingers with well-trimmed nails. They fascinated her. She wondered what they'd feel like in a moment of tenderness. Closing her eyes against the image her thoughts conjured, she jerked her attention back to the question and swallowed. "Yes. Three others, to be exact. This is the second time at a remote site."

The Scotsman smiled. "Well, at least we get down to the village some weekends."

"Might not feel the need to visit as often, now." Cyril grinned at Karin.

"Don't let Maggie hear talk like that," someone said.

Karin broke into a smile at the guffaws of the others.

Rowan did not join in. Instead, he pulled Jack aside, and the two stepped to the other end of the room. They spoke in low tones, and an occasional glance Karin's way indicated the discussion centered on her.

Because of the teasing Derrick received from the other men, Karin directed most of her questions to him, again sensing Rowan's gaze on her. When Thorny cleared the dishes and retreated to the kitchen, an uneasiness crept over her. Glancing up, she met the riveting force of Rowan's gaze.

Hostile. Definitely hostile. Damn him! she thought. Couldn't she even get acquainted? Deliberately, she turned again toward Derrick. "What were you saying?"

He gulped. "I—I asked if you play chess."

"I do."

"Perhaps you'd like to play sometime?" He voiced the question hesitantly, but the telltale crimson had faded from his face.

Rowan loomed beside them. "Don't you think you'd better let Miss Williams have an early night? She'll be up at dawn tomorrow." His tone was bland, but to Karin the warning was unmistakable.

"Oh, sorry," Derrick mumbled, his face reddening once more. "I should have realized you'd be tired."

"It's perfectly all right. I'm not too tired for a friendly chat." She touched his arm. "Tomorrow, perhaps."

Rowan scowled.

Karin rose, refusing to look at him. "Good night, all." Waving to the crew, she slipped out and jogged quickly toward the trailer. She certainly didn't need another go-round with her bad-mannered boss tonight, she thought wearily.

In her room, she hurriedly pulled on her ivory flannel gown and eased her tired body between the covers. Just as she closed her eyes, a sharp rap on the connecting door startled her.

"Miss Williams!"

Karin lay still. Couldn't it wait until morning? She'd be damned if she was going to argue with him tonight.

Her door opened quietly. Barely breathing, she feigned sleep. *Let him go away.* She did not want to see him, did not want him in her room. She did not want to think about him at her door—or in a tiny room four steps away, stripping his clothing off that powerful frame, sliding his lean body into that big bed.

Shocked at her turn of mind, her mouth went dry and her heart began a staccato beat.

Then, just as quietly, the door closed. After a moment, she heard him moving about on the other side, and then the sound of the shower.

She pressed her hands over her breasts and willed her heart to slow down. What was the matter with her? Rowan Marsden was an old-fashioned, irascible, autocratic engineer who . . . who was the most attractive man she'd ever laid eyes on.

Oh, Lord. What did *that* have to do with anything? She couldn't let herself notice such things about the man. It was improper. Unprofessional.

Dangerous.

She had to perform flawlessly on this assignment, had to keep her mind on business, for Leonard's sake and for her own professional reputation. Leonard needed her here on this job. She couldn't let him down. She'd have to see it through, have to manage it somehow . . . Rowan Marsden or no Rowan Marsden.

The next morning, Karin awoke to a raspy purring in her ear and the tickle of whiskers on her cheek. "Stop that, kitty. No!" She pushed the cat away and turned her face into the soft pillow. Suddenly, her door swung ajar.

Her lids snapped open, and she jerked her head around.

Rowan thrust his head inside. He paused abruptly when he saw her still in bed. "Excuse me. It was so quiet, I thought you'd gone out. I seem to have lost something." His gaze dropped to the cat curled into a ball in the crook of her arm.

He advanced toward her, his jeans disturbingly snug over lean hips and well-defined thighs, and reached for the cat. "Did Marmalade bother you?" he asked, roughly disengaging claws from the blanket. As he drew the cat away, his fingers brushed against her gown and the unmistakable swell of her breast.

His eyes blazed and met hers for a heart-stopping instant before he jerked back. "Sorry."

The heat of his fleeting touch brought butterflies to her belly. Her nipples hardened, and she took a shaky breath. "No harm done," she lied.

He lifted the tabby to his shoulder. "There's a girl," he crooned, smiling and stroking the short, thick fur. His smooth fingers moved sensuously over the gravel-voiced cat. His gaze dropped to Karin, the aloof expression evident once more. "I'll see she doesn't trouble you again." He turned and started out.

"She's no problem. I like cats," Karin said to his retreating figure.

But he had firmly pulled the door shut between them.

She lay on the narrow bed, breasts tingling, her breathing ragged. Dear God, what was the matter with her?

* * *

Rowan set the cat down on the bathroom floor, where it delicately crunched a chunk of kibble. He stared down at the orange feline. A woman like Karin Williams could be dangerous, a menace to his carefully controlled existence. Ever since Claudia had walked out, he had vowed not to let a woman get close to him. For seven years he'd made good on that promise. Until now.

Now Karin Williams seemed about to shatter his resolve.

He pounded a fist into his hand. Damn! Remembered heat from her small breast as it brushed the backs of his fingers set up a rush of feeling, a need that settled instantly in his groin. He'd have to be extra careful to keep his distance. He would not run the risk of starting something that had no future.

Curiously, the thought left him feeling oddly bleak.

Marmalade meowed to be let out. Muttering to himself, Rowan tramped down the steps after the cat.

FOUR

Slate skies and a penetrating wind announced a weather change as Karin stepped outside the trailer and headed toward the dining room. The morning chill penetrated her Levis and blue turtleneck, so she kept her heavy woolen mackinaw on when she sat next to Derrick at the long table. Thorny slid a bowl of porridge in front of her, then set a platter of sausages and eggs beside a rack of cooling toast.

Karin glanced at Derrick's almost empty plate and wolfed down a few mouthfuls of the hot cereal. No way would she linger. She'd skip the damned meal before she'd let Mr. High-and-Mighty Marsden chide her for tardiness.

When the men drained the last of their coffee, they headed toward the trailer vans near the ridge. Gulping one more mouthful, Karin followed them out the door. Rowan's brusque voice cut in from behind her.

"Are you ready to start, Miss Williams?" He strode toward the trailers, carrying an armload of drawings and folders.

"Karin," she corrected.

"Yes . . . Karin. Are you ready?" His voice was just short of hostile, she decided.

At the office trailer he mounted portable steps,

yanked open the metal door, then stepped aside for her. He slapped the blueprints down on a drafting board. "You'll work here." A deep, rich timbre enriched his speech. His face was impassive. Karin found herself growing uneasy, yet was unable to look away.

He flipped through several drawings, then pulled a site plan from the stack. "Now, here are the plans," he snapped.

Karin's head came up, and she felt her cheeks redden. "I can see what they are," she said through her teeth. "You needn't patronize me."

He exhaled wearily. "Miss Wil—Karin. At Pickering, we move forward by listening and following directions. No movement, no progress. You're no exception."

"I would assume everyone at Pickering has an equal voice?"

"Naturally. We started with nothing, and we made a success of our operations by doing just that. Working hard. This company was built on mutual hard work and dedication." He turned away, as if to dismiss her.

Stung, she felt anger flare. She gave him a long, hard stare. "And you pulled yourself up by your own jock—er, bootstrap, is that it?" Good God, did she really say that?

He stared back for a moment, lips twitching, then resumed. "We're powered by a twenty-thousand-watt dynamo—generator, in your terminology."

She opened her mouth to ask a question, but he cut her off. "I want the power supply here, the equipment shed here." He jabbed the locations with a red pencil, then, tapping a desk drawer with the toe of his boot, added bluntly, "The electrical requirements are in this file. Come along. I'll show you the layout." Turning, he pushed the door open.

Karin followed, her eyes drawn to the ripple of muscle across his back where the gray chamois shirt drew tight. Her gaze moved down to lean hips and legs encased in taut black denims. He strode with an easy grace and purposefulness, reminding her of a tiger stalking its prey. A sexy, gray-eyed tiger. Such an animal could spell disaster.

Inside the adjacent trailer, Derrick and Robin sat at computer terminals, their heads bent over sheets of data. Derrick waved a paper in front of Rowan. "Have a look at what's just come in."

Rowan skimmed the paper. "Home office will be interested in this one," he said. "Nice work. Send it out as soon as you finish." Derrick nodded and turned back to his terminal.

"I understand you've been briefed on the technical aspects of the program," Rowan said. "What, specifically, were you told about our operation?"

Karin pursed her lips. "Not a lot. Leonard said I would be fully informed once I got here. He said the installation is new, the project classified. Also that you are monitoring satellites and transmitting data."

"He's partly correct. We do send data, but our primary task is to receive and decode communications, then process the data."

In front of them, Mac struggled with a mass of cables that snaked across the floor from one computer bay to another. Rowan bent to pull the connector end of a cable through a loop in the tangled maze. He handed it to Mac, and the Scotsman grunted his thanks.

Rowan explained how the antennas functioned and demonstrated their ratcheting movement, then guided her along the row of computer bays and equipment. He described in startlingly clear detail his plan for the completed operation. Karin listened to his depth of knowledge and precision, fascinated in spite of herself. It was obvious that he placed his crew in high regard; she saw his features soften when he spoke about them.

The door swung open, caught by a gust of cool wind, and Karin shivered. Rowan's eyes followed her movement and flicked to her chest. "I'll show you the outside setups later when it's warmer."

Karin's attention instantly shifted to her cotton turtleneck. Her mackinaw hung open, exposing the hardened pebbles of her nipples against the soft fabric. She jerked the jacket closed, uncomfortably aware that the cool weather was only partly responsible. Rowan gripped the door in one hand and slammed it firmly shut as they left. In silence, he led the way back to the office.

At her drafting board, Karin returned to the blueprint he had set before her. "Pickering will furnish each of the antenna-mounting footprints?"

He nodded. "That, and all the installation hardware. Your job now is to provide me with the list of construction materials."

She challenged him with a direct gaze. "Am I free to order what I consider necessary?"

His gray eyes held their usual coolness, sparring with hers. "After I've checked over the list." He pulled a ruled pad from the center drawer of the desk, dropping it on the board in front of her with a plop. "I suggest you begin with the load calculations." He stepped to the enameled metal door, one hand on the latch. "Accuracy is essential, Miss Williams. I demand it." Then he was gone, leaving her staring at the chipped green paint on the door panel.

In the silence that followed, Karin found herself pacing, remembering with surprise the warmth and gentleness Rowan exhibited to his men. But not to her, she acknowledged. *He may be a fine engineer, but as a man* . . . She pursed her lips and plunked herself down on the drafting stool again.

It rained off and on throughout the rest of the day. At noon, Thorny served a hearty lunch of a mysterious stew in which Karin thought she recognized bits of beef from last night's supper. Afterward, she gathered up her drafting equipment and books from the suitcase under her bed, and lugged them to her drafting board. For the next three hours, she pored over the codes and the blueprints, occasionally setting them aside and making notes in her neat draftsman's hand. Rowan burst through the door late in the day, while she was bent over her board, sketching a layout.

"You don't waste time," he observed, peering over her shoulder at the sheet of calculations by her elbow. He'd donned a heavy fisherman's knit sweater of natural black sheep's wool; its lanolin smell mingled pleasantly with his own masculine scent.

"It's stopped raining. Are you ready for an outside tour?"

"Sure." She rose and stretched, feeling the release of tension in her back. He pulled her mackinaw from the coat tree and held it while she slipped her arms into the sleeves. She quickened her pace to match his as he steered her over to the equipment storage shed near the trailer vans. Rowan pointed out the huge diesel-powered generator, then ascended a wooden catwalk that skirted the trailers. Karin climbed up behind him.

If he would accord her the respect he gave his crew,

or speak to her in the same resonant voice he reserved for his work, she might enjoy working for him. Clearly, he loved what he did, and, she had observed, he did it well.

"The present installations are performed from this temporary support. As you can see, it's far too unstable for our needs." He rocked back and forth a few times, and she felt a slight swaying. Before she could comment, he stepped off the platform, then strode to one of the gunmetal gray Range Rovers parked in the trees.

Karin trotted to keep up with him.

"In you get!" Rowan commanded. He maneuvered the car up the slight incline where the road ended, jumped out and unlocked a chain-link gate; then they bounced and rattled in silence to the ridge of the basin.

From inside the car, Rowan pointed across a valley to a lower ridge beyond, its slope a reddish purple. "We have another installation over there."

Rowan's voice faded as Karin gazed toward the ridge, squinting through a shaft of sunlight that cut across the horizon. The view was magnificent. "Heather?"

"Bilberries," he answered. "To the right of that pine is our thirty-foot reflector antenna."

"I read about it somewhere. It's one of the best of its type."

"It *is* the best."

"Isn't this a walking haunt for tourists?" Karin asked, remembering signs she'd seen in the village below.

"It is. Keswick promotes regular walking holidays during the summers. This ridge is off limits, of course, but there are several grade-A slopes in the vicinity." He turned, pointing south. "That's Muncaster Fell.

From there you can see across the Solway Firth into Scotland. And over there," he moved his arm a fraction to the east, "is where we've installed—"

"Do you do much fell walking?" she interrupted, watching the smooth skin of his tanned fingers, the corded forearms revealed by the pushed-up sweater sleeves. Dark silky hair shimmered over golden skin.

His eyebrows shot upward. "I do. But then, I'm from the North, and used to steep climbs. On the ridge here—"

"Where in the North?"

He gave her a curious look. "York. My family are in Knaresborough."

"Your wife?"

"My parents. I'm not married." His eyes glinted, and a shadow flickered across his angular features. "Surely there are more interesting things than my personal life," he said, his tone indicating irritation. "Come, I'll show you the rest."

They got out. He moved cautiously to the edge of the steep granite promontory, pointing to three white discs mounted into the hillside.

Karin edged forward, peering where he gestured.

"Stay back from the edge," he cautioned. He grabbed her arm and pulled her away from the precipice. "It's dangerous."

His voice was hard-edged, his grasp firm and warm . . . and unnerving. His fingers tightened as he drew her closer to him. The woodsy-musky scent of him filled her nostrils. She swallowed, feeling the current flow between them.

Oblivious, he went on. "Last year a hiker was killed. There." He pointed downward.

She turned out of his grasp, ignoring the black look

he accorded her, and followed the line of his forefinger. A ledge jutted out some fifty feet below. The vision of a hiker's broken body flashed through her mind. "How awful!" she murmured. She stepped back a foot or so and let her gaze follow the smooth, bare line of dark gray fells.

"It's really very beautiful here," she said finally.

"This is the best location in the country. Here we receive communications from as far away as Newfoundland. If you will notice . . ."

Karin listened to the rich cadence of his voice, yet could not focus on his words. As a child, she had collected rocks on each family trip to the mountains. Later, in college, she had been fascinated by the geologic wonder of ice-age formations and volcanic disturbances. The stark beauty and the solitude of the surrounding knife-edge ridges and crags tugged at her inner passions. She pivoted one way, then the other, mesmerized.

She made a quick motion toward him, pointing in another direction, toward a blush of gold against a hillside. "Look! There! That's aspen, isn't it?"

"Miss Williams . . . Karin. Could we stick to the subject?"

Angrily she turned toward him. "Is that all you can see up here?"

"Careful! You're too close to the edge."

"Oh, for heaven's sake! Lighten up, will you?" She stepped back from him, then felt her footing give as the granite crumbled away. She cried out.

A strong hand grabbed her wrist and pulled her back from the precipice. Large chunks of rock hurtled down the mountainside, breaking into smaller pieces as they dashed against the rock face. She heard the echo of pebbles chinking onto the surface far below. Karin gasped, then wobbled unsteadily as the ground rose up to meet her.

Rowan's arms encircled her, and before she could react, she was drawn into a rough embrace. Her mackinaw fell open, and her breasts pressed against his iron-hard chest. Shock waves tore through her as she felt his heat through her cotton turtleneck, felt the sharp, uneven thudding of his heart. His distinctive scent of clean pine and musk washed over her. Her throat tightened, and she pulled away. "I'm all right," she said huskily. She backed away from him, but when she put weight on her foot, her ankle buckled. "Damn!"

"I warned you." His face was white and set. "I suppose it's sprained?"

She reached one hand toward him to steady herself. A ring of fire girdled her ankle. "Yes. I think so."

His mouth compressed into a thin line. "Well, we'd better take a look," he muttered. "Hold onto me."

Leaning against him, she hobbled down to the car. He swung open the door, thrust her unceremoniously onto the fabric seat, and began to unlace her shoe.

She drew her foot back. "I can do that."

"Perhaps, but I'll just have a look." His tone cautioned her not to resist.

He slipped off her shoe and sock, then gently rotated the ankle. His hands were warm, his touch just short of intimate. She drew in a sharp breath as her toes instinctively began to curl. She moved her gaze upward from the tanned fingers cradling and stroking her foot, along his forearms with their sprinkling of straight, dark hair to the fine white line of a scar that ran from his right index finger to midforearm, and then to his chiseled features, the firm jaw, the well-modeled lips.

He raised his head. For one breathless instant, his eyes met and held hers. An emotion far more intense than annoyance flickered into his gaze.

Heat flooded her. She couldn't look away.

Rowan dragged his gaze from the liquid warmth of Karin's eyes. She was neither tiny, nor helpless, but he found himself at sixes and sevens, wanting at one moment to wring her slender little neck and, a moment later, to kiss her senseless. He urged his fingers to pull her white sock back on her foot and to stop caressing the silky soft skin of her trim ankle and shapely calf. His fingers shook as he untangled the shoelace.

Great bloody Christ in the morning! He wanted her.

FIVE

Rowan drew the shoe onto Karin's foot, laced it loosely, and rose. "We'd better get some ice on that." His voice, though quiet, held an ominous tone. "It's not a sprain, but I'd advise you to remain off it for tonight." He slammed the car door, then slipped behind the wheel. When he finally looked at her, a remoteness had settled across his features.

Her eyes lingered on his lean, hard profile as he turned the car around for the descent. He remained stony-faced and taciturn throughout the bone-shaking trip down the mountainside. When they pulled up beside the trailer, he tried to help her without touching her, almost as if he were afraid of the contact. She jerked away and limped on her own into the room.

Later, Karin huddled on the narrow bed, scowling at a dust mote in the corner. Her ankle didn't hurt nearly as much as her bruised pride. She had appeared awkward and helpless in front of Rowan. And why in God's name had she prattled on about the scenery? Now here he was, towering silently over her, no doubt wishing she were six thousand miles away.

But she wasn't in California, she was here. And, as if she didn't have problems enough just working with the man, now this! Apologies came hard for her. She'd struggled against prejudice every step of the way in her career, and Rowan's silence made it even more difficult. She shifted uncomfortably, forcing her gaze upward. "I'm sorry I put you out this afternoon. I— I'm not usually so careless. In fact—"

"That was a damn fool thing to do," he bit out. "You could have been severely injured. Never mind putting me out. But, yes, you have done that as well. . . ." His words trailed off. Then, in a suddenly softer tone, he said, "I'll see that dinner's brought over to you."

Surprised, she could only stammer, "Thank you."

He avoided her gaze, finding a book on the desk of sudden interest. He picked it up, glanced at the title, then set it down.

"Tomorrow is Saturday," he said, focusing on a spot somewhere between her head and the wall. "The men will be going into the village in the afternoon. If you're up to it, I suppose you may come along. But I'll tell you, quite definitely, you're not going to find the place throbbing with excitement." He turned, one hand on the door.

"I don't think that's a problem, I—"

Still facing the door, he cut in. "Be ready to leave at half-past four."

He shut the door carefully, and she heard him clump down the steps. Well, that was a reluctant invitation, she decided as she limped to the shower. But then, it didn't really matter what the overbearing Mr. Marsden thought. As long as she did her job well, why *not* go into town and have some fun? She lingered in the shower, letting the spray of the water massage her aching shoulders. Afterward, she drew on her cozy flannel nightgown and returned to her room.

On her desk sat a covered plate on an oblong metal tray. Lifting the cover and setting it aside, Karin reached for a crispy fish fillet, not bothering to sit down. The first bite of food proved she wasn't hungry. After a few mouthfuls, she replaced the cover, leaving the rest of the fish and the chips untouched.

Marmalade meowed softly outside, and she opened the trailer door a crack for the cat to skitter within. "I bet *you* never get a harsh word from him." She snatched her hairbrush from the desktop, then sat on a corner of the bed, the cat stretched full-length against her thigh, and pulled the bristles through her thick hair.

Marsden might not be enchanted with the idea of her joining his crew in the village, but even he couldn't expect her to confine herself to a cramped trailer twenty-four hours a day. She gave the brush another tug, continuing until her arm ached, then curled up with the cat. Its warmth against her belly comforted her in a way she couldn't define.

She found herself once more thinking about Rowan, remembering the feel of his arms around her, the touch of his hand on her ankle. He might be gentle at times, she thought darkly, but he was still arrogant. What made him so cold and on guard? Was he afraid to show emotion? Afraid to appear vulnerable? What a combination of hard and soft! Karin rolled over, savoring the soft warmth of the cat nestled under the covers beside her. The cat adored him; his men obviously liked him. She imagined Marmalade tucked up against Rowan's lean, hard thigh. Strangely, she felt a stab of satisfaction that he had no wife.

* * *

"Watch your coat," Thorny cautioned. "Squeeze in a bit more. There's a girl." The thickset cook slid in beside Karin, who was already jammed against Derrick, and Cyril also seated in the back of the Range Rover.

"I'd not object to takin' your place now." Paddy turned from his seat in the front and winked at Thorny. "She smells a hell of a lot better than this bloody Englishman." He punctuated his sentence with a playful jab in Cyril's ribs.

"Keep your comments to yourself, you crazy Mick," Cyril chided. He cast a surreptitious glance at Karin.

"Karin stays where I can protect her from the likes of you both," Thorny interceded. "Isn't it enough I have to put up with your natterings during working hours? Since I've been around the longest," he murmured to Karin, "I'm something of a father figure to the lads."

She shifted her cramped legs into a more comfortable position, then smoothed her beige cords down over the soft camel boots. "Have you known the men here long?"

Thorny nodded, and his graying hair flopped across his lined forehead. "Most of us have worked together before. Except for Derrick. He's new. Rowan I've known since he was a nipper." He leaned toward her and spoke in a low voice only she could hear. "He has an eye for the ladies, but he doesn't get involved— doesn't let it interfere with his work." Thorny's gaze softened. "If it hadn't been for Rowan, I wouldn't be here." He glanced out the car window. "Shhh!" he cautioned. "He's coming straightaway. I won't go on except to say that with Rowan, you're working for the best. He'll move the earth for his crew."

Karin focused on the tall form striding toward the

car. Rowan's hands were shoved into the pockets of
fitted whipcord trousers; her gaze fell to the fabric
stretched tightly across his muscular thighs. He walked
with a sinewy grace, and a vivid picture rose before her
of his nude form in full stride, all taut flesh and rippling
muscle. Flushing, she let her gaze drop to her lap. She
had to stop fantasizing about the man. So he'd move
the earth for his men, would he? She fought the desire
to ask Thorny if Rowan's devotion extended to both
genders.

Rowan opened the car door, focusing on each of
them in turn. "It looks like everyone's aboard who's
going." In one fluid motion, he slid his lean frame
behind the wheel and shoved the car in gear.

"What about the others?" Karin asked.

Rowan addressed the road ahead. "We never leave
the site without having at least two men here to monitor the equipment and the security system. But if
you're concerned about fairness, last week I stayed
behind."

Dusk had fallen when they arrived in Cairnbeck.
One by one, overhead street lamps flickered on, illu-
minating the curving road. Small, rambling gritstone
cottages swept up the hillside beyond the distant village green and stood, sentinel-like, in rows. A news
agent stepped out of his corner shop and locked the
door. Ahead of them, a large woman in a navy blue
suit purposefully pedaled a rusty bicycle along the cobbled street toward a whitewashed, spired church.

Leonard came from a town like this, Karin thought. She
recognized similarities between the village architec-
ture and pictures he had shown her of his Yorkshire
home. He'd always wanted to come back, but he never
had. It was odd how her thoughts so easily drifted to

Leonard. But then, he'd been like a father to her over the years. She smiled as she gazed out at the passing scenery. Everywhere, the shop fronts and row houses glowed with the warm reddish hue of local sandstone. Leonard would love it.

Rowan skirted the small village green, then parked in front of the arched doorway of a narrow, rough-hewn stone building. A curtained window advertised a local brew; another sign proclaimed that Guinness stout was good for you.

"This is the place!" Thorny clambered out and offered a hand to Karin.

Paddy ambled off in the direction of the church. "See you lads later," he promised.

"Mass," Thorny whispered to Karin as they stepped inside. "He'll join us after he's attained a state of grace."

"And then he'll drink the bloody lot of you under the table," Cyril said, laughing. "Except for Rowan, that is."

"Oh?" She looked innocently at Rowan, tall and dark at her side. "Does he outdrink you all?"

Cyril guffawed.

Rowan gave her a black look. "Contrary to what you might think, I remain sober enough to drive the rest of you safely back to the site."

"Well! You're a regular Johnny on the spit, aren't you?" *Oh, Lord,* she thought, closing her eyes as she felt her face flame. "I mean spot."

An amused smile played at the corners of Rowan's mouth. "Nervous?" he asked.

"Of course not!" she snapped.

"Of course not," he echoed blandly. "Follow me." He turned and strode inside, toward a booth along the wall where he slid into a wooden-backed seat. Thorny and Derrick seated themselves across from him. Karin stood, hesitating, and looked from Rowan to Cyril.

"Sit down, dammit. I don't bite," Rowan muttered.

"You draw the line at barking, do you?" She threw him a wide-eyed look, then lowered herself onto the hard upholstered bench as Cyril, the fifth member, pulled over a nearby chair and sat himself at the head of the table. She shivered at the sudden narrowing of Rowan's eyes. A muscle worked along his jaw. She steeled herself, wondering if she alone was to be the target of his anger. Well, she could play the game, too, if that was what he wanted. Looking at him, however, she felt far more confused than confident. Besting Rowan Marsden was proving to be as difficult as maintaining her indifference. He was the most maddening man she'd ever encountered. And the most attractive.

At that instant, a dark-haired woman appeared. "Now wouldn't it be the lads from the fell." Her richly accented brogue made the words poetic.

"Maggie, luv." Cyril swept the woman into his arms and kissed her soundly on the cheek. "Meet Karin Williams."

Maggie eyed Karin with suspicion, her hands knitted together over an abundant bosom. Shiny black hair framed a pale face with enormous blue eyes.

Rowan's crisp voice cut through the silence. "Karin is one of our engineers, Maggie. We thought she'd like to see how a fine English pub operates."

"Aye," Maggie said slowly. "Then I'll have to be on me best behavior, won't I?" She caught Karin's eye and flashed a tentative smile. "Welcome to Sullivan's. But he's wrong, you know. This is no English pub. It's Irish I am."

"Like Paddy's pig—ow!" Cyril's anguished cry erupted as Maggie landed a blow on his shin. "Woman, you're vicious," he moaned. Gingerly he nursed his leg amid a chorus of chuckles. "It's not funny at all."

"And what might you be having tonight?" Maggie asked, ignoring the wounded Cyril.

"Bring us a round of the usual, Maggie," Rowan said. He turned to Karin. "What would you like?"

"Whatever's the usual," she answered amicably.

"Mackeson's." Rowan gave the order.

When the drinks came, Maggie joined them, sliding her generous girth in next to Karin. Inching toward the corner to make room, Karin became suddenly aware of Rowan's thigh, warm and firm against her own. A giddy heat shot through her. He settled against the back of the booth, making no effort to move away.

Karin concentrated on raising her glass in both hands and taking a tiny swallow. It tasted smooth and sweet. And potent. She took another sip and tried not to feel the excitement skating through her veins. He was far too close!

Cyril scooted his chair a few inches closer to Maggie. "Have you been in England long?" Maggie asked Karin.

Karin watched Cyril's blunt fingers as they moved possessively over Maggie's shoulder, then slipped down to her thick waist. "No, not too long. I arrived just a few days ago." She tried to edge away from the warmth radiating from Rowan's body, but she was hemmed in between Rowan and Maggie. She ran her tongue over suddenly dry lips.

"Ah, you're a Yank." Maggie's brogue broke through Karin's thoughts. "We won't hold it against you. Fact is, I've not been here long meself."

"Maggie owns the pub," Rowan said. He kept his eyes focused on Karin as he lifted his glass. The message in their silvery depths had nothing to do with pubs.

Karin took another sip.

"It's more than just a pub," Maggie said defensively.

Rowan's rich laugh made the hairs on the back of Karin's neck stiffen. "She's right," he offered. "The inn was once a courthouse. Men were tried here for sheep stealing. And hanged here for the same." He inclined his head toward the stair at the end of the room. "The cellar there was the gaol."

Maggie nodded toward the window and the shadowy hill outside that rose above the village. "They used to take them up there and hang them on a gibbet." Karin's startled look drew a grin from the older woman. "But that's not what I meant, about the inn. I mean," Maggie continued, "it's also a bed and breakfast. There are six rooms upstairs. In the summer, I'm fairly run off me feet with the tourists."

Karin turned toward Maggie. "I suppose you get a lot of hikers. There are signs in the village."

"Oh, lots of them. Holiday Fellowship also has a literature week, and then there's the rush-bearing ceremony—that's later in the month. And, of course, we have the village history itself."

Rowan shifted in the seat and looked down at Karin. "Cairnbeck is an old market town. Been here since the thirteenth century."

His warm breath fanned her hair. Her pulse hammered, and she edged forward to take another swallow from her glass. Her tongue darted out to flick the foamy stout from her lips. She felt Rowan's gaze follow the movement.

"But that's not all," Thorny broke in. "Tell her about the Roman baths."

"Hey, Maggie!" a voice called from the bar.

"Hold on there. I'm coming." Maggie rose. "It's been lovely chattin' with you. If I don't see you again tonight, do come back."

"Thank you, I will," Karin promised. She scooted into the space vacated by Maggie, uncomfortable under Rowan's scrutiny. He took a long pull from his glass, a frown of concentration deepening along his brow. He looked as if he were passing a judgment. One not in her favor. What could he be angry about now? She shifted her gaze to Thorny. "What about the Romans?"

Thorny smiled. "Rowan is our history expert. Tell her about the baths," he prodded his boss.

Rowan looked thoughtfully at Karin. "I doubt you'd be interested in a discourse on early settlements. Perhaps another time."

"Actually, I—"

"Uh, Karin? Would you care to try your hand at darts?" Derrick interrupted.

A scowl darkened Rowan's face.

"That sounds like fun." Karin's gaze followed the rigid set of Rowan's jaw. If the man wanted to be in a pique, then she'd damn well let him be!

"Here, use mine." Thorny shoved a polished wooden box across the table.

Karin followed Derrick across the room to a vacant dart board.

"Have you played before?"

"Not for real."

"What, then?"

"Oh, when I was a kid my father set up a board in

our garage. He and Leonard, my boss, used to play. I tried to learn a few times." She laughed. "It was hopeless."

Derrick opened the wooden case and selected a dart, then held it up. "This is the shaft, and this is the barrel." He moved his finger along the length. "The balance is very important." He pointed to the feathered end. "This is called the flight. Now, watch how I do it."

He positioned the barrel between his fingers and thumb, stepped up to a line drawn on the dark oak floor, and took aim. He released the dart with a snap of his elbow; it hit the target, just off-center. "Now, you try it."

Karin stepped forward and aimed as she had seen Derrick do. The metal tip flew out of her fingers and dug into the wooden support beam a foot above the circular board. "Uh-oh." She sighed.

"Try again," Derrick encouraged.

She stepped forward and eyed the target, shifting her stance several times.

"Ey, luvvie," a man's voice called out, "yer moves yer arm, not yer bum!" Laughter echoed.

Karin stiffened and flung the dart toward the bull's-eye. It glanced off the metal strip at the edge of the board and bounced to the floor. "Damn!" Impatiently, she selected a third dart and stepped forward to take aim.

"Not that way," Rowan's cool voice echoed behind her.

She startled and turned around, relief flooding her when she saw his smile.

"Like this." He stepped close to her and encircled her with his arms, clasping his tanned hand over hers. His warm, hard body fitted around hers and sent her pulse into overdrive. Unaccountably, she began to tremble.

"Hold the shaft lightly and release it when I tell you. Now, practice the motion."

Karin arced her hand back and forth, guided by his fingers over hers, his opposite hand cupping her shoulder. Concentration became more and more difficult as his musky scent swirled around her. Oh, why couldn't she keep her hand from shaking?

Rowan paused, frowning. "You *have* to throw with a steady hand."

She stiffened, unable to keep her mind on darts while her heart pounded. Slowly, he reached up and drew her arm back so that her body rested against his chest for a fraction of a second. Then he flicked his wrist lightly. "Now."

She opened her fingers. The shaft arced, and the point dug into the target.

"Double score ring! Not bad." He selected another dart. "Let's try it again."

Rowan's arms closed around her once more. She felt his chin rest on her hair. Her back warmed to the heat of his chest. She stared at the long fingers closed over hers. They were smooth, tapered and sensitive looking, with a light dusting of dark hair across the backs. She had never given a thought to a man's hands before, but Rowan's were decidedly . . . *What?* she wondered.

Exciting.

Abruptly, she wrenched her gaze away. She didn't want to find anything about him exciting. Her heartbeat increased to an irregular staccato, but she steeled herself to remain calm. The very fact that he was here with his arms around her rather than snapping out words in his usual brusque way made her even more unnerved.

"Relax," he breathed into her ear. "Move with me." The smell of his skin dizzied her senses as he rocked her back and forth against his lean body, urging her arm forward, then slowly drawing it back.

Suddenly Karin's hand flexed, and the dart clattered to the floor. Embarrassed, she swerved out of his embrace. "I—I think I've learned enough for tonight." She fled on unsteady legs to the safety of the booth and sank onto the bench.

"Are you all right?" Derrick asked.

"I'm fine," she lied. "I'm not used to heavy beer."

"What *are* you used to?" Rowan asked, sliding in quietly beside her.

"I don't drink much."

"Not even when you go out with your boyfriends?" he prodded. His cool gaze searched her face.

"I don't have any— What I do on my own time is my own business," she shot back. His eyes gleamed with interest and she stammered. "I usually have white wine or herb tea."

His gaze glinted with mocking humor. The silence lengthened. Finally, Karin scooped up her coat. "I'm going to walk for a bit."

"I could show you around," Derrick offered.

Instinctively, Karin glanced at Rowan. He looked up, with eyes that were suddenly cold and frowned. "I'd like that," she said to Derrick.

"Stay put," Rowan ordered Derrick. "I'll show her around."

SIX

They strode beneath an arch and Karin found herself propelled into a cobbled alley, past row houses with brightly painted doors and lace-curtained windows. Television sets flashed dancing patterns of light behind the gauzy barriers, flickering into small rooms already old before the onset of the century.

She was struck by the incongruity as they meandered down the narrow opening: Cairnbeck itself was an anachronism. The same might be said for her companion, she reflected as she walked beside the tall Englishman.

Rowan slowed his pace to hers. "Feeling better?"

"Yes," she admitted. A barn owl hooted in the distance. The night air washed over her, cool and calming. Coal smoke curled upward from a dozen chimneys. Faintly acrid, it stung her throat. "My head feels clearer."

As long as you keep your distance, a tiny voice inside her warned. Beyond the last house, the alley opened to a low stone wall overlooking a darkened meadow. Pinpoints of light glinted through the trees. Karin hesitated, unsure of her way over the uneven terrain. Rowan closed the gap between them and cupped her elbow, guiding her over the rough stones.

At the wall, he drew her into his arms and lifted her onto the flat surface. His hands lingered around her waist, warm against the patch of exposed skin where her sweater had hiked up. His fingers moved lightly over her flesh, and she edged fractionally away, only to find herself hauled back to rest against his chest. Heat radiated from his body to hers, and little by little she relaxed into its comfort. Her heartbeat steadied as she stared out into the blackness. Stars twinkled, then dimmed, tucked behind fast-moving clouds.

"There's no need to hide it, Karin," he said with deceptive calm. "It wasn't the stout, was it?"

The low cadence of his voice was a caress. She did her best to remain calm, but it was impossible when her pulse pounded in double time. She gazed into the black depths of the sky, her voice fading to a hushed stillness. "No."

This . . . awareness was something that had never before happened. She was exhilarated and at the same time puzzled by her body's physical response to him. Why *this* man? He'd scowled and glowered throughout the entire week, and yet she couldn't help admiring him. Liking him, even.

He leaned one hip against the wall, a dark form towering above her, remote and silent. A tremor shook her, and his grip tightened. Karin felt her resistance waver.

"Do I disturb you?" he asked at last.

His tone was like smooth, dark silk. His breath ruffled her hair, and she felt his lips at her temple. With uncharacteristic shyness she lowered her eyes. "Yes." Huskiness reduced the word to a whisper.

She swallowed as silence closed around her, pressing down like a crushing hand. He was a very sensual man. He shattered her ability to concentrate; he made her workdays a study in sheer determination, her nights an exercise in willpower.

For the first time she could remember, Karin was at a loss for words. Aware that she wasn't—had never been—"one of the guys," she had maintained an aura of reserve on the job. Co-workers had flirted casually, but she'd never taken time to begin a relationship; there was no room for romance in her busy life. Furthering her career had taken every bit of diligence she possessed, and none of the men she'd met had been remotely interesting enough to detour her pursuit.

But she'd never met anyone like Rowan before. He tested her resolve, made her feel things she'd never felt.

He eased his long legs over the wall and stood facing her. With a sweep of fingers, he tilted her chin upward. For a long moment his darkened gaze locked with hers, then he lowered his head, seeking her lips. What began as a brushing of mouths developed into passionate hunger as his lips moved urgently over hers. He splayed his fingers into her hair and cupped her head, drawing her closer.

She offered no resistance, moved fully into his embrace. This, *this* was what she wanted, what she longed for. His tongue teased against her lips and, when she granted access, dipped inside. She tasted him and wanted more.

A sigh whispered on the breeze. Hers. She wrapped both arms around his lean torso and pressed closer. Her nipples pebbled against him. A tingling started behind each sensitized tip and spiraled to her woman's center. No man had ever kissed her like this, made her feel such need. In answer she melded her tongue with his.

He pulled her forward, holding her so that she stretched along the hard length of his body. His arousal produced a shudder that ran deep into her belly. For the first time in her life, an unidentifiable feeling threatened to overwhelm her. Her knees turned to rubber. Oh, Lord, she thought. Let it go on.

When he finally lowered her to the ground, she tightened her arms around his waist. "Stay," she whispered.

"Karin. Oh, God."

He lowered his mouth to the hollow of her throat. His freshly washed hair skimmed her cheek, and she was vaguely aware of its tickle. He slid one long-fingered hand beneath her sweater and found the soft fullness of her breast. He stroked it to a peaked nub as she moaned against his jaw.

He groaned, then wrenched himself away. His eyes blazed. She sensed his internal struggle, and then in an instant, as if they'd been strolling on a tour of the town and had now reached the end, he resumed his earlier reserve.

"We'd best be getting back," he said in a voice thick with emotion. His eyes held hers, hooded and wary. His hand shook; he glanced at it for a fraction of a second and then thrust it in his pocket.

Karin staggered, her entire body aching from his touch. Good God! What was wrong? He had started it, and now he left her suspended, shaken. Did he suddenly remember his homily about not mixing business with pleasure?

The chill night air hit her like a slap in the face. Her skin cooled, mercifully slowing down her breathing.

She could not fathom his mercurial moods. He laid the ground rules, then promptly broke every one! She almost wept in exasperation. Well, so be it. If that was what he wanted, she could be as changeable as he.

Tossing her head, she struck out for the pub, two strides ahead of him. She'd show him just how unconcerned *she* could be.

At the site, Rowan pulled the car into the parking pad next to several tall aspens silhouetted against the pale silver moon. His hair brushed the collar of his jacket, partly concealing his face. He appeared composed, but when he turned to get out, Karin noted the fixed line of his jaw.

She shivered, partly in anticipation, partly in anxiety. The latter won, and she bolted out of the cramped Range Rover. If she was quick about it she could be in her room, safe in her bed, before any kind of encounter.

" 'Night, guys. Thanks for the ride." She trotted toward the trailer.

"Karin." Rowan's measured strides overtook her at the trailer step. "I want to talk with you."

Wary, she turned her gaze on him.

"Inside." He unlatched her door and stepped in after her.

She stood rigid, and fixed him with a stare. "So talk."

He frowned. His gaze traveled over her fitted trousers and upward to the slight curve of her breasts faintly visible beneath the loose, cream, knitted sweater. Finally, his eyes rested on her face. She flinched under his intense scrutiny. The silence hummed.

"I thought I made myself clear the other night."

"About what?" Her voice sounded tight.

"No fraternizing. I can't put it any plainer than that."

"For heaven's sake, Rowan. You're the one who's 'fraternizing,' as you put it."

His dark brows slanted downward, and the room seemed to grow colder by several degrees. "Was I? Then let me apologize. I assume you won't let it happen again."

"Me!" Karin challenged. "It was *you* who kissed—" She stopped suddenly. My God, half the evening she'd been trying to forget the feelings his embrace had evoked in her. He could not possibly have forgotten.

"That's different," Rowan said, giving the cosmetics jars neatly arranged on her desk a quick perusal.

"Different? How is it different?"

"I don't allow myself to become emotionally involved."

She ignored his unsteady voice, the hungry expression in his eyes. "You mean it's okay for you to kiss me because you're not emotionally involved, but it's not okay if I respond?"

With a rush, something Thorny had said hurtled back at her. *He has an eye for the ladies, but he doesn't get involved.* Well, if Rowan Marsden thought he could sit back and play games with her, he could think again. He'd been marching to the wrong drummer, and that was going to stop. Now.

She faced him, both hands rigid at her sides. "I'm adult enough to decide—" Suddenly she stopped, noticed that he'd somehow maneuvered her into a corner. She stood silent, unable to think, she was so angry.

He stepped forward and reached out, tilting her chin

so she could not escape his dark glare. "To decide what?" he asked in a silken voice. "Is it a lover you want?" His eyes glinted with barely concealed anger and something else . . . a predatory gleam. He loomed before her, a hunter stalking his prey. "Why not me? As long as you understand the ground rules—no attachments."

Her breath caught, and she stumbled backward against the desk. "You! I wouldn't choose you any more than I would—" Trembling, she stopped, her voice no more than a hoarse whisper. "The day I choose you is the day when—when pigs fly! Please leave my room!"

A deep, throaty laugh rippled through the air, and Rowan turned away from her, toward the connecting door. "We'll see, Karin. You might choose me yet." He stepped into the bathroom beyond. The panel door rumbled shut, and his muffled laughter faded.

She was still shaking when, a moment later, she heard the surge of the shower. The arrogance of the man was too much! In fifteen seconds, he'd reduced her from a professional engineer to a love-hungry female. "I'm just a body to him, not a person," she muttered, yanking her nightgown from a drawer in the desk and flinging it onto the bed. Sex only, that was what it boiled down to. Coupling bodies. No involvement. He had no right to speak to her like that. Who could have thought an English gentleman could be so uncivilized?

She closed her eyes. Underneath her anger she recognized a truth. She knew she had never, *never*, experienced a kiss like that. Even her knees had ached for him. What about him? Could he really have no feelings for her beyond simple gratification?

She pulled off her sweater and folded it on the bed, then unzipped her trousers. With a whoosh, they shimmied to the floor. She bent, retrieved them, and slid them onto a hanger. A thought struck her. Maybe Rowan didn't dislike women. Or her. Perhaps he disliked "liking" women.

Well, she could certainly remedy that. She could stay away from him. Or at least as far away from him as she could manage. In this situation, the job was more important than anything else.

The sound of the water ceased. The trailer vibrated as he stepped from the shower out onto the floor.

Karin drew the gown over her head, her mind made up. Keeping her thoughts on her work would be difficult with a naked, virile Rowan Marsden just one room away. But she would do just that. She could be a real ice maiden if she had to.

She snapped off the light.

Rowan turned off the shower and stood in the cramped stall a moment while the water sluiced off his body. Then he wrapped a fluffy white towel around his hips and stepped onto the cotton mat. What the bloody hell did he think he was doing? Wanting Karin Williams went against everything he'd sworn to avoid. Once he'd trusted women, believed in happily-ever-afters. But Claudia's betrayal had put paid to that account. The anguish he'd suffered at her hands had changed everything. He would never, ever, get close to a woman again.

He brushed his teeth and tried not to think about Karin—that mass of silky russet hair and the soft, inviting lips. Oh, hell, he might as well try not to breathe.

No doubting the feeling that had enveloped him. He had been shaken by that kiss as much as she. And, dammit, he hadn't wanted to be.

He slipped the towel off, wiped the moisture off the mirror, and tossed the damp towel into the hamper. Then he threw on his blue terry robe and strode into his room, jerking the bathroom door shut behind him.

He'd been without a woman too long. Perhaps he'd drive down to Blackpool at the weekend. Plenty of women there who'd be satisfied with dinner and a few drinks. A few kisses and no commitments.

He drove his fist onto the desk. A journey to Blackpool would solve nothing. Only Karin, with her quick intelligence and intuitive perception, could ease the ache inside him. And he'd be damned if he'd let that get started. He'd learned his lesson long ago.

Early Sunday morning, Karin hunched over her drafting board, scanning a page in her notebook. She yawned and reached for the cup of coffee that sat on the board's edge. She'd been on the job since before dawn, and her shoulders ached. But the preliminary layout was complete. Rowan should be pleased. With a sigh, she returned to her notebook.

The office door slammed against the side of the trailer, and Rowan filled the narrow opening. Startled, Karin snapped her book shut. The movement jostled the contents of her coffee mug onto the layout on her board. "Rats!" she muttered. One-handed, she groped for the box of tissues on her desk while raising a corner of the vellum to keep the pool of liquid from spreading.

"Allow me." Rowan thrust several sheets into her hand.

"Thanks." Carefully, she blotted all traces of the spill.

He peered over her shoulder at the drawing. "You wanted to see me?" His tone was detached, his eyes focused on the drafting board.

"Yes." She swiveled around to face him. "I've been thinking—"

"Mmm," he broke in. "You've left out the detail for the secondary supports."

"It's not needed. If you'll notice here"—she pointed to a sketch in the upper corner of the drawing—"I've designed one all-purpose support for each of the vertical beams and added horizontal bracing for the long sections."

"That's not the way I would do it."

She stiffened. "You're not designing this structure. *I* am. And I know what I'm doing. I've made calculations for each variance in elevation." She tapped a sheet of figures with her pencil. "It's all covered, right here."

She leaned back on the stool while he ran a practiced eye over her layout. He took the sheet she had completed and scanned the neat columns of numbers.

She focused on his straight dark brows, the deep cleft in his chin, the faint shadow of beard. He was good-looking to a fault, but constrained and cold. *Except for last night.*

Such a waste, she thought, shifting her gaze to his fingers as they moved slowly down each column. They were smooth and tanned, with neatly trimmed nails. Did those fingers touch other women as sensitively as they stroked the paper? As sensitively as he'd touched her? She rimmed her lower lip with the tip of her tongue. Was this maddening, mysterious man ever less than perfectly controlled?

He examined the drawing once again, then handed her the sheet of calculations. "I agree," he stated in a tone that held reluctant respect. "Your concept is competent, if unique."

"Thank you. But it's not my design I want to talk to you about." She took a deep breath. "I've decided to move to the village."

He shifted his attention to her with a startling directness, his eyebrows drawing inward. Instantly, she felt a tightness in her chest, felt her breath turn shallow. A lump lodged in her throat.

"*You've* decided?" he repeated. His gray eyes held hers. "And what mental perturbation caused this?"

She dragged in a lungful of air. "I'd like to stay at Maggie's. She has rooms available. Besides I need—"

"You're being rather shortsighted. I've no extra car available, and I damned well can't spare the time for someone to be ferrying you up and down the mountain merely on a whim."

"It isn't a whim," she stated, keeping her voice steady. "I'll do my fair share. I'll stay on the job as late as I'm needed."

"You jolly well will!" he exploded, bringing a fist into his palm with a thwack. "Just like the rest of us. Through the night if it's required, and it often is."

"You have no right to order me about."

"I have every right," he snapped. "This is my project."

The authority in his voice made her wince. Damn him! She was angry enough to crunch nails, but she managed to clamp her mouth shut. She could argue with him forever, she realized, and he would remain implacable. Losing her temper would only strengthen his resistance and damage Leonard's business relationship with Pickering. She turned away. For the thousandth time she regretted her decision to come to England.

Rowan placed a booted foot on the half-open lower drawer of the desk and watched her. Karin's eyes blazed, her lower lip thinned. She looked as if she were about to give him both barrels. But she didn't, he marveled. Once she knew he wasn't going to change his mind, she backed off. Her acquiescence pleased him. Underneath, Karin Williams might be a spitfire, but she was also sensible.

"Karin," he said with forced calm, "I can't permit you to leave the site. It's critical that we get this structure up before the autumn winds come." Again he bent toward the drawing. "If you don't like this type of working environment, why did you volunteer for the assignment?"

"I didn't volunteer," she muttered. "I was commandeered. Someone else was supposed to come."

His gaze slanted down and locked with hers. "Ah, yes. Geoff Ellis. Why didn't he?"

"His wife is terminally ill. He couldn't leave."

"Understandable. But what about you? Didn't you leave someone behind?"

"My mother," she said, in what he knew was a deliberate misunderstanding. "But she doesn't need me around all the time. She's quite capable."

He took a deep breath and asked the question that had niggled at him since she'd arrived on-site. "What about your boyfriend? Did he not object?"

She hesitated. "I don't see that my personal life has anything to do with this."

He picked up a pencil and examined it closely. "Your Mr. Dalkey thinks rather highly of you."

Karin brightened. "You've spoken to Leonard? When?"

"This morning. He said to tell you he's sending the specs you requested."

"Good. Then I won't have to hunt for duplicates here."

"He also said he's including your slippers." He stared again. "Is Dalkey a *close* friend?"

She glared. "You're out in left field. Leonard Dalkey is old enough to be my father. He's interested in my mother, if you must know, not me."

"He's English." Rowan stated matter-of-factly, surprised at his relief. What the hell difference did it make whether she was attached or not?

"Leonard left Yorkshire thirty years ago . . . in the sixties. . . ."

Her words faded as a dozen thoughts crowded into his mind. How could a woman who looked like Karin not be romantically involved with someone? She was beautiful, and not just on the outside, he acknowledged. When he wasn't baiting her, she answered his questions with freshness, humor and a candor he'd not expected. And she was damned bright as well as eager to please. Would she, he wondered, be equally eager to please in an intimate situation? Would she express her pleasure as directly as she expressed her opinions?

He drew himself up short. What the devil had they been discussing? He blocked his thoughts, straining to hear only her words.

". . . with the wave of aircraft designers," she finished.

"Ah, yes, the old de Havilland crew. A pity we lost

them. Some of England's top engineers.'' His thoughts corralled, he set the pencil back in the tray and turned to leave. At the door he stopped. "I have to make a trip to York tomorrow. If you've finished with the bill of materials, perhaps you'd like to meet the home office staff? You can look over the list of approved contractors while you're there and pick up anything personal you might need."

Karin turned solemn eyes on Rowan, wary at his sudden softening. He'd been so adamant about not fraternizing. And here he'd just invited her to accompany him to York. Maybe he regretted his decision not to let her stay in the village. "As a matter of fact, I *do* need some shampoo."

Now, why did I say that? she thought with a trace of irritation. *I could pick it up in the village.* Still, it would be nice to get away for a few hours. But with him? *Oh, what the hell! Even* he *can't keep me from buying shampoo.* She glanced once more at her notebook. "I should have this finished by noon."

"Fine. We'll leave after breakfast tomorrow. And Karin"—his tone held an unexpected warmth—"ordinarily we don't work a sixty-hour week. After the platform is under construction, you'll have some free time."

"What?"

"Free time. You've been working day and night. Even the most conscientious engineer needs some time off."

"Well . . . I *would* like to see the area before I leave."

"Fine. Tomorrow, then." He closed the door behind him.

Some free time, he'd said. She sighed, remembering all the plans she had made while still in California. Like

a ray of sunlight after a storm, her burden lifted. So
many things to do. First she'd visit the village, then drive
to the coast. She'd explore some of the Roman ruins,
spend a night fell-walking by moonlight, arrange for
her mother to visit. They could travel to the castles and
ruined abbeys in Yorkshire. She smiled. Athena would
have a field day taking photos for her paintings.

That night Karin dreamed of cool gray eyes and a
tall, lean body with dark chestnut hair. An owl hooted,
and she awoke in the blackness full of an intense longing for something she could not explain.

And in the morning, she wasn't sure free time was
such a good idea after all.

SEVEN

Despite the threat of rain, Rowan put the Jaguar's top down the next morning as they set out for the Pickering home office.

"I like to live dangerously," he said, a hint of challenge in his eye.

Karin glanced warily at him, retrieved a woven scarf from her handbag and loosely knotted it over the collar of her mackinaw. She settled into the leather passenger's seat while he fussed with the cover.

As they gathered speed on the motorway, the wind whipped her hair around her face.

"You're not frightened, are you?" Rowan's shouted words were nearly obliterated by the squeal of tires as he guided the roadster into an outside turn.

"Not at all!" she yelled back. A lie, she thought. The truth was she was petrified, but she'd never admit that to him. The fierce look on Rowan's face declared his love for speed and his expertise with the sleek vehicle.

Once she'd felt that way, too. A lifetime ago she had thrilled to the power of a high performance car—a thrill that ended suddenly and tragically the day her father was killed. The following week she'd sold the Jensen-Healey he'd given her for her birthday and settled for a sedate Volvo. Now, with Rowan behind the wheel, she hovered between terror and exhilaration as the powerful car sped toward York. The village was but a speck in the distance, and on the motorway to Penrith the telephone poles whipped by in a blur. Karin lowered herself in the seat and hung onto the door grip as the cold wind sluiced down the collar of her jacket.

Rowan introduced Karin to the office manager at Pickering's, a fussy little man who patiently trotted out the files she requested. Seated at a long table, she flipped through the papers until she located the documents she needed. She made copies, tucked them in her leather folder, and waited while Rowan went to search for the contractor list. After careful scrutiny, they agreed on three, which drew a measure of surprise from Karin. Each one had been her suggestion. For once, Rowan had listened to her.

"Are you satisfied with their work experience?" Rowan kept his eyes on the bid sheet and wrote in the last of the three selected companies. "If not, I can arrange for another list to be made up."

She stared at him. "Why ask me? I thought you wanted to make the final decision."

"I'm curious to see what types of choices you make, when you have a choice," he replied, his manner offhand.

"I believe my selections can stand up to any scrutiny you care to give them."

"Spoken with conviction," he said in a tone that left her wondering why he'd turned agreeable all of a sudden. He capped his pen and rose.

She gathered her things and followed him out. They headed back. Several miles outside York,

Rowan turned to her. "It's after two. I imagine you're hungry."

"Well . . . yes."

"We'll be stopping in Knaresborough shortly. My mother will have tea laid."

"Oh, I—I wouldn't want t-to trouble your mother," she stammered. Why in the world would he take her to see his mother? Karin ran her palms down her green woolen slacks. They were none too fashionable, a relic from her college days. Not exactly the proper garb for tea. But they were warm, and they fit her long-legged figure. Still, he might have told her before they set out.

She gave him a sidelong glance. "Are you sure? She might not appreciate unexpected guests."

"She won't mind. I'm afraid the stop is necessary. The bloody carburetor's malfunctioning, and I have tools there. It won't take long."

Karin sighed. Car trouble. She might have known. He wouldn't want to stop and introduce her to his mother for any other reason. She swallowed an odd sense of disappointment. "You do your own car repairs?" She risked a glance at his scrupulously clean fingernails.

His mouth curved into a smile. "Of course."

"I thought working on Jaguars was a specialized art."

He shrugged. "They're more complicated than some cars. But I rebuilt this one, so I know how to fix it."

"It's an older model, isn't it? A well-preserved one," she added, looking around the inside of the car. The wood trim was a rich walnut, the gauges and knobs polished to a patina.

"The last E-type roadster like this was manufactured more than nineteen years ago," he said, quiet pride in his voice. He pressed down firmly on the accelerator. The car hesitated, then roared up the next hill and crested the top. Suddenly a vista opened in front of them, and in the distance castle ruins rose out of the mist. In the foreground, a viaduct arched over a river that shone like beaten metal, and bright red and blue rowboats floated serenely on the water below. "How absolutely breathtaking!" she exclaimed.

"Yes, it is, rather, though I'm quite used to it. You can become a bit jaded to beauty when you're faced with it day after day."

Jaded? Was that how he regarded women? Did he tire of them and move on? Or did he . . . ? With a sigh, Karin turned her attention to the scenery. It didn't matter. She didn't figure in his life, nor he in hers.

"My mother would love this," she remarked dreamily. Rowan quirked a questioning eyebrow and she went on. "She paints. Cover art for publishers. Historical novels mostly. She's always looking for photos of castles or old manor houses."

"Possibly she would find my parents' home a worthy subject. It has all the right ingredients, including"—he raised his voice in a perfect Vincent Price imitation—"a sense of mystique." He swung the car onto a graveled drive, accelerated past a wrought-iron gate flanked by two enormous granite columns.

An avenue lined with beech trees stretched along the approach, their smooth gray-green trunks disappearing in a canopy of foliage. At the end of the drive sat a magnificent Gothic mansion, its turreted gables and brick chimney pots half-shrouded amidst the trees.

Karin gasped. *"This* is where you live?"

He shot a quick look at her face and chuckled. "My family have been here six hundred years, give or take a few. Not in the same house, mind you. This one's relatively modern, built in eighteen twenty-one. But the grounds have been in my family since the fourteenth century. There's even a chapel on the property. Miraculously, it survived the dissolution of the monasteries under Henry the Eighth."

He slowed as they approached the house. "Look, there's Mother now." He pointed across the sweep of impeccably manicured lawns.

A slender, silver-haired woman in a tweed skirt, silk blouse and sensible shoes, walked two black terriers fifty yards away. Rowan brought the car into the circular drive, then braked near the house entrance and climbed out.

The woman looked up at the sound of the car and waved. Straining at their leashes, the terriers barked their welcome. They raced for the car, pulling Rowan's mother into a trot behind them.

"Rowan," she exclaimed, her face alight. "Dear, it's wonderful to see you." She glanced toward Karin and stopped short, a mask of uncertainty replacing her warm expression. Her puzzled gaze darted to Rowan.

"Mother"—he pronounced the words carefully—"this is Karin Williams. She works for me." He swung long legs onto the gravel, stood and walked around the car to open Karin's door.

Karin found herself eye to eye with the older woman. She squared her shoulders and put on a brave smile. "How do you do, Mrs. Marsden."

"Why, you're an American! And much taller than Claudia. Oh, I—" She paused abruptly, frowning at her gaffe, then mustered a small smile. "How nice to meet you," she said politely before looking anxiously at her son. "You will be staying for tea?"

"Of course. If you could show Karin around a bit, I'll take the car to the garage."

Mrs. Marsden nodded and waved toward the polished granite steps. A large, pear-shaped diamond glittered on her finger. "Do come in, Miss Williams. I'll just ring for Mary."

Karin followed Mrs. Marsden into the beautifully appointed sitting room, done in shades of celadon and peach. A fire blazed in the marble fireplace; the rich gilt clock on the mantel chimed the hour. A tall, white-haired man sporting a tweed jacket and a thick, bushy mustache sat reading in a wing chair facing the fire.

"Arthur," Mrs. Marsden said. "This is Miss Williams. She's working at the installation."

Arthur Marsden gestured to the sofa. "Sit down, girl." He looked her over and gave a satisfied "Humph" as she settled on the cushions. "So you work for my son. Eh, what do you think of his little adventure?"

Karin groaned inwardly. It was certainly apparent where Rowan got his bluntness. Beneath dense white brows, Mr. Marsden's pale blue eyes probed hers. "Has Rowan given you any trouble?"

First Rowan's mother, now his father, too! Karin hesitated. "I'm . . . not sure I know what you mean."

"Is he working you too hard?" he asked gruffly.

"N-no," she stammered. "I like a challenge."

"Well, girl, don't let him bully you. He can be very demanding. In fact, decidedly obstinate at times."

"Like his father," Mrs. Marsden remonstrated gently.

"Humph." He turned to his wife, sitting opposite. "Where is that boy?"

"Here, Father." Rowan stepped into the sitting

room and held the door for the maid. "I'll take that, Mary." He set the tea tray on a serving trolley, then rolled it toward his mother.

"It wouldn't hurt to let the help do the jobs I pay them to do," his father growled. "Where were you just now?"

Rowan settled on the sofa beside Karin. "In the garage. Adjusting the carburetor."

"That damned automobile again! When will you get yourself a real car, not some antique you have to be tinkering with day and night?"

With a half-smile, Rowan bent toward Karin. "Father's idea of the right car is a good Daimler—though he doesn't drive one himself."

"Rowan, don't antagonize your father," Mrs. Marsden chided, her tone belied by the twinkle in her pale blue eyes. She handed each of them tea-filled cups, then offered a plate of tarts.

Karin smothered a grin.

The elder Marsden snorted, helping himself to a tea cake. "Drive? Why should I drive? That's why I employ Cassidy." He leaned forward. "Tell me, Miss Williams, what do you think of a son who has a comfortable life handed to him, yet insists on going off to work in the wilds?"

"Arthur!" Mrs. Marsden put a finger to her mouth.

Karin paused. She disliked being put on the spot, but liked even less the idea of not sticking up for what she believed. "For most people," she said carefully, "a life like this would be beyond their wildest expectations. But for others, Mr. Marsden—myself included—it takes creating something with your own hands to feel a sense of fulfillment. A purpose for being."

"Well! You're not one to mince words, are you, girl?"

For several seconds Karin heard nothing except the thudding of her own heart.

"I like that in a woman," Mr. Marsden boomed at last. He glanced smugly at his son. "Rowan, I think you've got a woman here who'll give you tit for tat."

Another tense silence. Rowan pretended not to have heard. He flipped through the pages of the *Country Life* magazine on the coffee table while Karin concentrated on her tea.

"Miss Williams," Mrs. Marsden asked, "might I ask where you are staying?"

Karin's heart leaped. "I—"

Rowan broke in smoothly, fastening his gaze on Karin. "Karin's quarters are . . . quite near mine, actually."

Karin choked on her sip of tea. "Well," she hastened to clarify, "not too near."

"Near enough," Rowan said, his voice silky.

Mrs. Marsden arched a delicate eyebrow and shot a look from Rowan to Karin.

Karin swallowed. "What I mean is—"

"What she means, Mother, is that Karin sleeps—"

"Soundly," Karin blurted.

"Just on the other side of the—"

"Camp." She groaned inwardly at the look on Rowan's face.

"That's nice," Mrs. Marsden murmured, seemingly reassured.

They conversed amicably for another half hour, both Marsdens expressing interest in Karin's work and her activities in California. Karin relaxed, enjoying their questions. Finally, Rowan rose.

"I'm sorry, Mother, but we must leave if we're to get back before dark."

The Marsdens walked them to the car. Heavy clouds had gathered overhead, and Karin noticed that Rowan had put the top up on the Jaguar.

Mrs. Marsden drew her aside. "Do come again," she urged.

"I will. If I'm in the area."

In the car, Rowan turned to her. "Sorry to have put you on the spot. My father can be a bit brash."

She leveled her gaze on his profile, calm in the August afternoon light. "He's just showing fatherly concern. He *was* referring to you, wasn't he? The one who doesn't want to have life handed to him?"

Rowan nodded. "Guilty as charged."

"Why?"

Abruptly he pulled into a turnout and stopped. Fishing through an assortment of cassettes, he selected one and shoved it into the tape player.

"You saw for yourself. What do they *do*? That life is just one dinner after another, one hunt after another. They're the moneyed gentry, acting out their lives apart from the real world." His mouth thinned. "My father never had to work. He inherited the estate from his father, and his father before him. Not one of them ever did a day's work in his life."

He hesitated. For a moment, his gaze assessed her. "That's the problem with this country. On the one hand you have the layabouts on the dole who think the government owes them a living. On the other hand you have the wealthy who don't need to work and spend their time in pleasurable pursuits without doing a damn bit of good for the country." His voice, though low, had a hard edge; his expression was tight with strain. "And you ask why I left? I want no part of that life."

Karin found herself agreeing. They were both individualists, it seemed, seeking—no, driven to find—their own fulfillment. And often, she acknowledged to herself, such a decision meant traveling a lonely path.

A silence fell, during which she kept her eyes on the road and considered his words. Finally, Rowan said thoughtfully, "Don't misunderstand. I love them both, and I love the estate, but I simply cannot be a bystander in life." He looked deep into her eyes and reached over and tucked a tendril of hair behind her ear. His fingers brushed lightly, intimately against her jaw.

She froze. His gesture seemed out of character, oddly tender. She felt off balance, confused. Perhaps it was those probing gray eyes that unsettled her, but a glance at Rowan suggested that he, too, was affected. With a rapid release of the clutch, he jerked the Jaguar back into the lane of traffic.

Karin dragged in a lungful of air, and clasped herself about the waist, letting her gaze fall on the blur of larches lining the motorway. Maybe coming with him had been a mistake.

"Did you mean what you said to my father?" he asked in a voice gone strangely soft. "Would you have given up a life like theirs?"

Karin closed her eyes, remembering why she had come to England, pushing aside thoughts of tall Englishmen with probing eyes and dangerous smiles. "Yes. My fulfillment comes from my work."

"Only from your work?"

She had no answer for his question. It was too private to discuss, this thing she had only recently discovered.

She was a good engineer. The praise she received from Leonard and her coworkers had always been the fuel that fired her. Her job had been everything. Not even Athena knew that she drove herself on the job because she felt adequate in that environment, accepted as a professional on her own merit. And, beyond that, she felt compelled to work because the other part of her life, the personal part, had never jelled somehow. "Yes," she finally answered. "From my work."

He raised an eyebrow in disbelief.

They drove in silence. Now and again, Karin let her gaze drift over to his straight profile. Finally, she voiced the question that had been at the back of her mind since their visit. "Who is Claudia?"

Rowan stared at the road ahead for several seconds before speaking. "Claudia was my wife," he said in a flat tone.

Her breath caught. "Do I remind your mother of her?"

A long moment passed. "You look something like her."

"I didn't know. . . . Is she dead?"

"No."

"You're divorced?"

He kept his face averted and said in a carefully neutral tone. "If you must know, she left me." His jaw muscle quivered. "Look. Could we drop this? I don't wish to discuss her." He gunned the car, eyes intent on the road.

Karin sat in tense silence, her heart thrumming. He didn't like women working with him, that she knew. Yet he was beginning to respect her, or at least her work. He'd said as much. And she looked like his ex-wife.

She forked her fingers through her hair. Was he still

in love with Claudia? Was that why he——? That would explain his attraction, and his anger and coldness. And why he hadn't wanted her there in the first place. Thoughtfully, Karin eased her tense muscles against the back of the contoured leather seat. Oh, Lordy, what a mess!

But did it explain that night at the pub playing darts? Or his kiss? Something told her *that* was something else again.

Rowan pushed another cassette into the tape player, and the throb of Stravinsky's *Firebird* filled the space between them. She closed her eyes and tried to think. She couldn't leave until the structure was completed. What did she do now?

She turned her face to the window and gazed at fields of black-faced sheep. If she could manage to last a few weeks more, the task would be done. She'd keep her promise to Leonard, and the firm's future, and her own, would be secure. She'd finish the job whether or not Rowan found her presence disturbing. His problems with women didn't enter into it.

And her difficulty with him couldn't matter, either. Karin squared her shoulders. She'd do it. She had to, no matter what.

She'd like to believe she was indifferent to him, but the prickly warm sensations that flooded her whenever she thought about him made that impossible. She felt her heart race when around him. Like now. Or when he touched her.

Well, okay, she wasn't indifferent. Rowan Marsden was the most dangerously seductive man she'd ever encountered. But from now on, she'd be all business.

EIGHT

From her bird's-eye view on the old wooden platform, Karin surveyed the progress of the auger as it bit into the earth's granite mantle. A still-warm sun slanted onto the sweating workmen through wisps of clouds dappling the late August sky. The din of the mechanized posthole digger rumbled through camp, its steady *thump, thump, thump* blurring the sounds of voices below.

Perspiration trickled onto Karin's cheek from beneath the yellow plastic hard hat she wore for protection. Absently, she wiped the dampness with the sleeve of her flannel shirt. Almost finished, and then she'd take a break. Her back and legs ached. She longed for a shower.

She checked her watch. When the lumber shipment arrived, the contract crew could begin setting forms for the vertical supports. She had fought hard with Rowan in favor of using the tubular support system. And she'd won. A sense of satisfaction surged inside her. She'd fought similar battles with opinionated engineers back home, but none as single-minded as Rowan. Nor as forceful, she acknowledged. He'd bowled her over when she'd presented her arguments; he had backed off and allowed her free rein on ordering supplies. Just the same, it angered her that, even in her field of expertise, he automatically questioned her judgment simply because she was a woman.

Since his trip to York nearly two weeks ago, Rowan had seemed far more agreeable. Good-natured, even. No, she wouldn't go that far. But certainly less imperious. He joked with the men as always, and was pointedly civil to her. On two occasions, a rare warmth had penetrated that hard surface. On one, he'd taken her side in a technical matter, and had actually revealed a fair-minded objectivity. Maybe he had a heart after all! If one just peeled away the layers, did a charming, possibly warm and caring, man lay beneath?

A man she could grow to love? Good lord, that would be a dangerous man in her chosen life. It was fortunate that he kept that part of himself hidden most of the time.

But more than once she had noticed him looking at her with studied interest, an expression in his eyes far more intriguing than courtesy. Was it preoccupation with her performance? Her resemblance to his ex-wife? Or . . . did a latent desire hide beneath his cool exterior? Whatever it was, it bothered her. She could not risk his thinking of her as a woman. She was an engineer. Period.

Nor, she once again reminded herself, did she want to think of him as a flesh-and-blood man.

When the auger shut down, only the constant drone of the generator broke the stillness. At that moment, the laden lumber truck clattered into view, and Karin gathered her papers and started down the steps.

Rowan and Thorny unloaded the cargo. Rowan's sweater, pushed up above his elbows, exposed heavily muscled forearms brown as the rawhide gloves he wore for protection against splinters. He leaned forward, stacking the two by fours into a neat pile, and Karin's eyes lingered on his broad shoulders and tapering waist. When he straightened and turned toward her, she jerked her gaze away. She refused to be caught ogling his backside.

He lifted his hard hat and wiped the beads of sweat with the back of one glove, his eyes twinkling.

Flushing, she scrawled her name across the bill of lading and handed it back to the driver.

At lunch, Rowan pulled his chair up beside Karin's. "Looks like they'll be pouring concrete next week."

"That's what I hoped," she said between mouthfuls. "If the rain holds off for a day or two while they're setting forms. Now I can relax a bit until they're ready."

He shook his head. "Uh-uh. Tomorrow we run a maintenance inspection of the antennas on the far ridge. They need to be examined for stability before the autumn storms make the road impassable. It shouldn't take long." He paused. "We'll be near some interesting Roman ruins. Thorny mentioned that you wanted to see them."

Karin studied her plate. "I do, but you needn't take the time to show me."

He shot her a whimsical half-smile. "You'll earn your visit. The antennas aren't easy to reach. We'll leave after breakfast." He shoved his chair back. "I'll ask Thorny to pack a lunch. Wear something serviceable." His gaze meandered slowly over her plaid shirt and denims. "Like that. And bring boots. It's a bit of a climb."

Karin watched his retreating figure. He hadn't asked her if she wanted to go along, just announced that she would. But at least he'd been friendly. That was some progress.

As the afternoon wore on, she found herself antici-
pating the outing more than she should.

Karin flopped down onto a grassy patch opposite
Rowan. "You weren't kidding. It's a long way up here."
Her gaze took in the narrow, steep trail they'd traveled
for the better part of an hour. "How often do you
check the antennas?"

Rowan glanced casually at the white reflectors
mounted on a ledge just below them. "Once a year.
But we have to start up the generators every month
or so to make sure they're operational, especially after
winter." He handed her a sandwich. "I don't know
what Thorny's concocted, but after our trek, I'm beyond caring." He took an enormous bite.

She lifted a corner of the bread. Sniffing the oily
filling, she wrinkled her nose. "Sardines?"

"Kippers. They're very nice," he mumbled, his
mouth full. She must have flashed him a dubious expression, judging by his huge smile.

"Don't eat them if you don't want to," he murmured and reached into the sack to produce an apple.

Karin shrugged it off. "No. Kippers are fine."

Rowan wolfed down the remains of his sandwich
and settled back against a flat rock. The sun cast bur-
nished highlights on his chestnut hair and intensified
the rich golden color of his face and hands as he
tented his fingers behind his head. He studied her.
"You're stronger than you look. I don't suppose secretly you're one of those body-builder females?"

Karin chuckled at the thought of herself slicked
down with oil, pectorals extended, preening in front

of full-length mirrors. "Afraid not. It comes from years of climbing."

Gray eyes flashed with interest. "On or off the job?"

She laughed. "Both. I hike in the hills near my house."

"Ummm. What made you take up engineering?" he asked, quietly shifting the conversation.

Karin studied a tiny black ant as it moved along a striated blade of grass. "My father and Leonard Dalkey were partners. I was good in math, and summers I used to work in their office as a draftsman."

Memories warmed her as sun shafted down on the smooth patch of green between them. Those days had been heady. She had reveled in her father's praise. She had never been the son he wanted, and eventually he'd realized that she could never be the china doll he had expected. If she had not wholly pleased him as a daughter, at least she had pleased him as an engineer. He'd said little, but the fact that he had turned some of the more difficult designs over to her had shown his satisfaction in her performance. But it wasn't the same as telling her he loved her, that she was important in his life.

Her independence became the driving force that sustained her.

She would never know if he had loved her for herself. One rainy night, a careless trucker had skidded across the median directly into oncoming traffic. The driver's side of the black Porsche had folded in on itself, killing her father instantly and paralyzing her mother.

Rowan's polite cough startled her. "You were telling me about your father. But if I've touched on a sore subject, I'm sorry."

Oh, Lord, where was she? Her brows knitted. "After

Dad died, Leonard encouraged me to stay in school and get my degree. He was a big help.''

"In your job?" Rowan asked casually.

Her head snapped up. "Absolutely not! I earned that on my own merit. I've worked hard for everything I've achieved. Harder than most engineers.'' She forced herself to take another bite of the pungent sandwich.

"Why was that?" His tone was wary. She'd definitely pressed one of his buttons. But, she realized, that was one of her buttons, too. Why did she have to treat such things as a challenge? Why couldn't she just let it go?

"So it wouldn't look like I was handed the job because of my father," she said in as calm a voice as she could manage.

His mouth twitched with amusement, and he raised a hand in surrender. "Just asking." He reached for their lunch bag and shoved it into his rucksack, then withdrew a Thermos of coffee. He unscrewed the top and poured the fragrant dark liquid into it. Curling one large hand around the sturdy plastic, he handed it to Karin.

Their fingers brushed, and she hesitated. A force like an electric current arced between them.

A probing query lit his eyes as their gazes locked. He reached for her hand and pressed the cup into it, his face impassive. She managed a quick nod, took a few self-conscious swallows from the cup and handed it back to him.

Still watching her, he drained the cup and capped the Thermos. "Would you like to see an eagle's nest?"

She flashed him a smile. "Yes! I've never seen one before."

Fifteen minutes later they stood on an enormous

granite outcropping. He pulled off his heavy sweater and stuffed it into the rucksack. As he balanced on a ledge slightly above her, she stared at the ripple of muscle across his back, visible beneath the close-fitted black turtleneck. Her gaze lowered to the faded denims stretched tight across his buttocks. He was lean and fit—quite compelling, if you liked that sort of thing. Which, she realized with surprise, she did.

"Look. There!" Rowan pointed in the direction from which they'd come.

Karin stared hard at the top of the high, rocky crag. "I don't see any—" She stopped midsentence as Rowan stepped up behind her and rotated her toward the east. He pointed again.

Aware of his long fingers curled around her shoulders, Karin felt her pulse hammer. Suddenly an eagle glided into view. The sun changed the hackles on its back into gold, silhouetted the slender, gold-tipped wings. The bird caught a surging downdraft and rode it into the valley below.

"I see it!" she cried. She turned her focus away from the warmth of his body and onto the beauty of the magnificent bird.

It reminded her of Rowan. He was an eagle—bold, predatory, elusive. What was it he hunted? she wondered. And why did he hide away in this remote location?

"People think you have to walk miles to see a golden eagle. But not if you know where to look." His whispered words fanned her cheek.

In spite of herself, she leaned back into the muscled hardness of his large frame and closed her eyes. She heard his sharp intake of breath, felt the momentary tremor of his hand. He released her slowly and stepped back.

She caught her lower lip between her teeth and dusted off her jeans lest he see her face. Her arm felt chilled where his had lain.

For a long moment he stared at the horizon. "Ready to leave?" His voice sounded forced.

An hour later, they drove into Cairnbeck. Rowan parked the Range Rover in front of a quaint shop on the edge of town. A varnished red sign over the door read, "Pennyworth's Antiques." Its bow-fronted window sported an unusual display of pottery and artifacts, harnesses and well-worn boots, their wooden soles shod with curving strips of iron. Rowan reached in the backseat for a green canvas tote.

"I'll just drop this off. Come in, if you wish."

Once again he was the consummate professional, evidently unmoved by what had happened back on the ledge. He was an enigma. She shrugged and followed him through a weathered oak door.

On one side of the room stood a refectory table, its top covered by a jumble of jugs, ornaments and bottles. A pile of polished wooden, metal-tipped objects, shaped like miniature boats, tumbled in disorder at one end. Karin picked one up and ran her fingers over its smooth surface.

"Old shuttles from the mills." A wizened shopkeeper came forward, his slight frame bent. "They carried the weft across the looms. All plastic nowadays, of course." The little man's eyes gleamed as he adjusted his round pince-nez glasses. "And what have you for me today, Mr. Marsden?"

Karin stifled a laugh. The shopkeeper stood rubbing his hands together in anticipation. Rowan emp-

tied the tote onto the counter and carefully un-
wrapped several pieces of crockery.

"I gathered this lot near Ravenglass," he said.
"Mostly from the old cottages." He held up part of a
bridle, the leather rotting away from its silver hardware. "This is older . . . Spanish, no doubt. Notice the
spade bit, and the etching."

"Oh my, my," purred the shopkeeper, his eyes dancing. "Our usual arrangement?"

Rowan nodded. "Get me a date for the bridle. From
the design, I'd guess late eighteenth century." He
looked hard at the shopkeeper. "And see that you
keep it for the museum." He folded the tote and
shoved it into his jacket pocket. "I have no interest in
the other items."

"As you wish, Mr. Marsden. I'll have an appraisal
done for you this week. You'll receive your usual fifty
percent on the rest." He began wrapping the items.

"I'll stop by next time I'm in the village." Rowan
glanced at Karin. "Shall we look at the ruins?"

Once out of the village, Rowan headed west, toward
the sea. Karin pondered Rowan's exchange with the
shopkeeper.

"Something bothering you?"

Her eyes met his. "Shouldn't the things you found
be turned over to a historical society or something?"

"They were abandoned. Only the bridle is of value.
The crockery's only twenty or thirty years old." His
tone was dismissive, his eyes focused on the road.

"But . . . you're taking money for it. Surely you
don't need funds?"

He let out a thin laugh. "Of course I don't need
the money. My arrangement with Pennyworth is that

I *give* the pieces to him to sell. Half of what he receives, my half, is turned over to the Cairnbeck Mill Society."

She fell silent.

"You really don't understand, do you?"

She flinched at his tone. "What you choose to do with your findings is entirely up to you."

Quick anger blazed in his eyes, and he muttered an oath. "That's a cheap shot. The Mill Society is putting together an historic village . . . of bygone days when the linen mills operated here." He exhaled harshly. "Not that you care, but several of us have funded their venture. My findings are from my rambles in the areas near here, and I see no reason why the pieces I find can't be used for the living museum."

Heat rushed to her face. So his reason had been altruistic after all. She should have known. "Sorry. I thought—"

"You didn't think!" he bit out. "You're quick to pass judgment. You need to accept some things based on the person's credibility before jumping to a conclusion."

She swiveled toward him. "Isn't that what you did with me? Isn't that like locking the barn door after the fire is out?"

"Horse," he offered. "You mean horse."

"I do not!" she insisted. "I mean fire." She hesitated. "Isn't it fire?"

Rowan's mouth curved into a barely suppressed smile. "Not in the barn, surely. Someplace else, possibly, but not in the barn!" His smile deepened into laughter.

Karin stared at the road ahead, her face flaming. What was it about the man that got her so tongue-tied? Mixing her metaphors was not something she normally did. But she wasn't behaving normally at all. If she were, she'd never have agreed to accompany him. In fact, she hadn't felt normal since her first night in England, the night she'd met Rowan. He'd never laid a hand on her since that night at the pub. But just now on the ledge, she knew he wanted her. Moisture pooled between her thighs. For a long moment she sat, squeezing her knees together. She stole a glance at his rugged profile, usually so shuttered, but now relaxed, his eyes merry. What kind of woman could ever have left him?

Rowan suddenly slowed the car. "Look! To your right." Out of the mist, a ruined wall rose before them, lime-whitened but mostly intact. Rowan braked at a turnout and turned off the engine. "Care to inspect it?"

Enthralled, Karin stared at the ruined wall in the expanse of field. Old things held a certain fascination for her. "Oh, yes."

They strolled along a well-trodden dirt path to the ruin. Rocks jutted up in the surrounding field, partially obscured by lush, thick-bladed grass. Clumps of tiny blue harebells and purple knapweed massed along the verge, fluttering in the breeze as smokelike mist swirled down from higher crags. It was like another world.

Lower, beyond the first wall, several wall fragments arched against a staggeringly beautiful backdrop of ascending slopes. In silence, Karin watched the fog roll in, listening for some sign of habitation. All she heard was the low whine of the wind. She closed her eyes and imagined ghostly Roman legions marching over the fells.

Rowan's voice behind her was soft. "The solitude

isn't confined to the fell-tops. This is only a few miles from the village, yet it's a place where you could think the world had passed you by."

She shivered at the timbre of his voice, wishing suddenly that time would indeed pass them by, that this moment might last forever.

"Peaceful though it seems, don't forget that the winds here can quickly build to gale force. And coupled with the rain . . ." His voice trailed off into an odd silence, broken only by the low moan of the wind.

"Don't ever come up here without an escort."

Karin flinched at his voice, suddenly hard and demanding. "I wonder how the Romans adapted to the wind and cold?"

Rowan paused, scraping at a toadstool with the toe of his boot. "They didn't. Roman administration was always economical of its own manpower. Those who held Britain in the conqueror's name were more likely to have come from the Celtic West than from the Mediterranean."

"Did they build forts? Or castles?"

"Forts, yes. But many sites of early Roman occupation were successively used and abandoned." He laughed. "We like to think we've a rather complete picture of Britain through the first five centuries, but most of it's just conjecture."

"Thorny's right, you *do* know a lot about the area, and its history." A chill rippled over her as she took in his words.

Rowan directed her attention to a rectangular wall, sunken below the surface of the buildings, and they tramped down to get a closer look. "That's the remains of a Roman bath." He drew a line across a wall with his finger. "Notice here. A plaster surviving more than two thousand years of Cumbrian weather is something modern technology might care to take a look at." He turned, facing her. His eyes glinted in the golden afternoon light.

Her thoughts sped light-years away from archaeological exploration. *I wonder what it would be like . . . a Roman bath,* she thought. *I wonder what it would be like if he touched me . . . if he undressed me, made love to me here. . . .*

She brushed a stray lock of hair behind one ear, aware of how her fingers shook. Did he notice? "Seems odd for an aeronautical engineer to be so interested in antiquities," she murmured in a voice not quite her own.

He gave her a long, considering look. "Perhaps. Before I decided on flight mechanics, I planned to specialize in geology. I still do a lot of exploration. This part of the country is fascinating—every aspect of natural geologic occurrence since the Ice Age is here to discover." He motioned toward the ruin. "There are some stairs beyond this wall that lead to a lower level. The decoration is impressive."

She imitated his huge stride, placing her feet where he had stepped in case of crumbling rock. The cavern below was deep. Dangerous. Not a place to visit at dusk, or alone. She shivered, and drew the collar of her jacket high on her neck.

"Cold?"

"A little."

"We'll leave soon. Have a look here." He turned her toward the wall, at the same time slipping his jacket around them both.

His clean, musky scent enveloped her. Her heart flip-flopped in her chest. He pulled her closer against his lean body, and his warmth penetrated through her clothing. They stood unmoving for several moments, the only sound his ragged breathing.

Karin's pulse raced. I want him! she thought. A languor spread over her. Her feet and body seemed rooted to the earth, robbing her of movement. She longed to slip her arm around his waist and lean her head against his shoulder.

Three weeks ago she'd thought she'd be happy if Rowan accepted her as a co-worker, an equal. Then, after meeting his parents, she wanted to get to know Rowan as a person. She'd hoped the two of them, like Thorny and Derrick and the other men on the crew, could become friends. Just friends, nothing more, she had told herself.

Now she knew she wanted more.

NINE

Hesitant, Karin laid a hand on his arm. "Rowan." She gave him an uncertain smile. "Could we start over again? Could we be friends?" It had to start from there.

He burst into harsh laughter, then sobered. "No, Karin," he said thickly, "we cannot be 'friends.'"

He took her face between splayed fingers. Before she could react, he roughly slanted his mouth down on hers. His lips moved over hers as he hauled her hips against him. His loins pressed against her belly. His arousal filled the space between them, and a frenzied longing whipped through her. She knew she should resist, but her body refused to obey. She trembled, the strength ebbing from her limbs. Her lips parted.

Instantly, he thrust her away from him.

Her eyes flew open. He towered over her, his own eyes dilated. "I didn't mean for that to happen," he rasped. He balled one hand into the other, the knuckles whitening. "Let's get back."

Turning on his heel, he took the stone steps two at a time and stalked toward the car.

Karin felt as if a bucket of ice water had been dumped over her. What was wrong? Her pulse pounded as she scrambled after him over the rough stones. In her haste, she missed the top step, and the edge bit into her shin. She righted herself and hurried on, despite the dull throb in her leg.

She slipped into the seat and made a pretense of fastening the shoulder harness while Rowan slotted the key in the ignition. Her face burned. Unwilling for him to see her shaken state, she kept her face averted.

Why had he kissed her so urgently and then stopped so abruptly? Was it because they worked together? What did he want? she thought angrily. Was there something wrong with her? She forced her gaze on the road ahead and sat in stony silence.

He did not speak until they had driven some miles. "If you're concerned about what happened back there," he said in an even voice, keeping his eyes on the road, "you needn't be. It won't be repeated."

"Am I supposed to feel relief?" she challenged.

His head jerked toward her. "What the hell kind of remark is that?"

"It takes two to percolate," she snapped, suddenly aware that her words could be misconstrued.

"Why, Miss Williams," he drawled, "I'm flattered."

"Don't be," she snapped.

He shot her a glance. "You admit to enjoying my . . . er . . . advances?"

"That's not what I meant!"

"Yes? Do go on." One corner of his mouth turned into a lopsided grin. The campsite flashed into view. Rowan stopped the Range Rover a few feet from the trailers, took his time pocketing the key and then settled back against the door, eyeing her with casual amusement. "Dare I assume that my previous offer meets with your favor?"

"Your— What offer?!" she exclaimed.

"Surely you don't have so many lovers that you've

forgotten?" His lips curved into a smile, but his eyes were deadly serious.

Heat flooded her face. She remembered his words.

"If it's a lover you want, why not me?" he repeated.

God, he even had the nerve to say it again! And in that same supercilious tone. Her blood boiled.

"Oh, go to hell!" She tore off the seat belt, flung the door open, and stormed over to the trailer without a backward glance. She knew without looking that he was still sitting in the vehicle.

Cyril rounded the doorway into the office as Karin sat at her desk. "Call for you," he said. "From the States."

Leonard. She'd been expecting his call.

All week she'd been pointedly ignored by Rowan except when he'd come by to check her work. Even then, their conversation had been strained. Well, she could play the game his way, if she had to. She hadn't overestimated her ability to cope. Not at all. What she had done was underestimate Rowan.

A flush of warmth stole through her. She shrugged out of her sweater as she picked up the receiver on her desk. "Hello," she said, hastily brushing a hand through her hair.

"Karin." Leonard's voice boomed above the static on the line. "Everything going okay?"

She paused. That depended on what he meant by 'everything.' "The contract crew is ready to pour concrete tomorrow if it doesn't rain. We're down twelve feet. The ground is stable. So far everything is going as planned."

Everything except her relationship with Rowan.

"How are you getting on with Marsden?" Leonard

asked as if reading her thoughts. "He giving you any trouble?"

Interesting choice of words, "trouble," she thought. If he only knew. "Well, ah, he lets me handle the work myself."

"That's what he told me. Seems you've convinced him you know what you're doing. But"—Leonard hesitated—"are you having any personal problems with him? Marsden seemed reluctant to discuss your position there."

"Well," Karin admitted, "Rowan's a very private person. And he's not too friendly."

Leonard sighed. "I was hoping that wouldn't be the case. Never mind," he said, "relief is in sight."

Karin stared at the telephone. "What do you mean?"

"Geoff's wife passed away two weeks ago."

The line crackled in the silence. "I'm sending him over to help you. He needs to get his mind on something else. Be a good girl and look out for him, will you?"

Leonard had dropped a bombshell. Geoff Ellis had been one of the most condescending of Dalkey's male engineers. She sank onto the desk chair. He was not too admirable an engineer himself, and besides, he was a bit of a drunk. Now, shattered by his wife's death, Geoff could be a basket case, which, she reasoned, was why Leonard had decided to send him.

She wanted Geoff on the job about as much as she wanted a case of cholera. How the devil was she going to tell that to Leonard? Karin closed her eyes and took a deep breath. "Have you told Rowan that Geoff's coming?"

"He thinks it's an excellent idea. Says he can use the extra hand."

Damn Rowan! Why should he suddenly think she

needed help? She was managing just fine, and she certainly didn't need a heckler like Geoff Ellis around. Ever since he'd come to Dalkey, Geoff had ingratiated himself with Leonard, working behind the scenes to undermine her position. She could barely stand the man, and now she was supposed to look out for him? If she didn't look out for herself, Geoff would have her job. And, given the present state of their relationship, Rowan would be only too happy to give it to him and get rid of her.

"When is he coming?" she asked at last.

"In a few days. I'll let you know. Karin," Leonard said quietly. "Your cooperation means a great deal to me. Now, someone is here who'd like to tell you some wonderful news."

The line crackled again.

"Karin, darling?" Athena's voice caressed the air waves. "Leonard tells me you're doing splendidly. I knew you would." She talked on about her work until Karin interrupted.

"Leonard said you had some news."

"I do. *We* do." Athena's laughter pealed over the line. "Leonard finally convinced me that we'd have a much better arrangement if we were together full-time. We're going to be married."

Married! Leonard and Athena married? Karin sagged in disbelief. Could her mother really be happy giving up her independence? Athena had always been so outspoken about retaining her freedom. And though she truly adored Leonard, and Karin knew he loved her mother, she wondered what had happened to make Athena change her mind.

Athena's voice broke into her thoughts. "Karin?"

"Yes, Mom?"

"Aren't you going to congratulate us?" There was a hint of reproach in the lovely voice.

"Oh, sorry, Mom," she amended hastily. "Yes, of course I'm pleased for you. And I know that Leonard is delighted."

Athena laughed. "He says he almost gave up. I'm glad he didn't," she murmured.

"Me, too, Mom," Karin echoed. Her sentiment sounded hollow. Had her mother noticed?

Long after she rang off, Karin pondered her mother's words. Evidently, independence had its drawbacks, too. That was something new to think about.

But hadn't she been feeling the same thing about her own life? That independence wasn't all there was to life.

And all because of Rowan. He was the cause of her frustration.

Oh, damn. Everything seemed to happen at once. Just when she was convinced Rowan was the most untouched man on earth, he cranked up the charm and had her hormones playing tag. She knew he was attracted to her, but he blew hot and cold. When she was dizzy with need, he held her at arm's length. And now, after she had the project going to Rowan's satisfaction, he welcomed Geoff's arrival. Nothing made any sense.

She stared at her drawing board. Suddenly she couldn't sit still a moment longer. She marched to the trailer door and gazed out at the barren fell. She needed a walk. A long walk.

In her trailer, she pulled on an extra pair of socks and shoved her feet into her green kangaroo boots, lacing them securely. She snatched a commando sweater from the bathroom shelf and drew it on over her turtleneck. It had belonged to her father and, though worn, it was warm. She hugged herself, felt the prickle of the coarse wool on her fingers. How she wished they had shared the closeness she had with Leonard. Leonard had a lot of love to give. Athena's decision to marry Leonard would have pleased her dad.

On the trailer steps, she ran headlong into Rowan. He frowned and looked at his watch. "Where are you going?"

"For a walk."

"It's a little early, isn't it?" His eyes narrowed. "Exactly where do you plan to walk?"

She gave an expansive wave of her hand. "Out there."

"On the fells?" His voice rose sharply. "Not bloody likely! I told you before, it's not safe." He shifted his stance and faced her. "I have to go down to the village. We'll talk when I return."

Without further explanation, he turned on his heel and disappeared into the trees.

"Oh, no we won't, Mr. Marsden." Karin sniffed at his retreating back. "I don't need you to tell me where I can walk. Or anything else, for that matter!" She slammed the door of the trailer and stalked toward the office.

Seething, she stood at the step and focused on the ascending cloud of dust as Rowan gunned the red Jaguar down the road to the village. Did he actually believe she would obey him? Stay in the trailer like an obedient child while he wandered off at will?

Like hell she would! She'd had enough of this infuriating man.

Her gaze followed the Jaguar until it disappeared; then she started off for the ridge. She needed a good, long walk.

TEN

Karin strode purposefully along the path until she knew she was out of sight. Only after she'd gone another twenty minutes or so did she pause to look around.

She found herself on a narrow path not twenty yards from an embankment. Brooding gritstone cliffs dropped sharply away on one side; to her left, a chasm gaped between the ridge and Great Gable Mountain beyond. Gaunt peaks rose ahead of her, blue-violet in the filtered afternoon light. A gentle breeze blew wisps of cloud around her, which, just as quickly, wafted away.

She trudged on, climbing upward where the path narrowed and rose above a crag-circled tarn, the ground barren. The water's mirrored surface reflected the naked wall of granite that jutted toward the heavens. It looked like a pock-marked moon crater, eerily dark where clouds shadowed it; then turning silver, reaching for dark thunderheads. Awestruck, Karin slowed for a better look.

She marched on. It was easier now as she descended into another valley. Here, spongy moss covered the path and wet grass lapped at her boots. Golden larches and wild mountain ash, conspicuous with its red berries, dotted the hillside. Somewhere below her the faint burble of a stream broke the stillness. She began to relax as her leg muscles started to burn. Just a little farther; then she would turn back toward the camp.

The path forked. Off to her right an area of flat rocks beckoned, and she headed in that direction. She slumped down on one rock and set her back against another. Breathing hard, she laid her head on her knees to rest. Thoughts swirled in her mind, thoughts she could no longer banish by walking. Too many questions demanded answers.

She cupped both hands over her ears, and listened to an inner voice. Why was Rowan so prickly at times? What had she done to make him so changeable? Tomorrow she'd demand an apology. And she'd talk to him about Geoff. She was the structural engineer on this project. Geoff Ellis could work as her assistant.

Athena, however, was another matter. Karin sighed. Now her mother was marrying Leonard. Perhaps her mother was independent and *also* lonely? Still, Karin had to admit Leonard was good for Athena. He didn't coddle her the way her father had. Leonard simply supplied strength when Athena needed it. Strange she hadn't thought until now that her mother might want more than independence.

She plucked a blade of grass and nibbled on it. There were a lot of things she hadn't thought about until lately. Was *she* lonely? She had never thought so before coming to England, and during the first few weeks of work at the camp she had been too busy to give it much consideration. Proving herself to Rowan had demanded all of her time.

But now, shut up in that tiny trailer room with nothing to do but read and think, she was growing restless. True, work-related things were satisfying. But poring

over a technical brief wasn't very warming on a winter
night. And there was no lazy afterglow when you finished. Had she filled her life with only equations and
books? Work, she realized with sudden clarity, was a
cold lover.

Maybe she was hungry for something else. Maybe
she was hungry for . . . Good Lord, was it possible?
Could she be lonely for a man? For Rowan? The breath
whooshed out of her, and she sat motionless, staring
at the grass.

Fate played cruel tricks, all right. After years of being alone, successful now on her own, she'd found a
man she could lose herself over, and he had to be the
world's biggest chauvinist. Rowan acted at times as if
he didn't even like her! And yet, she could tell he
wanted her.

And, dammit, she wanted *him*. She wanted him a
lot.

She had never been so completely mesmerized by
anyone before. Rowan was charming with his suave
manners, and compelling with his strength of character. She loved his passionate declaration about needing to be engaged in challenging work. His ideas
matched her own.

Fat lot of good it did! For reasons he kept to himself,
Rowan evidently did not act on his feelings. That this
left her off balance was another problem; one she'd
deal with tomorrow.

Karin settled her spine more comfortably against
the rock, leaned her head back, and closed her eyes.
She took a deep, cleansing breath. A few moments
more, and then she'd have to start back.

* * *

Karin lifted her head uneasily. A gray, murky darkness crept around her; the wind hissed and whined through the swaying trees. She rubbed her eyes and looked around. How long had she slept? Her sweater and jeans were sodden with drizzle. She was freezing.

The clouds opened, and rain splashed down.

She bolted from her seat, threaded her way between the trees toward the path. It was barely visible in the sheeting downpour.

Branches slapped her face. A sharp twig raked her cheek. A gust of howling wind brought rain lashing down her neck and under her sweater, pelting her hair into her face, blinding her.

Karin squinted through the rain. It was growing darker by the minute, and she had no idea where she was. Worse, no one knew she had left camp. She had to get to shelter or she'd freeze.

Panic lent her a spurt of energy. She began to run, fell headlong over a tree limb blocking the path. Pain jolted through her shoulder.

Choking on a sob, she tried to swipe dirty leaves and mud off her jeans, then checked for cuts and sprains. A dizzying ache spread from her crown down to her forehead, and her shoulder throbbed.

Head down, Karin staggered to her feet. She jogged determinedly in the direction of the camp as the rain, carried by gale-force winds, whipped into her face. She slowed to a walk, checked by the tree limbs falling in her path.

Her head ached as though a sledgehammer had split it open, and she tasted a saltiness on her lip—blood. A bolt of lightning lit the sky, splitting a dead tree in her path. She recoiled as the old wood thumped onto the ground ahead of her. After a moment, she trudged around it, then stopped again.

The embankment should be on her right, but it wasn't. There was no embankment. She'd been walking on the wrong path. Oh, Lord, she was lost!

Her soaked sweater dragged at her shoulders. Suddenly fear slashed through her. She was cold—colder than she'd ever been in her life. Her body shook. She couldn't survive a night on the fells in weather like this. Even if the men had known where she'd gone, they could never find her in the dark. She had to do something, but what?

Oh, God, why had she been so headstrong? The fells were for experienced walkers, not tourists. She knew nothing of the vagaries of Lakeland storms where the wind quickly built to gale force. Rowan had been right. *Don't be without escort.* He had known what could happen.

The sky lit up with another bolt of lightning. Still no sign of the embankment. Oh, where *was* she?

Just ahead on her left, a large outcropping of rocks jutted. She lurched toward it and steadied herself with outstretched hands against the wall. Groping her way slowly along the rock face, she came to an opening. Instinctively, she ducked into the sheltering gap.

A cave! Another bolt of lightning flashed, and in the brilliance, she glanced around. She had stumbled into a cavern, its walls and floor irregularly chiseled gray-green slabs of what looked like slate. At least it was dry.

Outside, the thunder reverberated, and the wind-driven water lashed against the rocks. Karin's head pounded with every pulse, and she felt the rise of a stinging weal where the branch had raked her cheek.

But more than anything, she was desperately cold. The chill penetrated her jeans and sweater, numbed her legs. She shook so violently she could barely stand. Exhausted, she sank down onto the icy slate and curled into a ball, resting her head on one bent arm. She might not sleep, but at least she would be protected from the rain. Thank God for the cave; it was probably a cavern from an old slate quarry.

She thought again of Rowan. When she did manage to get back, he would be furious. He had accused her before of acting on impulse, and that was exactly what she'd done. Well, it was too late now. She would just have to wait out the storm. She curled up tighter. In spite of the cold, she said a small prayer and fell asleep.

"Kaar-in?" A voice echoed from somewhere in the darkness.

Karin's eyelids snapped open. Someone was out there. She strained to hear. In the distance, a thin light flashed. Again the voice called. "Kaar-in!"

Rowan. Thank God! She could hear his voice nearby. She struggled to her feet and stumbled on stiff legs toward the cave opening.

The pale gleam of a flashlight slashed a ribbon of light on trees in the valley below. The rain had stopped; she heard only the sound of water drops slopping onto the ground, then the squelch of leaves as footsteps tramped beneath the outcropping.

"Here," she croaked. "I'm up here."

The light beamed upward.

Rowan scrambled up the steep incline to the mouth of the cave, ducking his head under his arms to protect himself as rocks tumbled down the mountainside. Karin swayed forward.

"Karin!" Rowan reached out and pulled her against him. His strong hands clenched her shoulders while he murmured her name. Suddenly he thrust her away from him and shone the light in her face. "Where in hell have you been?" he thundered! His eyes narrowed to angry slits.

Then he focused on her cut face. "Karin! My God, what happened? Are you hurt?" He pushed the sodden hair off her forehead, and began running his hands over her face and body, searching for injuries.

At the touch of his fingers, the starch went out of her. She collapsed against his chest, sobs wrenching her body.

Rowan lifted her in his arms and carried her toward the back of the cave. He set her down gently and rocked her against his chest, holding her while he smoothed large hands over her damp, matted hair.

When the flow of tears subsided, her teeth began to chatter. "I'm all right," she answered. "I fell, but I'm not hurt. I'm just awfully c-c-cold."

"You're soaked through!"

Abruptly she felt her sweater being stripped from her body, his hands then fumbling with the buttons of her flannel shirt. Finally, in desperation, he tugged hard and the buttons sprayed across the floor of the cave. Tossing the shirt aside, his fingers groped for the fastening of her damp bra.

"In front. It opens in the front."

His warm hands moved over her body, skimming the soft curves of her breasts, grazing them while he worked the hook loose. The tissue-thin garment parted, and the straps slipped from her shoulders. She was dimly aware of his hands touching her sensitive skin.

He drew away, and seconds later tugged his anorak over her head. A comforting cocoon of warmth enveloped her. His scent, permeating the fleecy garment, made her head spin.

"Put your arms through," he whispered, holding the sleeves out. Listlessly she obeyed, then snuggled against the secure warmth of his chest and closed her eyes. She kept her face pressed to his chest, the coarse wool of his sweater scratchy against her bare flesh where the anorak was pulled up.

She began to tremble, and his hands encircled her, touching her bare skin. She heard the sharp intake of breath and felt him tense. The heat from his fingers seared her flesh.

A wave of feeling, like tiny fingers of fire, migrated from her flesh to a spot deep within her. In an instant, a flood of longing suffused her.

Karin grasped his arm. Splaying her hand over his much larger one, she drew his fingers to her midriff. He groaned and slid it up under the anorak to cup one small breast. His other hand followed.

Needles of desire rippled through her. She wanted to feel his hands on her body, needed to belong to him, if only for this moment. She wanted . . . Her thoughts tumbled, and she burrowed closer.

"Karin." He spoke her name in a throaty voice. His lips skimmed her forehead. He pulled his hand away from her flesh and grasped her shoulders, dragging her closer. "Have you any idea what you're doing?"

She raised her head, arching her neck upward. Her lips grazed his jaw. The tender skin of her mouth scraped across rough stubble. She drew in a ragged breath and moaned.

He hesitated a moment, then sought her mouth, capturing her lips beneath his in a kiss that seemed endless.

Karin floated, mindless of the cold and damp, heated by the desire that flamed between them. His mouth moved over hers in a sensual, bruising litany. His hands caressed her skin, sliding again to her breasts. With a wild surge of longing, she wove her hands under his sweater. Hesitantly, she skimmed the mat of hair on his chest.

His fingers found a nipple and began stroking it. Her throat constricted. The nipple puckered, and a tightening sensation radiated from the erect tip straight to the core of her being. She licked her kiss-swollen lips as a warm, delicious heat flowed through her.

"I want you, Karin," Rowan whispered, his voice husky against her cheek. "I want you." He moved his mouth back to hers. "And I'm going to have you, make no doubt of it." He rimmed her lips with his tongue, then dipped it into her mouth.

She felt a spiral of heat flame in her belly. A current of desire surged through her chest, her limbs. Her heart pounded, and she arched mindlessly against him. She wanted him. She needed to feel him beside her, inside her!

He drew back. Tilting up her chin, he said hoarsely, "Not here. Taking you here would be a reaction of the moment. When I make love to you, it will be in a comfortable bed, where we can both fully appreciate each other."

A cold wind penetrated her mind. He wanted her,

but not here. Not now. His measured, sensible words swept the fog from her brain. Not here, but in a bed.

She glanced around, remembering where they were, the foolish thing she'd done. She'd got herself lost, then had thrown herself at him in a cave, of all places.

Heat flushed her face, and she moved out of his arms. "Leave me alone, Rowan. I can manage myself."

"We both know that's a lie." He laughed, a short, tense outburst.

Karin rose from the cave floor. Thank God he couldn't see her face. She *did* want him. But if she never learned another thing, she would learn not to let it control her. Oh, God, if only she could tell her body that.

"Can you walk?" he asked, after a pause.

"I can walk," she muttered.

"Then shall we start down? I've the entire crew out after you. No sense wasting their time." He shone the light on the floor, picked up her wet clothing and stuffed it into his pack.

He'd sent the men out looking for her? On a night like this? She'd apologize to them later. But no way would she admit her error to Rowan. Not with his I-told-you-so attitude.

Rowan pulled her up and cradled her shoulder, steering her toward the cave entrance. When they stepped outside, Karin edged away. He dropped his hand and they began to walk in silence, Karin following him down the narrow path.

A mile outside the camp they met Derrick and Cyril.

"Hoo!" yelled the latter. "You've found her. Thank God." They clustered around Karin, interrupting each other with their questions.

"Derrick," Rowan broke in harshly. "Have you the Very pistol?"

"Yes."

"Well, dammit, fire it!" Rowan demanded. "Tell them we've found her. We've wasted enough time."

Karin heard the pop and watched the blue-white flare arc skyward. "Come on, then," Rowan growled. "Let's go meet the others."

The four headed down toward the trailers. Soon Thorny, Paddy and Robin joined them. "Jaysus," muttered Paddy. "We'd about given up."

Thorny clapped a comforting hand on her shoulder when they reached camp. "I'll bring something to warm you."

"Back to your posts, lads," Rowan commanded quietly as the men clustered around Karin. He turned his attention back to Karin, his expression grim. "Now, may I suggest that you get yourself inside?"

She met his sharp look with a stubborn tilt to her chin.

After a curt "Good night," he strode away.

Karin sank onto the bed, too weary to move to the shower. A tap on her door broke the stillness. She did not bother to look up. "Come in."

Thorny poked his head inside. "I thought you might be needing some nourishment. I've heated some broth." He lifted the plastic cover from the tray. "Here's a treacle pudding for dessert. And," he added, eyes twinkling as he pulled a flask from his apron, "a tot of brandy to cheer you."

Karin smiled at the cook's perception. "The cheering I could use, but I'm not sure brandy's the answer."

Thorny lowered his ample frame onto the bed beside her. "Don't let Rowan get you down, missy. He means well. Sometimes he gets short, but it's just his way of hiding his concern."

"I— It was my fault. I shouldn't have gone out alone without telling anyone. We argued, and he ordered me to stay here." She turned away. "I was angry."

"I know, lass. I know more than you think." Thorny smiled and gave her shoulder another pat. "You had our man really worried. Thought he'd keelhaul the lot of us when he'd heard you'd gone out on the fells by yourself."

Karin looked into Thorny's blue eyes, crinkled at the corners, and saw both concern for her and respect for Rowan written in them.

"You told me once that if it hadn't been for Rowan, you wouldn't be here," she said.

"That's true."

"Why? What did you mean by that?"

Thorny fingered his graying hair. "I'll tell you while you have your broth."

Karin set the cover beside her and began to spoon the warm liquid into her mouth.

"I worked as cook for the Marsdens while I was goin' to school . . . studyin' engineering at the local technical college," Thorny stated somberly. "Rowan was just a young lad at the time—used to hang around, watch me cook, come up to my room while I did my studies. Lonely little fellow, needed a friend. We became regular pals, he and I." He brushed wiry hair out of his eyes. "After I sat my exams and left, we didn't see much of each other. Then we lost touch altogether. About eight years ago he found me, but this time the shoe was on the other foot. I needed him—in the worst way."

He shuffled his boot against the floor. "I lost my wife and son in a boating accident. One day we were a happy family, the next, they were gone. Without a trace. The Royal National Lifeboat Institute never did recover the bodies." Thorny's voice shook. "Only a spar from the *Mary Anne*—that's all they found. . . ." His voice trailed off, and he stared at the floor.

Karin swallowed, unwilling to disturb him as he relived the moment. Her heart constricted.

He went on in a subdued tone. ". . . couldn't seem to concentrate on anything after that. I moved from job to job—drank heavily—even drifted into drugs. After a while, nobody would hire me. I came desperately close to ending it. Then Rowan offered me work here with him." He focused on her, held out trembling hands. "I'm no longer an engineer, but I'm a damn good cook. And, thanks to Rowan, I have my self-respect again. God bless him." His voice broke.

So he'd been rescued by Rowan, too, Karin thought. That explained why Thorny knew so much about him. No wonder the two were close. She was glad Thorny had confided in her. Somehow it made Rowan's harsh remarks more understandable. She laid a hand over his. "Oh, Thorny. I'm sorry."

"Nothing to be sorry about." He stood up. "Have a hot shower and a brandy. Do you a world of good." He peered at her face. "I'll see that you get some dressing for that cut."

Karin rose, clasped her arms around his stocky frame and pressed a kiss on his rough cheek. "Thanks for being here."

The door snapped open and Rowan's tall form appeared. "Am I interrupting anything?" His voice held a dangerous edge.

"Only thanks from the prettiest engineer you're likely to see," Thorny said, giving Karin a swift smile. He gathered up her tray and clattered down the steps.

"What was that all about?" Rowan growled when the door closed.

She met his penetrating gaze and sighed. He assumed so much. "Something that doesn't concern you."

"No, I suppose it doesn't," he answered, "unless you plan to add Thorny to your list of conquests."

"Skip the accusations," she said, her voice crisp.

"Then don't provoke them. Now, get yourself off to the shower. I've brought dressing and salve for your face."

"Leave it on the desk. I'll deal with it later."

"I'll stay."

She shrugged. "You're the boss." She slipped through the connecting door and stripped off her jeans and Rowan's anorak, then stepped into the shower. The spray of hot water warmed her instantly, stinging where the branch had gouged her face. She shampooed her hair, then let hot water run through it to rinse. Uneasy at the thought of facing Rowan again, she lingered. No doubt he was livid, now that she was safely off the fell. Oh, well. She was beyond caring. She dried herself and pulled a flannel gown over her head, then opened the door to her room.

"You look like hell." He spoke matter-of-factly, his examination a searching, penetrating assessment strangely at variance with the anger he'd exhibited earlier. He thrust a tumbler in her hand. "Drink that." He poured one for himself and took a long swallow.

She settled on the bed while he tore a strip of gauze from a roll. He tipped her head toward the light, brushing the hair away from her cheek. "This might smart," he muttered. He upended a bottle of rubbing alcohol onto the wadded gauze and laid it on her cheek. It burned like fire, and she gasped. Somehow she sensed he was enjoying her discomfort.

He smeared salve on another strip and placed it on top of the cut, then secured the ends with adhesive. "Now, let's tuck you up."

She hesitated. "I can manage, thanks."

Impatiently, he yanked back the bedcover. With a sigh, she wriggled underneath. "I don't want to go to sleep just yet." She sat up and struggled with the pillow, and he pulled it away and propped it behind her back.

"Do you want a book?" He stepped to the bookshelf.

"No. I . . . I . . ." Her voice trailed off. He looked as imposing as a five-star general.

"What, then?" He moved toward the desk, turned around again and faced her.

"I want to talk."

He said nothing but kept his eyes focused on her face. She read several emotions in his steady appraisal. He must be furious with her for leaving the camp on her own. The silvery flecks in his irises stood out like icy shards in a sea of stormy gray. She knew that a part of him wanted to leave, wanted to get away from her, but the gaze he leveled at her also said he found her desirable. A warmth pulsed through her that had nothing to do with the brandy.

She plunged on. "I don't understand you."

He paused momentarily, and his dark brows rose. "Is that a requirement?"

She ignored his sarcasm. "Yes. It is for me."

He turned the desk chair around and straddled it,

his arms rested across the back. "What do you want to know?"

"What's bothering you?" She saw his eyes grow dangerously dark. She hastily added, "Is it me? Or is there something about the way I do my job?"

"Aren't you being oversensitive?" he interjected, contemplating her with a critical squint.

"No! I'm talking about my job, my performance." She was rambling, deliberately avoiding the real issue—why he was so changeable. And he knew it, too. She took a deep breath and hesitated, weighing her words. "And about—"

He leaned forward. "There's nothing at all wrong with your 'performance.' Why would you assume there was? Aren't you aware that I've given you almost complete responsibility for construction of the platform?"

"Yes, but that's not what I meant." She lowered her gaze to the comforter, then let herself be pulled back to the seduction in his silver-flecked eyes. "I meant to ask you—"

"What are you *really* hunting for, Karin? What is it you're curious to know?"

"I—I'd like to know why you don't like me," she blurted out. "Why you didn't—"

His expression turned from anger to amused appraisal. Hot-faced, she sought to amend her words. "If it's because I look like your ex-wife—"

"You're nothing like Claudia," he said quietly. "Nothing at all."

She stared up at him, and as casually as she could manage, she asked, "Are you sorry I'm not?"

"Lord, no!"

Relief flooded her. Thank God for that, she

thought. But still there was something very wrong. He was too tense. "Was she an engineer?" she persisted.

He shook his head. "She was a rich man's daughter. Her father owned a string of woolen mills from the Pennines to the border. I was twenty-one and had been out of school a few years—had a few seasons at the hunt. . . ." He flashed an oblique smile that never reached his eyes. "I played polo when I met Claudia Preston. She was nineteen. We married two months later." Pain sounded in his voice.

Rowan's mouth hardened. "Once the initial attraction was over, I discovered there was nothing else. We had nothing in common. Claudia liked spending money on expensive clothes and jewelry, going to parties. I hated that. We drifted apart when I decided to do something constructive with my life."

He drained his glass, then stared thoughtfully at it, turning it in his fingers. "I finished my degrees. I bought the Jaguar and rebuilt it." He laughed harshly. "She refused to ride in it. By that time, we were barely speaking to each other. I was twenty-three when I enrolled at university. While I studied, she partied. Sometimes she hadn't gotten home by the time I left for classes the next morning." He set the glass down on the desk, poured it full again and took a swallow.

"I warned her, but it never mattered. She kept on partying, kept a string of lies ready to satisfy my curiosity as to why she was gone all the time, why she could never make time for me—for us. Finally, one day she left. Not a word, nothing. Later I learned that she'd been sleeping with most of my friends. I'd been the laughingstock of the campus. The cuckold of cuckolds." He stared into space as the minutes ticked by.

Karin squeezed her lower lip between her teeth. "Rowan, I'm sorry."

"Don't be," he said shortly. "I'm thirty-eight. It happened a long time ago, when I foolishly entrusted my heart—" He rose abruptly, and set the chair aside. "I, however, am not going to make the same mistake twice."

He clumped through the connecting door, turned and murmured, "That, however, has nothing to do with our enjoyment of each other." He slid the door closed.

Karin squeezed her hands into fists. For a long moment she stared at the closed door. Rowan wanted her. Possibly as much as she wanted him. She could not, however, use sex to assuage his body hunger—or hers. For her, sex had to be based on feelings. Respect. Trust. She sighed, and switched off the bedside lamp.

She stared into the blackness. Going to bed meant more to her than just physical release. How she wished it did for him, too!

Rowan closed the book he was reading and snapped off the light. The clock on his desk read midnight. He was bone tired, but sleep eluded him. Long after Karin's even breathing told him she slept, he tossed, wide-eyed and tense. A moment ago he checked on her, and she was curled up with the cat. He winced at her still form. The weal on her head ought to resemble an egg by tomorrow.

He'd never been as frightened as when he'd returned from the village to find her gone. The little fool! Despite his warning she'd gone out anyway. Thank Christ, she was safe.

He thought again of their earlier conversation.
Odd, how he'd been able to talk of Claudia without
rancor. If he were honest, he'd assume the lion's
share of the blame for the breakup of their marriage.
Claudia had never pretended to be anything other
than a wealthy, utterly spoiled young woman. Only
he'd been too besotted at the time to see it. Or perhaps he'd hoped marriage would change her. It
hadn't, and he'd let his anger speak out in bitter
accusations. He'd hated the parties she thrived on,
but he'd been the one to withdraw. She'd salved her
ego with shopping sprees and more parties. And
men.

He was surprised Karin had understood that part,
the pain. He'd seen real compassion in her eyes. It
brought a warmth to his heart he thought he'd lost
forever; in a small way it helped ease the hunger.

But Karin Williams wanted too much from him. And
if he were honest with himself, he knew he had nothing left to give.

ELEVEN

Karin lingered at the long trestle table after breakfast, reluctant to leave the dry, cozy mess trailer with its tantalizing smell of fresh-baked scones. Derrick, Cyril and the others had long since stomped out of the dining room to go to work, and Thorny clattered back and forth into the kitchen, arms laden with dirty dishes. She yawned and swallowed the last of her lukewarm tea.

For the past fourteen days straight she had worked late into the night to complete her revisions to Rowan's satisfaction without delaying the workmen. It had been difficult. Her mind had churned as she strained to focus her thoughts, and often she found herself staring off into space.

Now, she watched as the leaden sky outside the window emptied itself with the kind of sullen, persistent rain that promised a sea of mud. Thorny set a steaming mug of fresh tea in front of her, grabbed his own and took a seat opposite.

"How's the project going? Rowan tells me you're nearly finished installing the load-carrying supports." His eyes shone with interest.

"Yes." She was mentally jolted into the present. "I'm ready to have the contractor put up the cross braces.

Then we can start laying the decking." She glanced at her watch and sighed. "I'd better get a move on before Rowan sees me enjoying myself."

Thorny spooned sugar into his tea. "He's not here. Went to Manchester early this morning to pick up someone, a chap from your California office."

Her heart plummeted. "Geoff Ellis?" She took a scalding mouthful of the tea and grimaced. Damn. She sucked in a mouthful of cold air. Tomorrow her tongue would be sore.

Karin frowned. No one had told her Geoff was arriving today. In fact, lately, Rowan had communicated very little with her. Since the night of the storm, he had avoided her except for those brief occasions when he'd stopped by the engineering trailer to oversee her progress. Even though they shared a trailer, she rarely knew whether he was in his room or not.

Except last night.

Past midnight, Karin had awakened to Marmalade's scratching at her door. The inquisitive bundle of orange fur might be Rowan's, but since her arrival, the cat had firmly ensconced itself in her bedroom.

Karin crawled from the warmth of her comforter, tiptoed to the door and opened it just wide enough for the cat to squeeze past. She latched it as quietly as she could.

With a muffled thump, Marmalade landed on the bed and settled in the center. Karin smiled, scooted the compact orange body to one side, and slid between the warm flannel sheets.

"It's damn well time you showed up," Rowan's gravelly voice thundered through the partition.

Karin bolted upright. "What on earth are you talking about?" she called. "I've been right here all night. In fact, I was asleep until—"

"Where were you?"

What on earth was he talking about? She lowered both feet to the floor just as the bathroom door shot open. Karin's retort froze on her lips.

Bared to his waist, he lounged against the jamb, his tall form backlit, his chest gleaming in the trail of light. Swirls of dark hair matted his pectorals and tapered provocatively into black silk pajamas. His eyes glittered oddly.

Karin forced a smile. "Derrick and I played chess until nine." She glanced at the clock on the desk. "I've been here ever since."

Rowan pierced her with a brittle glare. "Don't play innocent with me, Karin. It won't wash." He lunged forward, knocking into the chair, which clattered to the floor at his feet.

Karin had never seen him like this. He was compelling, and a little frightening. She made a dash for the door.

He snaked a hand forward, halting her flight. "You're not going anywhere. Not tonight." He rocked backward, pulling her with him.

Her breasts pressed against the hard wall of his chest. Her breath whooshed out, and for a long, delicious moment she let herself rest against him. His heated flesh scorched her skin. He smelled of scotch.

She stood, paralyzed, then took a quick step backward. "You've been drinking."

"Of course," he rasped. "I intended to get drunk."

"That's not very intelligent."

He muttered something she couldn't make out, then lunged for her and fell facedown on the floor of her room, missing the corner of the desk by inches. Karin knelt beside him, raised his head up. "Rowan, can you hear me?"

"Perfectly," he mumbled.

"Rowan, for God's sake, get up."

He rose to a sitting position, then swayed onto his feet. "Put your arm around my shoulder," she commanded. They staggered toward his room. Halfway to the doorway, he stumbled. His arm tightened around her shoulder, warm fingers moving on her flesh. She looked down. Merciful God, her nightgown was unbuttoned to the waist! She jerked it closed.

They inched along until they reached his bed, and Rowan lowered himself onto the mattress. She drew the comforter over him and was starting to leave when his arms curled around her.

"Karin? Karin, don't go. Don't . . ." He muttered something she couldn't understand.

She pulled against his grip, but he held her fast.

"Rowan, let me go, now. Please." Rowan turned his head, brushing a peaked nipple with his mouth.

"I want you," he groaned against the soft areola. Liquid fire surged through her. She was helpless, burning. Suddenly she wanted him to go on, to ease the ache deep inside her.

She turned toward him.

He lay still, his breath whispering against her bare skin, his tongue wet and seeking on her flesh. Her breasts throbbed. She knew he wanted her. And she wanted him, yearned for him to go on, to touch her. Everywhere. *Don't stop,* she wanted to scream. *Don't stop.*

But he did.

As if by magic, he sobered, rolled to one side and rose up onto one elbow. He looked up at her through eyes dark with emotion.

Fear and some unnamed feeling struggled with the desire in his expression. She sensed his withdrawal before he spoke.

"Karin," he said huskily. "Go back to bed. Now."

Her heart shriveled. "But—" She gasped. She fought her churning emotions.

There was a note of pleading in his voice. "I've had a bit to drink, Karin. Some scotch, with Thorny, and later, here in my room. Much more than I should have had. Don't stay. . . . It's not. . . ." He turned away, the sentence unfinished.

"Not what?"

He groaned. "Not right. Not yet. I want to be cold sober when we make love."

Trembling, she leaned toward him for a moment, an ache deep in her belly. He knows how I feel, she thought. He knows I want him. The next time . . . Oh, God, what would she do the next time?

She drew away and switched off the light to avoid his eyes.

From the doorway, she looked back at the bed where he lay, one arm flung over his head, his breathing deep and ragged. Karin's heart thumped uncomfortably, loud in the darkness. She found her own bed and curled up small under the covers. Eventually, she had achieved a small nest of warmth, but sleep did not come.

Now, Karin took another careful sip of tea. "Thorny, did Rowan say when he was coming back?"

"Late this afternoon," the cook replied. "He said he's left instructions in the office. If you need some help—"

"No," she said, rising, "I have everything under control." *Everything except how I'm going to deal with Mr. Know-It-All Ellis,* she thought.

"Thanks for the tea, Thorny." She gathered her

dishes and carried them to the sink, then stepped thoughtfully down the stairs and walked toward the office.

On her drafting board she found a note in Rowan's thick scrawl. He would meet Ellis in Manchester this morning and had arranged for him to double up in one of the other trailers. Which part of the project did she want to turn over to Geoff?

A dull flush of anger stole over her. Great! Not which part would Geoff help her with, but which part would she hand over to him?

She flipped through the files in her desk drawer, grabbed the ones for the calculations on the main platform, and slapped them onto the gray surface of the desk. She'd give Geoff that. At least she had done all the stress work. "He can hardly screw up my design," she muttered.

She hesitated. Could she be blowing this out of proportion? After all, Geoff hadn't actually done anything wrong at Dalkey and Williams. But he hadn't done anything right, either. He got by, that was all. He always stuck his nose into her projects, and she knew he coveted her job.

At noon she peeked outside. The rain continued to sheet past the pine trees in front of the door, the first storm since her disastrous walk on the fells. She shuddered. If Rowan hadn't known all the footpaths . . .

The wind gusted, shaking the small trailer. She reached for the door handle and another blast almost tore the knob out of her hand. She slammed it shut. These sudden storms would be her undoing.

Her stomach rumbled, but she'd wait until it cleared a bit before venturing over to the mess trailer. Thorny usually set something aside for her if she failed to show up at mealtime.

She settled back on the stool and continued to sketch a layout of the decking. Diamond plate would meet the needs of the project and provide the nonskid surface Rowan requested. She added it to her detail. She tried to concentrate on her drawing, but the howling wind slapped rain against the trailer wall. She found her mind miles away.

Rowan's cool exterior had to be just a facade, protecting the man beneath. For all his haughty demeanor, was it possible he hid a heart as sensitive as her own?

This sensitivity wasn't confined just to his heart, she thought. Under that layer of bravado, she sensed deep sadness and pain. It intrigued her, drew her to him like a moth to flame. What else had happened in his life? His ex-wife had probably been the real reason he didn't allow women on-site. No wonder he hadn't wanted her here.

And now this attraction sizzled between them. Her breasts tingled even now as she remembered the heat of his hands against her flesh, how expertly his fingers had stroked her to arousal that night in the cave. And last night . . .

Her pencil dropped and rolled into the tray. All she had resented about his coolness, his indifference, had been obliterated when she'd had a glimpse of his real self.

What should she do? How was she ever to sleep again, separated from him by only a thin fiberboard partition? On the other hand, the trailer wall was nothing compared to the barricade he'd erected around his heart. Chances were nothing more would happen between them.

At five o'clock, Karin gave up all pretense of work, covered her board and slipped into a hooded yellow slicker. She made a dash across the clearing and caught a glimpse of Rowan's red Jaguar in its usual spot near the trees.

He was back.

Inside her room, she sponged her face, applied a dusting of color to her cheeks, then pulled a heavy cream knit sweater over her head and ran a comb through her thick hair. As an afterthought, she went back into the bathroom and skimmed her naturally rosy lips with gloss.

The mess trailer bustled with commotion as the men tramped up the steps for dinner and Rowan distributed pay packets and letters. Geoff Ellis sat at the end of the table. He looked ten years older. Dark circles rimmed his eyes, and tiny red veins darted over his nose and gaunt cheeks. He nodded to her as she stepped into the room.

Rowan shoved a gray envelope into her hand. "Mail from home?" he asked politely.

Her gaze dropped to the neatly penned script. Athena's. She nodded, and looked across the room at Geoff. He looked terrible. The loss of his wife had taken a greater toll than she'd thought.

Geoff pulled a cigarette from a crumpled pack and lit it with the stub of one still in his hand. Then he rose and shuffled toward her. "Karin," he said shakily. He pulled her close with his free hand and planted a moist kiss on one cheek. He smelled of whiskey.

She drew back, the old distrust welling up. "Hello, Geoff."

"I understand we'll be working together." Geoff blew a stream of smoke skyward. "Just like the old days."

Not if I have anything to say about it, she thought. She frowned at the cigarette in his hand. "Would you mind putting that out? We aren't allowed to smoke on-site."

His lip curled. "Damn! Well, all right." Sulking, he slid a tea mug in front of him and ground the cigarette into it.

Rowan motioned Karin aside. "Show a little sympathy for him. He's going through a rough period." He spoke tersely, his expression dark.

She gave him a careful smile. "I'm very sympathetic for his loss," she said quietly. "I just don't sympathize with his working habits, or his tendency to usurp my jobs."

Rowan's mouth tightened. "You're being childish."

"And you're being arrogant. Again." She whirled and stalked over to the table, leaving him standing by the door. She plopped onto the chair Derrick held out for her.

Rowan scowled, then seated himself at the opposite end of the table, next to Geoff.

After dinner Karin accepted Derrick's challenge of a game of chess, while Rowan went off with Geoff to show him where to stow his gear.

An hour later, Karin's bishop captured the pawn guarding Derrick's king, and she gleefully watched as he toyed with his remaining knight, unaware that his flank lay exposed.

Rowan stalked through the door and into the kitchen, returning with a beer. "If you're wise, you'll move your king," he drawled to Derrick, flicking his gaze over the board. He raised his eyes fractionally, and his gaze locked with Karin's.

Derrick reddened and angled the teakwood chess piece away from danger.

Karin's mouth tightened as she focused on the board. Replotting her strategy, she cornered the hapless king two moves later.

"A rematch?" Derrick asked, a hopeful expression in his brown eyes.

"Early day tomorrow. Another time." She rose and bid Derrick good night. Giving Rowan a determined look, she scooted out the door.

Karin got up before dawn the next morning and slipped into a pair of moss green cords and a warm ivory, knit sweater. She jogged over to the mess trailer, the crisp air burning her lungs. Alone in the kitchen, she boiled a kettle of water and poured a cupful. She spooned instant coffee from the container into a mug, then carried the warm beverage outside and strolled along the edge of the ridge.

The earth was soggy from yesterday's rain, but the air felt clear and crisp. The valley floor disappeared beneath fluffy white clouds, and a line of fence posts loomed out of the mist and disappeared into the clouds. The hilly peaks to the west jutted up like black islands in a pale sea. The peaceful scene clashed with Karin's roiling thoughts.

The platform would be finished soon, and she would return to the chaos of California and her job. And her loneliness. The thought of leaving England—and Rowan, she acknowledged with an unexpected pang— left her more bereft than she cared to admit.

Karin stretched her gaze toward the hills. The fells stood wild and beautiful, with their windswept peaks and tiny lakes pocketed in green valleys. This was Rowan's milieu, a land as unique and untamed as the man himself. And almost as fascinating. Her gaze wandered out across the chasm.

Inexplicably, she sensed another presence.

"Is this a private interlude?" Rowan asked, suddenly materializing beside her.

Startled by his noiseless approach, she found herself staring up at his finely hewn, even features. He towered over her, dark hair tousled, as if he'd dressed hastily. She noticed his freshly laundered shirt and jeans, breathed in his clean scent of musk and pine. Dark tendrils of hair peeked out from the vee neck of the blue and burgundy madras plaid. Once more, he physically overwhelmed her.

The silver-flecked eyes gleamed provocatively in the half-light; he seemed almost hungry for the sight of her.

Which, she reasoned, was absurd.

"You're up early, Karin."

She glanced at her watch. "I was just leaving."

"Stay." He motioned to her. "I want to talk to you."

She stiffened. "Now, what have I done?"

"Not what you've done," he said dryly. "What you might do."

"If you're referring to Geoff," she blurted out, "don't bother telling me. I'm well aware of his situation, and I'll see that he gets his share of the workload." She tossed her cold coffee to the ground. "But I'll be damned if I'll play nursemaid to him." Tension made her voice harsh.

Rowan continued to stare, offering no comment. His expression showed no reaction whatever to her outburst. He would be a good poker player, she thought, wishing she were more adept at hiding her own feelings.

"You don't much like him, do you?" Rowan said at last.

"No."

"Would you care to tell me why?"

"No. I . . . ah . . . it's personal." She had no intention of demeaning herself, or Geoff, no matter how much he might deserve it. She turned to leave.

"Not so fast." He snaked out a hand and latched onto her arm, spun her to face him. "I haven't finished." He looked down at her, pale eyes blazing.

Then his mouth twisted into an odd smile, and he pulled her to him, seeking her mouth. The kiss went from a gentle brushing of their lips to a heated exploration of passion. He forced her lips open, his mouth hungry and demanding.

His kiss ripped away her reserve, banished thoughts of all but him. In moments, her body ripened under his touch.

She could give in—fall in love with him so easily. And that would be the most dangerous thing she could do. By his own admission he did not, would not, allow himself to care. All he wanted was a casual affair. A quick roll in the hay. The breath whooshed out of her.

"I know you want me, Karin," he whispered against her mouth. "Say it."

His words scorched like a blast of fire. Want him? Yes, she wanted him, but . . . she wanted more than just sex.

She pulled out of his grip. "*You* say it, Rowan," she said slowly. "Say it. Tell me you want me, that you—"

"You know that already," he murmured. "There is no need for me to tell you that, is there?" He bent toward her, his eyes dark and knowing.

"Yes, but that's not what I mean. I want you to—" She stopped. His face was so carefully masked.

"Oh, go to hell!" She turned toward the trailer. He was the most unnerving man she had ever known. A man who clearly desired her, but who refused to get involved on any level but the physical. He didn't want a relationship; he just wanted a sex partner.

But she wanted more than that. She knew that now. He could make love to her and leave her, but if she let herself get close to this man, she knew he would break her heart. It was *she* who feared involvement now. She wanted more than he could give her.

The week dragged on. Karin extracted a portion of the design task for Geoff, but he was as overbearing as ever. She answered his questions with as much diplomacy as she could muster. When Rowan strode in to explain some phase of the work to Geoff, he stayed and listened with apparent interest to Geoff's dissertation on how he perceived the project. Karin had a mind to tell them both they could have the job and good riddance. But she wasn't going to be accused of not completing her assignment, no matter how angry Geoff made her. She owed Leonard that. Nor would she allow either of them to walk all over her. She owed that to herself.

In midweek her mother telephoned from Ripon. The wedding, a brief ceremony in Judge Thompson's office, had gone without a hitch, and she and Leonard were on a leisurely honeymoon tour of Yorkshire. Could they get together for dinner in Cairnbeck on Saturday?

Despite her objections, Rowan insisted on driving Karin to the hotel. They arrived at seven and entered the restaurant, a study in dark paneling and beveled glass. In one firelit corner, Athena sat in her wheelchair next to Leonard.

"Mother!" Karin kissed her cheek. "You look wonderful." Beautiful under the most ordinary circumstances, Athena now radiated an inner glow. Self-consciously, her mother fingered the wide gold band on her left hand.

Leonard stood as Rowan materialized behind Karin. "You must be Marsden." He offered his hand. "Dalkey here."

"Dalkey," Rowan murmured, grasping the older man's hand and nodding. Then Rowan bent to Athena, his handsome face warmed by a smile. "And you must be Mrs. Dalkey? Karin's description doesn't do you justice."

Karin started. She had never described her mother to Rowan, only told him she was coming to England. Wasn't he spreading it on pretty thick?

Athena laughed.

Karin gave a tight smile and laid a protective hand on her mother's shoulder. "Thank you for the lift," she said pointedly to Rowan.

Athena looked up through a sweep of lashes. "Yes, you're very kind." Smiling, she turned to her husband.

"Won't you join us, Marsden?" Leonard asked suddenly. "There's a matter I'd like your opinion on."

Karin's heart stopped.

"Of course." Rowan's eyes flashed her a gentle but firm warning. "Thank you."

"After you," he said silkily. He ushered Karin into the booth, then took the end seat closest to Athena.

"You're here on holiday?" Rowan asked.

"Well, yes. Actually, we're on our honeymoon. But I suppose Leonard has told you that." Athena gazed across the table at her husband.

"He mentioned something about a wedding the last time we spoke."

Leonard patted Athena's hand. "I thought to show

Ath—my wife the part of the country where I grew up," Leonard said proudly. "She has a penchant for castles."

Karin watched as Rowan's gaze shifted back to her mother. "Karin tells me you paint," he said. "Cover art, is it?"

Leonard broke in, beaming. "She does cover art for novels. Beautiful work."

Athena glanced at Leonard, then back to Rowan. "He's prejudiced, of course. But, yes. I'm currently doing cover art for Columbine Publishing, and I've been looking for a medieval manor house to photograph."

Rowan regarded Athena with warmth. "I know just the place. If you've no plans for tomorrow, perhaps you'd like to visit?"

What on earth was he talking about? Karin wondered. He knew perfectly well tomorrow was the day they planned to mount the first antenna.

Athena captured her husband's hand in hers. "Oh, Leonard, could we?"

"I don't see why not," he said, his tone jovial.

Rowan shot Karin a look of satisfaction. "Excellent. I'll make the arrangements."

"Uh . . . where is this house?" Leonard asked.

"Knaresborough."

Oh, no, Karin groaned. An image of the Marsden estate flashed into her mind. He wouldn't take them there. Would he? She stirred uneasily on the hard seat. Much as she enjoyed her visit with the Marsdens, she didn't want to spend an afternoon with them, didn't want to like them too much.

"Bless me. I grew up near there." Leonard scratched his head thoughtfully. "There was one fine old place near the river. I remember climbing the wall once to steal apples. There was a magnificent chapel on the grounds with stained-glass windows."

"That's the one."

"Do you know the owner?" Athena asked.

"Rather well." Rowan flashed a lopsided grin.

"Mom," Karin interjected, "his parents own the estate."

Rowan extricated himself from the booth. "Please excuse me while I make a telephone call."

When he had gone, Leonard leaned toward Karin and whispered, "How is it going with Geoff?"

Karin shrugged. "So-so."

"I was sorry to ask this of you, Karin. I know Geoff can be a trial." He smiled, his eyes warm, yet tinged with sadness. Somehow it comforted Karin. Leonard always showed so much concern for his employees. A twinge of guilt fluttered in her heart.

Leonard went on, still smiling. "Geoff's okay at heart. If anyone can help him, you can." He nodded in the direction Rowan had gone. "Good-looking chap, Marsden. Family's loaded, I hear."

"Rowan refused his family's inheritance. He says he wants to accomplish his goals without the advantage of his family's means."

"Rather foolish of him, isn't it?"

"Certainly not! I think it's . . . noble." Karin's quick defense brought a flush of color to her cheeks.

"What are you two chattering about?" Athena broke in.

"Nothing," Karin muttered. "Just business."

Leonard laughed. "I think your daughter is developing a passion for . . . things English. Not that I blame her, of course." He sent Karin a perceptive look.

Athena gave him a conspiratorial wink. "Must be genetic."

"Oh, Mother, for heaven's sake!"

A moment later, Rowan returned, a pleased smile

on his lips. "I've arranged transport. We'll leave your hotel at ten o'clock." He turned to Karin. "Oh, yes. Mother asked that you come along, too."

Her heartbeat quickened at the almost hopeful glint in his eyes. She wanted to ask him whose idea it had been, his mother's or his? Instead, she murmured, "Fine. I'll be ready."

At a little past twelve the next day, they pulled up in front of the Marsden estate. Rowan escorted Athena and Leonard around the grounds, leaving the Marsdens to entertain Karin. The three of them trailed after Leonard and Rowan, who pushed Athena's wheelchair along the smooth, flagged path. Lord, he can certainly be charming when he wants to, Karin thought, listening as Rowan chatted and laughed with her mother and Leonard. Just look at him—he's genuinely enjoying this.

At the point where the path ended, Rowan scooped Athena up into his strong arms and carried her easily over the spongy, moist grass. Leonard strode alongside, maneuvering the empty wheelchair. He made a comment to Rowan, but his answer was muted by Athena's lilting laughter, pealing over the sounds of birdsong.

At the gate of one small stone building, Rowan shifted Athena in his arms and pushed on the latch, then set her gently down into the chair Leonard held for her. The two men waited while she snapped a picture.

Watching the interplay from a distance, Karin's breath caught. Rowan was very much in command, yet he appeared so gentle, so caring. Had he given this tour to other visitors? To other women? *To lovers?* a small voice asked. Did he express to them the same tenderness and concern when he took them to bed?

A sharp chill knifed into her. How many women had he invited to share his bed? Her mouth suddenly went dry, and she pivoted toward the manor house.

During tea, Rowan lavished attention on Athena, suggesting the best angles for photographs and asking penetrating questions about work in the publishing business. Occasionally, Karin caught him stealing a surreptitious look at her, but as soon as her eyes met his, he turned to Leonard or Athena and continued his discussion.

Damn the man! Her hand shook, sloshing her tea dangerously close to the edge of her saucer and an elegant wine velvet footstool beneath. Rowan gave her a bland smile, then turned again to Athena.

"We have some excellent examples of seventeenth-century stables if you'd care to see those." He balanced his teacup in one hand, his slim fingers curled possessively around the delicate bone china.

"I have a fine old volume of Wordsworth and some original Malory," Arthur Marsden said to Karin. She met the older man's gaze.

"My son seems to be taken up with his tour-guide duties," he whispered with a smile. "Come, let's have a look."

Karin followed the elder Marsden into the library, leaving Leonard and her mother deeply engrossed in conversation with Rowan.

"I must commend you, girl. We haven't seen Rowan so relaxed in a very long time." Mr. Marsden peered at her, a kindly smile on his pale face. "My son and I have had our differences over the years. But only recently has he expressed interest in the old place." The elder Marsden gave her a long look. "I think that's due, in part, to you, my dear."

Karin hesitated. "But I only work for him. I have no contact with him outside my job."

"That's a pity, because I think you could do so much to help him. He's had a difficult time since— Well, since he's been alone."

"Mr. Marsden, I don't think—"

The elder Marsden flashed her a sad smile. "You ought not to be listening to an old man prattle, is that it? Perhaps, but I don't mind telling you that I think you can—are—doing a world of good for my son. And if you can keep on doing it, well, I would be most grateful."

Mr. Marsden stopped at a pair of double doors, pushed one open, and stepped aside for her to enter. "This is the private collection I want you to see. But, before we go in there's one more thing, my dear. Let this little talk be between the two of us."

All the rest of the day, Karin watched Rowan and remembered his father's words. If only he acted the same way around her that . . . She glanced at Leonard, bent attentively over her mother. Oh, God, she thought in desperation. If only Rowan cared about her as Leonard cared about her mother.

Late in the afternoon they gathered in the drawing room. Athena turned to Mrs. Marsden. "Leonard and I have certainly had a wonderful time. Thank you for allowing us to visit."

Mrs. Marsden smiled. "My dear, the pleasure was entirely ours. We're so happy to meet you—and delighted to see Karin again."

Athena then faced Rowan. "I think I have all the photos I need. Thank you so much, Rowan. It is an unusually beautiful house. I especially enjoyed the chapel." She looked up at Karin. "Don't you agree?"

"I haven't seen it." Karin explained in a low tone. "When I was here before, we were in a hurry to get back to the site."

The quiet clip of Rowan's footstep echoed behind her. "We aren't in a hurry now," he said. "Come along if you've a mind to."

Karin glanced at the elder Marsden, who gave her a nod. They strolled down a cobbled path behind the house, past a drystone wall. There, enclosed by a tall, manicured privet hedge, stood the chapel. Ancient round-topped tombstones leaned crookedly in the tiny graveyard, and at the altar end a medieval lancet window hung as if suspended in the building stones, its reds, blues and greens alive in the sun's rays. Inside the curved oak doors was a small antechamber, and in the thick stone wall, a font of holy water.

"It's a Catholic chapel?" Karin asked. "I thought they disappeared with Henry the Eighth."

"Most of them did, but several powerful families remained loyal to Holy Mother Church. During the Dissolution, masses were held in secret in a number of great houses. My family have worshiped here for six hundred years."

He led her inside the sanctuary. "My first project after graduating was to completely renovate the interior. If you look carefully, you can see how we reconstructed the new materials to match the old."

He pointed toward the altar, built of heavy, dark oak and covered with a length of hand-embroidered linen.

Rowan mounted the step. "The wood for this altar came from a ship wrecked off the Grimsby coast. Craftsmen in my great-grandfather's time did the carving along the front."

"That's beautiful workmanship," she said. "The altar cloth is lovely, too."

"A gift from my grandparents when Father and Mother were married."

"Here?"

He nodded. "All the weddings and baptisms in our family have taken place right here."

Karin's heart thumped. "You were married here, too?"

His expression became impassive. "No, not here." He made a half-turn away from her. "Besotted as I was, I think I always knew that she . . ." His voice faded.

He spun toward Karin, his gaze dark, intense. "To marry her here would have been a—a sacrilege." His voice cracked, a harsh echo in the empty chapel.

Karin opened her mouth to speak, licking lips gone dry as the Sahara. Suddenly she wanted to touch him, smooth his hair as she would a small boy's. Her hand moved in his direction.

"Don't," he said, drawing back. "I can manage anything but your pity.

"And if you touch me for another reason," he whispered, "this is not the time, or the place."

TWELVE

The faint light of evening hung in the sky when they reached Cairnbeck. For the last fifty miles, Karin had listened to Rowan's skilled conversation with Leonard and Athena, heard the soft murmur of words that passed between her mother and her husband in the backseat, and heated to Rowan's occasional probing glances. His eyes seemed to strip away her clothing. Under her shirt, her breasts ached. She felt like a desert traveler, suddenly discovering an oasis but forbidden to drink. Thank God, it was dark, and Leonard and Athena could not see her face, could not guess her thoughts.

Outside the hotel, Karin hugged her mother and Leonard. "Have a wonderful time in Scotland."

Rowan drew Leonard away in conversation, and Karin perched on the car seat beside Athena. "I'm happy for you, Mom. Really. I can see now that you and Leonard need to be together."

"Yes. We do." Athena's eyes glowed. "And so do you." She gazed at Rowan as the two men peered beneath the hood of the Jaguar. "I like him, your Rowan. I like him a lot."

Karin made an impatient swipe at a stray tendril of

hair on her forehead. "Mom, he's not 'my Rowan.' I just work for him."

Athena captured her gaze. "Maybe that's how you see it, but the man's in love with you."

"You're crazy, Mom. Rowan doesn't believe in love."

"Well then, dear," Athena pursued in her matter-of-fact voice, "why did he work so hard all day trying to impress me? I know a man in love when I see him."

Karin's mind reeled. Could that have been his motive?

Suddenly Leonard's voice boomed. "Having a heart-to-heart?" He leaned against the door, the warmth of his gaze echoed in his voice. "Your mother's missed that while you've been away."

Karin clambered out of the car and hugged her stepfather. "I think you've managed to keep her fairly occupied."

"That I have." Leonard smiled. He grasped Rowan's hand. "Nice to have met you, Marsden. We'll have to discuss that new proposal further."

"I'll be in touch." Rowan turned to Karin. "Ready?"

She nodded and turned to her mother. "Have a happy honeymoon, Mom." She slipped into Leonard's embrace and gave him a peck on his cheek. "You, too." At the last minute, she clasped Athena tightly in her arms. "Thanks for . . . everything," she whispered.

When she climbed into Rowan's Jaguar, her nerves vibrated. *If he touches me, I'll come apart*, she thought. If Rowan was in love with her, as Athena said, how could she possibly finish this assignment and stay uninvolved? A flush swept over her. Who was she kidding? She was already involved.

"Your mother is quite a lady," Rowan said as they sped up the mountain.

"Yes," Karin responded. "Athena is a great lady. She has warmth, and she has courage."

"She has something else, too," Rowan said, his voice husky.

Karin looked at him. "Oh?"

His knuckles whitened as he gripped the wheel. "She has love."

Astonished, Karin stared at his profile. She had never seen him look so bleak.

Good Lord, maybe Athena was right. For all his play-acting, Rowan was involved, too. A small pulse hammered at the base of her throat. Okay, he's involved, she acknowledged. That doesn't mean he wants anything to come of it, anything even remotely resembling a commitment.

She turned toward the side window and stared at the specks of light in the valley below.

"Karin," Geoff said to her a week later. "I need to talk to you."

"I'm right here."

"It's . . . personal. Can you meet me in the village?"

"Rowan has made it clear that he doesn't want me socializing with the crew."

"This is different. We don't work for him in the same sense as his crew. Please. It's about work. It's important."

Seeing the pleading in Geoff's eyes, she relented. "All right. I'm off Saturday, and Rowan will be here working. I'll take one of the Rovers down on Friday evening and meet you at Maggie's. That way it'll be less obvious."

"You're a peach." Geoff clasped both her hands and held them a moment.

At that instant, Rowan burst through the door. At once he stopped, looked from Karin to Geoff, then back to Karin. He held her gaze, his eyes dark and brooding. After a long moment, he nodded slowly, then turned and thumped heavily down the trailer steps.

Blue-violet shadows stretched across the road when Karin parked the Range Rover in front of Maggie's. Cairnbeck lay silent except for the tolling of the Angelus from the church belfry. One by one, shades were drawn and lights dimmed in shop windows. Karin pushed on unseeing, her thoughts centered on Rowan's face as he had stared at her and Geoff yesterday.

She knew Geoff waited inside. If she'd followed her instincts, she wouldn't have come. But if Geoff needed help, she would do what she could for Leonard's sake. Even Geoff deserved a chance to turn over a new leaf. Rowan could not possibly object to that. Still, she felt uneasy as she brushed through the pub door.

Inside, she found Geoff slumped at the end of the dark wood bar. A bottle of scotch, two-thirds full, stood on the polished counter in front of him, along with an almost empty glass. One glance at his ravaged features revealed the truth. Geoff's plea was real. He caught her reflection in the mirror behind the bar and swiveled toward her, his expression petulant.

"You took your own sweet time getting here."

Karin pressed her lips together. Somehow, he always put her on the defensive. "I had things to do before I could get away, but if you're going to take that tack,

you can sit and sulk by yourself. You asked me to come
down here tonight." She took a step toward the door.

Geoff's countenance fell. He raised his glass and
took a gulp. "Dammit Karin, I'm sorry. But I've been
waiting almost three hours."

Her gaze settled on the bottle of scotch and the
mound of half-smoked cigarettes in the ashtray. "So
I notice. But the only way I could get a car was by
agreeing to pick up an order for Thorny. And then I
had to run errands for the crew."

"Yeah, that's what I'm supposed to be doing, too."
He poured another generous inch of the amber liquor
into his glass.

"Geoff!"

He paused while screwing the cap on the bottle.
"Ease off. I can handle myself. Don't need you to
nag," he countered with hands raised.

He leaned back against the bar. "Can I order you
something?"

She shook her head. "I'll order my own." After
speaking to the barman, she turned back to Geoff.
"You wanted to talk?"

His gaze flitted across the room. "How about over
there? It's more private."

"I'm sure that anything you have to say can be said
right here."

Geoff shook his head and stood up. "No, it can't."

She paid for her drink and reluctantly followed him
to the dimly lit corner booth.

Seated, Geoff drained his glass, fumbled for a cigarette and raised it to his lips. He paused in midair
when his eyes met Karin's. "Uh, sorry." He shoved
the unlit cigarette into his pocket. His hands twitched,

and for a long time he said nothing, seemingly gathering his thoughts. "I know you don't like me much."

She broke in. "That's not true." At least not entirely true, she thought. "But I don't like to feel that you undermine me each time we're on an assignment."

"Since when have I ever—"

"Come off it, Geoff. Ever since you came to Dalkey, you've been after my job."

Geoff raised doleful eyes. "Not true. But I have been after a share of the respect. Leonard always treated you as if you walked on water. Still does. But if I've done anything to offend you, I apologize."

"Forget it." She gave him a tight smile. "That's in the past. Besides, Leonard values you—he told me so."

He fastened pale eyes on hers. "Yeah, Leonard really cares about people . . . I understand that now. He figured by sending me over here I'd get over Alice's death a lot quicker. No familiar reminders. But"— Geoff's eyes clouded—"he doesn't know"—Geoff's voice broke on a sob—"nobody does."

Karin watched Geoff's face work, her own eyes misting. She would never forget that awful void when her father died, and the huge, empty house she'd wheeled her mother into after the months of therapy. The first days after the accident had been the worst. Helplessly, she had watched her mother struggle for life while a frightening assortment of tubes transported vital fluids in and out of her body.

She drew in a slow breath, then said softly, "These things take time."

Geoff poured himself another shot of whiskey.

She pulled the glass away. "You've had enough, Geoff. Drinking isn't going to solve anything. You have to want to help yourself."

Pain shadowed his face. "You don't understand, Karin. I killed her—I killed Alice. It was my fault."

"No, Geoff." Karin's voice rose. "She was ill. Nothing you may have done made any difference. You've got to remember that."

He went on dully. "I cheated on her. Lots of times. She found out and was going to leave me, but then she got sick." He dropped his head into his hands. "I wish to God it had been me. She was the only good part of my life."

Aghast, Karin stared at Geoff. "Why are you telling me this?"

"I need your help, Karin. I . . . need you to cover for me on the job until—until I can get myself together. It's getting better, but I need more time." He gave her a naked look. His revelation came as no surprise, but his depth of conscience did.

She said gently, "You need to stop relying on alcohol."

"That's not a problem, I can handle it." His mouth twitched into a smile, and a hint of the old Geoff passed over his gaunt face. "Karin, help me. Please?"

Impulsively, Karin reached across the table and cupped her hand over his. He was pleading; there was no way she could refuse a person in such pain. Even though he smiled, she was quick to catch the desperation in his eyes. "Okay. You have my word on it. I'll check everything you do before it goes out."

Relief shone in the look he flashed her. "Thanks, Karin. I knew you'd come through." He drew her hand between both of his and squeezed it affectionately.

From behind them a deep voice cut in, the tone velvet, edged with steel. "Is this a private rendezvous?"

Karin froze. She found herself staring up into narrowed gray eyes.

"Rowan!" She withdrew her hand from Geoff's and slipped it into her lap.

"Didn't know you were coming down to the village," Geoff said, making a weak attempt at hiding his surprise. "If I'd known, I'd have invited you along."

"Like hell," Rowan muttered.

Geoff swallowed, and gestured to the spot beside him. "Have a seat."

"Thank you, no." Rowan's eyes raked over Karin. "I gather you weren't expecting company. Is this the reason you asked for tomorrow off? To meet him?" He nodded toward Geoff. His flinty gaze slid down to her breasts, thrusting against the soft cotton T-shirt, then moved upward again to her face. "When I agreed to let you take the car, I had no idea you were having a tryst."

Heat flamed in her cheeks. "You're jumping to conclusions."

"Am I?" he said, his voice soft.

"Rowan, this is not what you think."

He flashed her a cold smile. "Maggie tells me you've engaged a room for the night."

She bristled. "I planned to spend the night—alone—and pick up Thorny's supplies in the morning."

"Spare me your explanations," he snapped. "I'm not interested. Report to the office Monday morning. On time." He turned and strode to the door.

Karin sagged against the back of the booth. "Oh, hell."

"Karin, I'm sorry," Geoff whispered.

"It's not your fault," she said wearily. She had nothing to hide. If he hadn't set such a stupid restriction, there'd be no problem. No, the problem was his. And when she got back, she'd tell him so. It had been only a question of time until she had it out with Rowan. Now was the time.

She rose. "I'm tired. I'm going up to bed. See you Monday."

Karin tossed fitfully for hours, her sleep filled with fragmented dreams. In one, she looked down at herself languishing in a heated Roman bath. Perfumed water swirled around her, along with a misty cloud of heavy, sweet fragrance that beaded on her face.

Suddenly, as if parting a veil, Rowan swept in out of the mist and stared down at her. A flowing, magenta-toned silk dressing gown draped his lean frame. It was open to the waist. Her gaze focused on the ridges and contours of his chest, the flat planes of his stomach. Her pulse leaped in quicktime, and a feeling so sensual, so intimate, swept over her, she felt a choking sensation in her chest. So, this was how one felt when consumed by passion. Unable to breathe, to think. Filled with a mind-numbing ecstasy of pain so exquisite . . .

Like a voyeur, spying on a pair of lovers, she then watched Rowan's eyes drink in her entire body, the small, upturned breasts tipped with delicate peach-tinted aureoles, the mass of thick russet hair swirling around her shoulders in the water, the darker triangle at the apex of her thighs. With one hand, he slowly pulled his sash free. The garment drifted to the floor.

Naked, he was beautiful. He descended the steps into the water, moving slowly but purposefully toward her. Her breath caught. With one hand outstretched, she welcomed him. He drew nearer, grasped her fingers and pulled her gently up out of the water.

His lips made a quick descent, but no sooner had their mouths fused than a strange, rhythmic music filled the air. It was a sound like none she had ever before heard, a sensuous throb, low and elemental, with the plucking of lute strings, the whine of an ancient horn, and the rich cadence of timbrel and drum.

Rowan stilled, listening. At once, he drew back, then released her and retreated, his eyes never leaving hers as he moved backward out of the pool and into the mist. She waited, but he did not return. Finally, the music ended with a cacophonous climax. Cold night air chilled her glistening body as she stood alone in the water.

Karin's eyes snapped open. Outside, rain pelted down, and from the open window beside her bed, the wind blew a fine mist onto the coverlet and over her arms and face. Shivering, she rose to close the window. From far off in the distance, the scream of a police siren tore through the stillness.

The dream abandoned, she drew the window down, shutting out the solitary, wailing sound.

Oh, God, she was lonely.

THIRTEEN

Shopping in Cairnbeck failed to offer the distraction Karin hoped it would. After her discussion with Geoff, and Rowan's unexpected intrusion at Maggie's, her interest in browsing flagged. As she moved from shop to shop, she puzzled over her dream.

Of course, she thought with sudden insight. Rowan's response in her subconscious mirrored reality. Just when she was sure he wanted her, perhaps even cared about her, he retreated, as if angry. And in the pub last night, his reaction was even stronger. He thought she was sleeping with Geoff. *If he's jealous,* she reasoned, *then he must care.* Was that why he was so angry? A glimmer of hope rose in her consciousness.

One way or another, she was going to find out tonight.

At Mr. Pennyworth's antique shop, she idly fingered one of the wooden bobbins, dropped it in her basket and added a tartan plaid neck scarf for Leonard. For Athena, she chose an arresting print of Fountains Abbey at dusk.

At the small boutique next door, she fell in love with a nightgown of delicate white lawn. Pale yellow appliquéd butterflies flitted across the bodice, and a row of tiny buttons held the front demurely closed. She pictured herself wearing the gown, envisioned Rowan's hands slowly undoing each button, his fingers brushing over her breasts as he worked to free them.

Heat suffused her body. Unconsciously, she moistened her parched lips with her tongue. Lord, if she didn't get her thoughts under control soon, she'd melt. She looked up to see the shop assistant staring at her.

Karin pushed the garment across the glass case. "I'll take this." Eyes lowered, she rummaged in her bag. Did the shopkeeper guess why she wanted the gown? Did all women in love feel so . . . exposed?

She strolled on through the village. A bookshop drew her attention, and she purchased the latest Tom Clancy thriller for Derrick. Next, a sweetshop for several doily-covered jars of bramble jelly. Thorny, she remembered, particularly liked the sweet berry spread. She shopped slowly, realizing she was deliberately delaying her return to the site because this was the night she'd confront Rowan. "Courage," she muttered to herself.

Finally, when she'd picked up the grocery order Thorny had asked for and had secured everything in the back of the Rover, she returned to the pub to have tea with Maggie.

Since meeting the pub owner, Karin had visited with her each time she and the crew came into the village. Now, upstairs in Maggie's pretty, wallpapered room, all lace and linen, she kicked off her shoes and relaxed while Maggie brought a tray of crustless chicken salad sandwiches and slices of whiskey cake. These were Maggie's private quarters, and here the Irishwoman's flair for decorating shone.

Karin sank more deeply into the down-backed sofa and tried not to think about returning to the site. They washed the food down with cups of strong, sweet tea while a stereo played Mozart in the background.

Maggie propped slipper-clad feet on a leather ottoman. "It's lovely to see you out and about," she said after Karin described her surprise meeting with Rowan. "And I wouldn't be overly concerned about Mr. Marsden. It's his manner, is all. Sort of uptight like. Sure and he'll be himself tomorrow." She paused, a reflective expression crossing her face. "Though it's God's truth, I don't recall seeing him that intense before. Why, he looked as if he wanted t' tear apart that gent ye were with." She laughed and poured another cup of tea. "I do believe he's jealous."

Karin arched a brow. Inside she secretly warmed to Maggie's assessment. "Jealous? Not Mr. Perfect Control No Matter What. In Rowan's view, I'm simply an employee who defied his orders." She sighed and bit into the whiskey cake. "He makes no secret of the fact that he thinks of me in only the most basic sense."

Maggie shot her a whimsical look. "Well, that raises a question about 'perfect control.' " Her expression grew serious, and she asked, "What about you? Do you like him?"

"Yes. But not just as a friend," Karin blurted out. "I mean—" she glanced away. Was she blushing again? She felt the heat, knew her cheeks were a telltale crimson. "He's not a likable person . . . most of the time. And yet"—she pushed herself from the back of the chair and leaned forward—"I find myself fascinated by him in spite of his aloofness. At times he can be surprisingly sensitive."

"Oh?" Maggie's eyebrows rose. "Do you like them aloof or sensitive?"

Karin's gaze veered sharply to Maggie, whose mouth curved in amusement. "I've . . . er . . . never taken time out for anything but a few casual dates since I left school. Never anything serious. I don't know much about men, really," she admitted.

"And why not? You're a normal, healthy young woman."

Karin shrugged. "My career. And no one caught my interest before now. No one ever—" She stopped short. Odd that she should ramble on about herself to this woman whom she'd only known a short time. Up to now, Athena had been her only confidante. Now her mother had decided to share her life with Leonard, and that changed things.

Maggie said delicately, "No men in your life, is it? Interesting. And I'm thinkin' you'd want to change that." She popped a sweet into her mouth, then focused enormous blue eyes on Karin as she chewed thoughtfully. "Are you in love with him?"

"In love?" Karin was jolted by the notion. "I . . . don't know. I certainly feel something." She dropped her gaze to the crisp linen tablecloth. "And I want him as a man, but"—her voice faltered—"I've never felt like this before . . . like I'd want any relationship beyond friendship. But now— Oh, I don't know! It's all so incomprehensible."

A grin spread across Maggie's face. "If I didn't have Cyril, I might be showing you some competition. Rowan is a gorgeous man."

"With ice in his veins."

"Not ice, lass. You're not looking in the right places."

* * *

When Karin pulled into the camp parking area at nine o'clock, all was quiet except for the hoot of a lonely night owl. Light shone from the mess trailer.

She climbed from the Rover and lugged her purchases into her bedroom, closing the door as quietly as possible. She unpacked her carryall, stowed it neatly under the bed, then slipped across the stretch of ground to the trailer kitchen. Inside, she set the jars of jelly on the counter. After she'd carried in Thorny's supplies, she walked slowly back to her trailer.

Rowan stood in the connecting room doorway. "You're back early. Didn't Ellis suit?" His stony expression made her flinch.

"What do you mean?"

"You're not simple, Karin. Wasn't he to your liking?"

Anger welled up. "That's my business."

"I'm making it mine." He took a step toward her, forcing her to retreat back against the desk. "I warned you before—you're not to get involved with the crew. That goes for Ellis, too."

"Rowan, there's nothing between Geoff and me. Besides, you don't dictate what I do in my spare time."

"Quite the contrary. On this project, I dictate everything. This isn't California. The men here can be coarse." His glittering eyes moved up her body. "You might find them a bit rougher than you like."

"Perhaps that *is* what I like," she snapped, goaded beyond sensibility.

He whirled. "Rough? You want it rough?" He pulled her forward, slamming her against his chest.

She pummeled his torso with her fists until he grasped them in his strong hands and pinioned them behind her, backing her against the wall. "That's not my style, but if it's what you like, far be it from me to disappoint." He gave a harsh laugh.

Karin shrank under his darkened gaze, wondered at his labored breathing. Had he been drinking? Or was he, as Maggie suggested, just jealous?

Her heart pounded against her ribs as he stared down on her. His head lowered, obliterating the light, and his lips descended on hers. He forced her mouth open, darting his tongue between her lips, driving the resistance out of her.

She stopped struggling. Sound roared in her ears, like surf crashing against rocks. Heat enveloped her body, and her limbs felt shaky.

He freed her hands, slid his fingers under her sweater, and teased one nipple. His mouth moved over hers, nipping at her lip, his tongue running along the inner edge of her mouth. A blade of heat stabbed through her belly.

He lowered his mouth still farther, to the pulsing softness of her breast, and Karin gasped. He pushed the vee of her sweater aside and pressed his lips against the rounded contour of creamy flesh revealed by her black lace bra. His breath warmed her skin, but she shivered.

"Did you wear this for Ellis?" he probed in a low whisper, slipping the satin strap off one shoulder. He cupped her breast, lightly kneading the hardened nipple between his forefinger and thumb.

"I dress to please myself." The words came out in a husky whisper. Her knees felt weak; a moistness gathered at the juncture of her thighs as she pressed against him. "I don't even like Geoff Ellis, Rowan."

Rowan straightened, looking down at her, the flames in his heated gaze searing through her. Pinned between the wall and the hard muscles of his chest, the last of her defenses crumbled. Karin trembled, and knew that he could feel it. Oh, God, she wanted him to touch her . . . wanted him to . . .

She raised both arms and pulled his mouth down to hers. He groaned and bruised her lips with his in a savage kiss, moving against her mouth with rising passion. The moist exploration left her breathless.

"I'm not Ellis," he whispered.

"I know," she breathed. "Rowan, it's not Geoff I want. It's—" Sweet, hot heat spread under his touch.

"What do you want, Karin? Tell me!"

"I want you," she moaned.

"Karin," he whispered. "Oh, God, Karin."

He gathered her in his arms, and carried her to the narrow bed. She sat trembling, her heart racing, waiting for his next move. She didn't trust herself to look up.

He drew her sweater over her head, then bent to remove her bra. He unclasped it with shaking fingers and flung it aside. Her engorged nipples ached.

Gently, he pushed her back on the mattress and spread himself over her, dusting her cheek, her neck and breasts with kisses soft as birds' wings. His voice was a low murmur. "Karin, show me what you want. Show me." He kissed her again, melding his tongue with hers.

Karin's heart leaped. Raw need surged through her, feelings she had not known she possessed. She reached for Rowan, crushing her breasts against his chest. Suddenly she wanted to feel him naked against her, and she moved her hands to the buttons of his shirt, unfastening them one by one in jerky motions.

He made a sound in his throat, and drew her hand away. He tore at the buttons, finally tossing the shirt on the floor. He lowered himself beside her and wrapped her in his arms. The crisp, dark hair of his chest tickled her breasts. He moved lower, covering each crested peak with his hands, finally pressing a kiss on one nipple. His warm breath fanned her delicate skin, and a sweet throbbing blossomed from deep within her.

He moved his hand to her jeans, pulled the snap loose and edged his fingers downward along the flat contour of her belly. His large hand rested atop her silken mound; then he slowly slipped his fingers beneath the elastic of her panties.

Instinctively she arched against his hand, gasping as he gently circled, his fingers searching. She was fully aroused, moist and hot. The throbbing that began as a tiny thread of feeling surged until she was engulfed in its vortex. She heard him groan as he thrust his finger inside and stroked her with exquisite sensitivity.

"Yes," she moaned, moving against him.

"Karin . . . is this what you want?" His voice was strained. He caressed her throbbing flesh with the tip of one finger. She shuddered involuntarily. Heat radiated through her veins, building upon itself until she thought she would go mad.

"Make love to me," she breathed against his lips.

"Oh, God," he said huskily. "You can't know how long I've waited to hear you say that." He reached for her zipper, yanked it down and pulled her jeans and panties off her smooth legs. Standing, he jerkily removed his shoes and trousers, then lifted her to her feet. Puzzled, she looked up at him.

His gaze pinned her, forcing her to acknowledge him. "My room, love. The bed's bigger."

The heat of his desire transferred itself to her. Her lips parted, and she licked their parched surface with the tip of her tongue. For a moment, he stared, transfixed. Then he gathered her up in his strong arms and pushed through the narrow passageway to his room.

Karin wound her arms around his neck and lay against his chest, listening to the harsh sound of his breathing and the uneven thudding of his heart. His warmth burned through her skin. Her heart pounded against her ribs, and she gulped in a giant breath, forcing oxygen into her lungs. She had never wanted a man before. But even if she had, she knew that this, with Rowan, was different. *He* was different. Or perhaps, now, she herself was different.

He laid her gently on his huge bed, and she moved toward the center. For the first time, she looked at him. A tremor shook her body as he gazed back at her. He was big and well muscled. A clear line of demarcation revealed where his tan ended below his neck. Lower still, his skin was a pale golden color. Dark hair dappled his legs and arms and spread across his chest; a fine line darted down to the elastic of his low-slung briefs. Her eyes remained riveted to the cotton fabric, drawn taut by his arousal.

His hand shook as he switched off the desk light, and Karin felt the mattress sag with the weight of his body. Breathing unsteadily, he drew her against him, all muscle, hard planes everywhere, while the swelling of his need pressed firmly against her groin.

All at once panic flamed inside her. She had never been with a man before. What if he didn't want what she offered? He was certainly experienced, but she wasn't. Somehow, the thought of him with anyone else made her crazy.

"What is it?" he murmured.

"Rowan, I . . . I'm frightened."

His head dipped lower. "I've waited so long for this . . . I'm a bit frightened, too."

He teased each swollen nipple with his tongue, lightly nipping with his teeth until her breasts ached with longing. Then he traced a path of slow kisses along her belly down to the mossy softness between her legs. He circled the sensitive nub with a forefinger, moving delicately until she writhed and arched toward him, drawing quick, shallow breaths. Rowan, Rowan, her mind screamed. Her body spun as spasms of pleasure shook her.

Suddenly Rowan stilled. He groaned softly, his quick intake of breath ragged. "Karin. Oh, God, Karin. I've wanted you for so long. You can't know how much I need—" He covered her body with his own, parting her legs with his knee and lowering himself until he was poised at the moist temple between her thighs. His penetration was quick and smooth, and she heard him utter a startled gasp.

Her breath caught with the momentary pain, her cry silenced as his mouth moved over hers, kissing her lips, her cheek, her eyelids. Rowan moved convulsively against her, his breath ragged, out of control, and Karin's thoughts tumbled.

Don't let it end, she thought. Please don't let it end. With a cry he moved against her. Then he was fully sheathed in her softness.

"Karin," he said roughly. "Karin . . . Karin." To her surprise, his voice had a sob in it. Slowly he began to move within her, his motions languid, sensual, as if he were savoring her body. As if he were savoring *her*, she thought in a flash of understanding.

A sharp, sweet tension built at the apex of her thighs. The blade of pleasure mounted into a spiraling crescendo that overwhelmed her senses, and instinctively, she wrapped her legs around his to deepen his penetration.

"You are mine, mine!" he murmured, his voice a low growl. "Karin!" Then, seemingly beyond lucidity, he spilled himself into her, holding her desperately against him. "Oh, God!" he cried.

He lay for a long time cradling her body, his face buried in her hair. At last he raised his head and looked into her eyes.

Tears glistened on his dark lashes.

Karin's lids fluttered open as a shaft of sunlight streamed through the narrow window and softly illuminated her face. She closed her eyes, letting her thoughts drift, savoring the dreamy heat that pervaded her limbs. The warmth came not from the soft comforter swathing her body, but from a sudden, delicious revelation.

Rowan loved her.

He hadn't told her in words; he hadn't needed to. His actions had spoken for him. The high-and-mighty Mr. Marsden had been as shaken by their lovemaking as she! Rowan held the power to ignite her with a single caress. Remembrance of his husky voice murmuring her name flooded her, and she felt her nipples harden. Later, he had taken her again, and then again, and she had encouraged his every touch.

Spent from passion, they had basked in the languid afterglow, bodies entwined, then had drifted off to sleep. Now, she trembled with the potency of her thoughts and edged closer to the center of the bed, seeking his warmth.

Her searching hand slid over cold sheets. "Rowan?"

He was gone.

FOURTEEN

Karin's eyelids snapped open. An indentation in the feather pillow revealed where Rowan had lain, but the room was empty. The trousers he'd discarded in her room last night were draped over a chair, the connecting door closed. He'd evidently taken care not to disturb her.

Her mouth curved into a contented smile. Unlike most men, Rowan was meticulous about his surroundings. It was she who struggled to keep their tiny shared bathroom up to his impeccable standards. As a roommate he rated top marks. As a lover . . .

Karin blushed at the memory. She had no one to compare him to, but on a one-to-ten scale, he must be well off the chart. Still smiling, she stepped lightly onto the cold linoleum. The clock on the desk read seven. She was late! And whose fault was that? she thought wryly, disregarding her normal inclination to hurry. She crept under the warm shower spray and winced at the soreness between her thighs.

She dried herself and dressed in a fresh pair of slacks and a blue chambray shirt, then opened the door to her bedroom. Her jeans and sweater, flung hastily on the floor the night before, lay neatly folded on the bed, her underwear on top, as if nothing unusual had occurred.

Had Rowan risen, dressed and folded her clothes, put last night's lovemaking out of his mind as he conveniently discarded other events in his life? A niggle of doubt threaded itself into her mind. No, she thought. He couldn't have done the things he did, said the things he said last night and not have felt something.

Karin stepped into the deserted dining room. As soon as she seated herself, Thorny poked his head out from the kitchen.

"There you are." He set a bowl of muesli in front of her, then brought a pitcher of milk. "I wasn't sure you'd be back for breakfast, but I saw the box of supplies on the counter this morning. Rowan said you'd got in last night." He shuffled off to the kitchen and returned with a mug of coffee, toast and a jar of the bramble jelly.

She waved it away. "That's for you."

Deep crinkles formed around his eyes. "So it is. And I'm sharing it with my friends. Come on," he urged when she spooned a small mound onto her toast. "Take some more."

"Not another bite, thanks. I'm full." She pushed her plate away and rose to leave.

At that moment, Rowan stepped into the small dining room. He met Karin's shy smile with a curt nod.

"You're up, I see. I went over to check." He motioned toward the door. "Let's go for a walk."

Rowan led the way along a path into a dense copse some distance from camp. Karin followed. He stopped beside a stream, where clear water burbled from under two giant, flat rocks. Rowan knelt on one and motioned to Karin to sit on the other.

He stared dispassionately at the tumbling water. "I'm sorry about last night. If I'd known you were"—he took a deep breath—"inexperienced, it never would have happened."

Karin's heart lurched. "What's that supposed to mean?" she asked in a steady tone, daring him to look her in the eye. A heavy mass settled in her chest.

His eyes darkened. "I don't make a habit of deflowering virgins. Had I known, I would have kept my distance."

Incredulous, she stared at him. "You mean you didn't want me unless . . . unless I was experienced? You sure had me fooled!"

He gave a tired laugh. "Don't be naive, Karin. Of course I wanted you. I think that was fairly obvious."

Anger swept through her. "And what about—what about the things you said to me last night?"

His eyes flicked over her face. "All men say those things. My God, Karin, do you think that I—?" He plucked a lichen-covered twig from a branch overhead, stared at it briefly, then dropped it into the water below. His expression turned vague. "We're quite good together, actually. The next time—"

"The next time? Wait just a minute. Are you suggesting that because we're—what did you call it?—good together, what you want is just a casual affair?" She rose and took an unsteady step backward.

"Sit down, will you?" He gestured toward the spot she had vacated. Karin remained unmoving, her chin set.

"Then we'll stand." He unbent, planted both feet firmly on the rock and stared down at her. The line of his mouth tightened. "Isn't your terminology a bit out of date? This is the nineties. When two people desire one another, as we certainly do"—he swept gray eyes over her—"it's not something to be brushed under the carpet."

Karin took another step back. "I'm not brushing it under the carpet. I just don't have casual affairs. And since when is being traditional considered 'out of date'?" Unexpected tears stung her eyes, and she blinked hard to keep them in check.

Rowan clasped one hand over her wrist and drew her toward him. In a rich, velvety voice he asked, "Don't you think some things transcend tradition? Things like this?"

Still gripping her wrist, he pulled her against his body with his free hand and kissed her, hard. His mouth moved over hers, urgent, demanding, until her lips parted. A pulse at the base of her throat pounded in a disjointed rhythm. His breath, warm on her skin, made her shut out everything but him. Reality tumbled away, and she locked her hands around his neck, pulling him closer.

Rowan made a low, feral sound in his throat and thrust his tumescent body against her groin. They swayed together, bodies locked. Karin felt herself drowning in a flood of sensation, sudden and overpowering. She wanted his mouth against hers, his body caressing her . . . loving her. She wanted him inside her.

Finally, Rowan lifted his head and, with hands that shook, held her away from him. His breathing was ragged and hot against her temple. His eyes burned into hers, and she noted the tiny lines that radiated out from their corners. He looked tired, but triumphant. "Shall I stop?" he murmured.

She trembled uncontrollably. "No."

"Can you deny that you want me, Karin?"

"You already know the answer to that." She kept her eyes averted, studying the top button on his shirt in an effort to maintain her equilibrium.

"Do you feel casual?" he asked, caressing her cheek with one gentle finger.

"No."

His eyes glinted. "Then there's no reason why we shouldn't enjoy each other." He swept her into his arms again and pressed his body against hers. Eagerly, he moved his hands over her buttocks, pulling her tight against him. His breathing grew labored as he kissed her cheek with moist, warm lips, then moved his mouth along the downy softness of her jaw.

She heard herself gasping for breath, felt herself slipping into a chasm as the ground began to whirl. He thrust his tongue into her mouth, inviting, torturing, stroking hers.

Sliding a hand forward, he found the button of her slacks, and before she could mobilize her drugged senses, he had worked it loose. His fingers roamed wildly over her midriff, across her belly.

A flood of moisture gathered at the juncture of her thighs. She slid her hands under his sweater and tee-shirt, into the coarse hair on his chest and rested her head against his breast. The rasping *crex crex* of a corn-crake echoed above the sound of their breathing.

"Karin, I— Oh God, Karin . . ." He stilled his hands and held her a moment, then pressed a light kiss on her reddened lips. "This can wait until tonight. If I don't stop now, I'll . . ." His voice trailed off.

I wouldn't mind, she thought. I love him. And he loves me, whether he admits it or not. All men do *not* say those things. She smiled to herself as the knowledge resonated, bringing with it warmth and an odd sort of abandon. He *did* love her, and he was afraid of his feelings.

Stretching to Rowan's height, she placed a lingering kiss on his lips. "Then perhaps we'd better get back to work."

He flashed her a surprised smile. "Perhaps we had."

Karin turned, hastily buttoned her slacks, and marched off in the direction of the trailers, leaving him to stare after her.

The rest of the morning, she labored over load requirements for the two large antennas. When the truckload of diamond plate for the flooring arrived, she signed the bill of lading and directed the men to unload it, then returned to the office, determined to finish her calculations. But each time she focused on her work, Geoff or one of the other men would stop by her desk and distract her with a question.

After the fifth such interruption, she shoved her laptop aside and stared at the wall, elbows on her board, her head propped between her palms. After a moment, she gave up trying to think about work and let her thoughts drift.

She'd been powerless around Rowan from the beginning, from that first day on the ridge when he'd pulled her into his arms to that night in the cave when he had kissed her, pulled her shivering body close to his, wanted her. Yes, Rowan wanted her as much as she wanted him. It had always been that way, she thought with a start. Always.

And last night . . . yes, she was sure. He cared about

her. He might not *want* to, and he certainly wasn't going to admit it, but he did. And she knew he knew it.

She smiled dreamily. Even when she hadn't *liked* him, she'd wanted him. Even when he was brusque with her, she knew he wanted her. He never bothered to hide his annoyance when any of the men spent more than a few moments with her. Plainly put, he was jealous. She relished the fact.

Absorbed, she jumped when Geoff swept in and paused at the door to kick mud from his boot.

"Karin, would you look over these figures?" He stepped over and dropped a sheet of paper on her desk.

She glanced down. "These are new calculations for the main platform. What's wrong with the old ones?"

"I reworked the north section," he explained. "Rowan's decided to add another antenna."

Her brows rose. "But there's not enough clearance here for a third reflector."

"There is for this one."

She scanned the sheet. "Good grief. You've more than tripled the loads. What's he putting up there, a skyscraper?"

Geoff grinned. "You got it."

"But why—?"

Rowan's baritone interrupted. "The low-frequency gain measurements are unacceptable. Too much broad-beam illumination."

Karin swiveled around. "So you're going up instead? How high?"

"The pedestal is six feet, and it sits on a fifty-three-inch positioner."

"But the requirements for a structure that tall will be more than four times as great. What about wind loading?"

"We're going to narrow the transmit beam so the ground isn't illuminated. The last data we sent were worthless." He gave her a calculating look. "If you don't feel like tackling this, perhaps Geoff will work it up."

Geoff's mouth twisted into a smug smile. "I already have." He picked up the yellow sheet of paper from the desk and handed it to Rowan. "Those are the figures you want." Rowan perused them quickly. "Very well. I'll get you the footprint straight away. One last item"—his gaze swept from Geoff to Karin—"the completion date has been rescheduled for October twelve. That's three weeks from now. The first article must be in place for test a week prior to sign-off."

He strode toward the door, tucking the paper into a binder. "Karin, I'll talk to you later." He paused at the top step and turned, his eyes lit by dark fire. "Tonight."

Karin turned away to hide the blush she knew colored her cheeks. Finally, she looked at Geoff and sighed. "So much for free time. We have a lot of work ahead if we're going to meet that deadline."

He shrugged and, without replying, shuffled toward the door.

"Geoff!" Karin said, her tone sharper than usual.

He whirled at the door, his features drawn into an indignant scowl. His face looked desperate, haunted, the pale eyes lusterless in his shrunken face.

She began again, softly. "Please, Geoff. I know you're under stress. I understand how you're feeling"—her voice lowered—"I'd be, too, given the circumstances, but you can't buckle now. We have to finish on time. Leonard's counting on us both." Without a word, Geoff stomped out.

At dinner she ran into Derrick. "I hear you got a bunch of new calculations dumped on you," he said, as they lounged in the mess room waiting for the rest of the crew to file in. "How's it going?"

She offered him a smile. "Okay. The mounting plates are ready. They'll be bolted in place tomorrow."

"Even the new antenna?"

"Everything's ready except for that one. Which means I have to speak to Geoff about it since he's now designing the main platform." She glanced down the row of chairs. "By the way, where is Geoff?"

Derrick looked away. "I haven't seen him since early this afternoon. Said he had to drive to the other ridge to check something."

Karin's brow furrowed. "There's nothing to see over there." Had she said too much to Geoff earlier? She didn't think so, but he'd left the office without responding. Lately he'd seemed preoccupied.

"Uh, here he is now." Derrick turned toward the door as Geoff, then Paddy, stepped inside. Geoff's eyes glittered, and a deep red suffused his nose and ears.

He's been drinking, Karin thought. She motioned to him, waiting until he sidled over, then pulled him out of earshot. "We need to talk. The workmen will be up to install the grating tomorrow."

Geoff turned dilated pupils on her. "Then let it wait until then. I have one hell of a headache."

Karin sniffed. "Gin, isn't it?"

"What are you talking about?"

"You've been drinking gin. Never mind rolling your eyes at me. You think if Rowan can't smell it on you, he won't guess. But I know what you're like sober, and you are definitely not sober tonight."

She touched his arm. "Geoff, wake up. You're only hurting yourself."

"Mind your own business," he snapped. "I don't have to listen to your nagging. You're blowing this out of proportion."

He lurched toward the door and stumbled down the steps.

Karin followed, heart pumping with alarm. He was dead drunk.

Near the pines, where his trailer stood, he stopped, shoulders slumped.

"Geoff," Karin said evenly. "You can't drink and do this job. There's too much at stake. Think about your future." *Dear God, let him wake up before it's too late.*

Geoff supported himself against a scraggly pine. "You know what you are? A damned, nagging female. I don't need you to help me with my life. Or my job." His mouth thinned. "Rowan trusts my judgment. He gave me the main platform to design, didn't he? That proves I don't need help from you."

He shot her a look of contempt. "Just like Alice. Always bitching about something," he muttered. He turned his back on her and strode off into the night.

Karin sighed. Geoff was just being Geoff. She'd seen it before. If he was unable to recognize that a problem existed, she could do nothing for him. But if he botched the job—her job—she'd have to tell Leonard.

She turned back toward the mess trailer. Rowan stood at the door.

"Anything wrong?" he asked. His gaze flickered from Karin to Geoff's trailer and back. "I heard you talking to Ellis."

She hesitated. "No—nothing's wrong. Geoff said he's not feeling well—a headache. He said he'd skip dinner." Karin grimaced at the lie. She mounted the steps, brushing past Rowan. "Coming in?" she asked. After a searching glance into the shrouded trees, he nodded and followed her inside.

She took a seat across from him. A moment later, Thorny brought in a steaming platter of sliced lamb and roasted potatoes. She helped herself, dug her fork into a mound of potato and pushed her worry aside. Geoff was right about one thing—she couldn't tell him how to run his life. But still . . .

Stop thinking about it, a voice urged. With a sigh, she dragged her thoughts back to the dinner conversation.

She glanced up to meet Rowan's heated gaze. His eyes flicked over her body, secretly undressing her. A pulsing knot formed in her stomach, threaded its way through her chest. Heat pressed in on her. Pushing her plate aside, she raised the teacup to her lips.

Across the table, Rowan listened politely to his friend Jack, but the smile he flashed to Karin, and the message in his silver-flecked eyes, caused her blood to race.

She let herself be persuaded into a game of chess with Derrick, but her mind wasn't on it. Instead of plotting her board strategy, she pictured Rowan's fingers moving over her body.

And she thought about the situation between them.

Could she risk it? What if Rowan could never admit he cared for her? Was he so frightened of commitment that he would let her go back to California, let her move out of his life forever? She licked dry lips and tried to concentrate.

"Checkmate," Derrick chortled, lifting her king from the board.

"Right," she declared. "I guess I'm not much competition tonight." She rose and stepped to the door. "Good night everyone."

Inside her room she leaned against the door. As darkness gathered, she realized she had been waiting all evening to be with Rowan, feel his arms around her, his lips on her body. Heat flushed her face and brought a trembling weakness to her thighs.

She stripped and folded her clothes and set them on the chair. She didn't want to think anymore—she just wanted to let it happen. Resolutely, she set aside her doubts.

She showered, smoothed on lavender body lotion and slipped into her new cotton lawn gown. It flowed in a smooth line from the bodice to the floor. The thrust of her breasts parted the soft shirring and displayed the row of tiny pearl buttons that closed to the waist. With languid motions she ran a brush through her hair and splashed Shalimar on her neck and wrists. She didn't feel like reading. Instead, she pulled a tablet out of her top desk drawer and began a letter to Athena. It gave her something to do.

Before she had completed three lines, she heard Rowan's door open, then close. A minute later, the spray of water from the shower beat a tattoo against the metal wall. She forced herself to continue writing until her door opened.

Rowan appeared in his pajama bottoms and a matching robe of deep burgundy paisley, loosely tied at the waist and pulled tight over broad shoulders. His exposed chest showed the dark hair glistening on his still-damp skin. Freshly shaven, he had a bit of tissue clinging to his jaw where the razor had nicked his skin. His musky fragrance filled the room. Excitement sizzled through her.

He stepped close, reached out both hands and pulled her to her feet. "Ready for bed?"

She made a quarter-turn and slipped an arm around his waist. "I thought you'd never ask."

The laugh began deep in his chest. "So impatient you are. Well, now, I never retire early, so I could hardly tear off after you without arousing suspicion." His gaze drifted downward. "Are you wearing that for me?"

"Maybe. Like it?" She dropped her hands, stepped back and pirouetted. He drew her back into his arms, answering with an affirmative growl deep in his chest. Then he tilted her chin and bent to her mouth.

His tongue traced her soft lower lip. His hands cupped her breasts, lifting them until he had gathered their fullness in each hand. "I wanted to do this all day. God, I could think of nothing else."

Suddenly he lifted her into his arms and carried her through the doorway and set her down on his bed. At once he began working the buttons of the gown. "You look lovely in this, but I think we can dispense with it." He managed three small buttons, then gave up in exasperation. "Oh, hell." Impatiently, he pulled the flimsy material over her head and sailed it across the room.

She laughed at his hurry, feeling a delicious power as she realized how hungry he was for her. Her nipples puckered in the chilly room, but in the next instant Rowan touched his tongue to one swelling peak, and desire flowed through her, coursing all the way down to her toes. She reached for the tie of his robe. "Stand still."

The garment parted. Slowly she drew it off, deliberately lengthening the ritual, watching his eyes grow dark. His chest was bare except for the coarse hair matted against the pale gold of his skin. Karin brushed her fingers, then her lips, over the small nipples.

Rowan trembled, sucked in a mouthful of air. He smelled of pine soap and musk. The crisp hair tickled her lips as she teased one nub.

He groaned. "Don't stop. Where'd you learn that?"

"From you." She smiled. "I'm waiting for tonight's lesson."

He drew in a ragged breath. "Ah, I don't think you have all that much to learn." He captured her hands and brought them to his pajamas. "But if you don't stop, I'm going to have a real problem."

She felt him through the silky fabric, swollen and ready, and suddenly her own need pulsed through her. She laid her hand on the fastening.

He pushed her fingers aside, stripped the pajamas off, and rolled with her onto the wide, soft bed.

She raised her body up and moved over him. He glanced at her, a question in his eyes, but his body stilled when she began to stroke him, first with her fingers, then her mouth, her breasts. He gripped her shoulders, the fingers of each hand splayed against her skin.

She ripened under his touch, and moving astride him, she took him wholly into herself. She moved with a gentle, deliberate rhythm, amazed by her own seductiveness, until his face contorted and he grasped her buttocks, stiffened and cried out.

He lay back, guiding her fingers over his moist skin. "Oh, God, Karin. You feel so good. I can't believe you're real." He pulled her against him, rolled her over and let the gentle motion of his body within hers ignite them both. He wound his fingers in the strands of her hair and covered her mouth with his, murmuring her name again and again as he increased the tempo of his thrusts. "Karin," he gasped. "Oh, Karin, I need you so much."

She moved as if possessed. Her mind floated unbound, aware only of aching tension and her hunger for him. Moments later, her body burst into exquisite, shattering sensation.

Afterward, she tucked herself into the hollow of his arm, resting her head against his chest. The steady beat of his heart lulled her. Being with Rowan felt so right.

"What are you thinking?" he asked lazily.

She flushed but remained silent.

His arm tightened. "Must be good. Tell me."

She planted a kiss just above his nipple. "I was wondering if we'd feel this way if we were married."

His lids snapped open, and he edged away. "What brought that up?"

"Don't you think it's natural to think about marriage, under the circumstances?"

He propped himself up on one arm and stared down at her. "There are no circumstances, Karin. We've been over that."

Her thoughts raced. Suddenly she sat up. "Marry me, Rowan," she blurted. "You're in love with me."

"I'm not—" he began.

She stopped his words with her lips. "Yes, you are! And you're scared."

He gave her a long, long look. "Yes, Karin, I'm in love with you. Unfortunately. But that's my problem— not yours." He edged away a fraction, watching her face. "I thought we agreed to enjoy each other in the time we have left. I made no mention to anything beyond that."

"In the time we have left?" What on earth was he saying? "Are you . . . asking me to sleep with you while

I'm here, and then go back to my job, back to my home in the States as if this . . . as if this were just part of the assignment?"

"It's all I'm prepared to offer, Karin. I made it perfectly clear—I don't make commitments." His gray, hooded gaze moved hungrily over her body and stopped at her face. "I've had commitment. Thank you, no."

He separated a lock of her hair and twirled it absently between his fingers. "Bernard Shaw said it succinctly: it is most unwise for people in love to marry."

"Bernard Shaw was dead wrong," she said flatly. "Where I come from, people in love *do* marry."

"Marriage is a state to which I do not aspire . . . again. Admit it, Karin. You want me, and I certainly want you. I enjoy your honesty. You're a good worker and a passionate woman. Surprisingly passionate. As I said, we're good together."

"That isn't enough for me."

He stared at her. "It's what I can offer."

She fingered the comforter underneath her. Other women would not reject his offer. But she wasn't other women. She loved him, more than she could have imagined possible. And he'd just admitted that he loved her, she thought with sudden clarity. Then she paused, rethinking what he'd said. Perhaps he really did want only her body? No, she acknowledged, that wasn't true. He loved her. Or he would, if he'd let himself.

She met his heated gaze, the silver flecks in his eyes like ice shards radiating outward from darkened centers. She knew trying to reach him now was futile. His mind was closed.

Oh, Lord. What should she do?

The answer came almost immediately.

She shrugged. "Then I guess we've said all there is to say." She slipped out of bed and walked deliberately to her room.

"Karin, wait!"

She latched the door and glanced at the desk. Three o'clock. She scanned the room for her nightgown, then remembered Rowan had flung it away in his room. She pulled on her robe and crawled between the chilly sheets into the cold bed.

She knew she was gambling. It was risky. Very risky. Her body ached for him. For a moment she considered going to him, reaching out to touch him. Maybe, in time, he'd change his mind.

And maybe he wouldn't.

The clock struck four when she heard Rowan's outer door close and his heavy tread down the stairs. Apparently he couldn't sleep either. Good. Let him walk it out. Maybe the cold night air would clarify his thinking.

Oh, Lord, she could use some clarity, too. Should she compromise? Make an exception in Rowan's case simply because she loved him? Wouldn't that guarantee that he'd never conquer his fear of commitment? On the other hand, if she gave in, accepted a short-term affair, what did she have to lose?

Everything. Her sanity. Her heart. And Rowan, too.

Oh, God, was there no way out of this?

She turned her head into the pillow. She'd try to sleep. Tomorrow her mind would be clear, and she'd think about what she should do.

FIFTEEN

Wind gusted through the trees, rattling the window glass in the mess trailer. Seated alone at the table, Karin toyed with her breakfast, unmindful of the warmth generated by the kerosene heater or the sharp sounds outside. Although she was normally hungry for the hearty food, breakfast had as little appeal for her this morning as sleep had had the night before. She glanced at the leaden sky outside, then at the wall clock. Five till seven. The crew had eaten and shuffled off to their tasks, and still Rowan hadn't returned.

Oh, God, what was she going to do? She wanted him desperately, but she wanted more than just his body. No matter what his feelings for her, all he was willing to offer was casual sex.

But there had been nothing casual about their lovemaking. A delicious quiver spiraled up from her belly as her mind relived the previous night. Yes, she most certainly wanted him. All of him. For her, nothing about her feelings for Rowan was even remotely casual.

Karin sipped her coffee and willed her body into submission. She'd done the unthinkable, allowed herself to fall in love with a man who only wanted an affair. But she still ached for his touch. She ached to be a part of his life.

She knew Rowan's often cold, arrogant manner was just a facade, his protection against his own vulnerability. She understood that now. And though it helped to understand him, it offered no solution to her dilemma.

How could she show him that he needn't fear involvement with her, that she wasn't anything like his first wife? But he knew she wasn't, had even told her she was nothing like Claudia. No, the problem was deeper than that.

Had he been so scarred by Claudia that nothing, not even her love, could ever heal him? Had she found at last the man she would love for the rest of her life, only to lose him to the impenetrable barrier he had himself erected?

She was at a complete loss. How could she get through to him, make him understand?

The truth was, she couldn't. Rowan was remote when he was frightened, and he was frightened now—of her. He was scared spitless because he *did* care about her; if he were less emotionally involved, he would not be threatened. How ironic.

She should count herself lucky—at least she had that, a small corner of his heart.

But it didn't ease the pain in hers.

Thorny began clearing the table. "You don't like the porridge this morning? Perhaps some eggs?"

"No. Thanks, I'm not hungry." She flashed him a thin smile, then gulped the last of her coffee.

In her office, Rowan stood with Geoff beside the drawing board, discussing plans for the day's work. When Karin stepped inside, Rowan gave her a cursory nod and resumed his explanation.

She seated herself at the gray desk and set to work

on the tables she'd begun the day before. A moment later, the squeal of brakes announced the arrival of the construction crew.

Geoff snatched his clipboard and shoved a tablet into the clasp. "I need to talk to the foreman. Be back in a minute." The door slammed shut as his footsteps thudded on the stair.

In the sudden hush, Karin stared at Rowan. Pain, distrust and hunger warred in his gray eyes, and in that instant she glimpsed the open window into his soul. Yes, he wanted her, loved her. But he could not risk it.

He looked at her a long, long moment without smiling, then turned back to the drawing board. He made a show of shuffling papers, finally slapped a set of drawings on Karin's desk. "I want these double-checked. There's a discrepancy between your figures and Ellis's."

The sharpness in his tone jarred her. She looked up, but the familiar mask of detachment had again descended over his features. "I suppose we're going to work through mutual antagonism again?" The words tumbled out before she could stop them.

He smiled without humor. "It doesn't have to be this way, Karin. The choice is up to you. I was sure that after . . . after last night we both knew what we wanted."

Karin forced herself to brave the cool cynicism in his eyes. "You make last night seem . . . simple. One might think it didn't mean much to you."

"It meant a hell of a lot to me. I simply put it in its proper perspective," he said with maddening calm. "You're the one who's making an issue out of it."

"Damn your proper perspective! We're discussing human feelings, not statistics on a chart."

"We are at that. And you've got yours knotted up into some female fantasy. This is real, Karin." He took a swift step forward and jerked her out of the chair into his arms. "This and nothing else." He pinioned her chin between his thumb and forefinger and lowered his mouth to hers.

At the first brush of his lips, her body trembled. She jerked away, but he caught her in an iron grip. Inexorably she felt herself pulled into the muscled circle of his arms, and he increased the pressure on her mouth until her lips parted; then his tongue dipped inside. Warmth curled around her as he pressed his hips into hers. He drew back and looked down with hooded eyes.

Her senses swam, and her breath constricted. She had to get away before . . . "No," she moaned, turning her head away from his descending mouth. "I don't . . . want . . ."

"Oh, but you do," he said in a low, hypnotic whisper, his breath hot against her cheek. "We both do." Again he brought his lips down on hers, moving over them until she stopped struggling. A sharp surge of desire pulsed through her, and she parted her lips, savoring the taste, the texture of him. She knew that in another minute she would be swept away. . . .

And she knew that he knew it, too.

His mouth moved demandingly over hers. She breathed in his musky, male scent, threaded her fingers into his dark, thick hair, and let her body take over. He gripped her shoulders, forcing her back against the desk. The thrust of his groin against her belly, the rough, taut fabric and the tumescence beneath sent her pulse skyrocketing. Instinctively she arched against him. Then abruptly, he pulled away, his breathing harsh, and stared at her, his eyes dark, unfathomable pools.

Without a word, he whirled and walked out.

Shaking, she slumped into the chair. She sat very still, hearing only the pounding of her heart while the minutes ticked by. He'd done it again, reached for her, kindled her hunger for him, then pushed his feelings away. She knew why now, knew she could not go on like this much longer. She knew she'd have to make a choice soon—love him on his terms or leave him, on hers.

Neither option would be healthy for either of them.

Finally, her breathing steadied, and she spread out the drawings he had dropped on her desk.

The lines coalesced into a beehive of black figures on the white paper as her mind struggled to focus. After a determined moment she garnered her powers of concentration and doggedly began to check the drawing. On the second run-through, she spotted the problem. Geoff hadn't adequately provided for the added weight.

Twenty minutes later, Geoff's footsteps rang on the landing. She drew him outside. "Walk over to the platform with me—I want you to see something." She handed him one of the drawings. "I don't trust those vertical columns. They're going to have too much deflection."

Geoff craned his neck toward her and scowled. "Rowan said you insisted on four-inch pipe."

Karin sighed. Geoff had never liked having his methods questioned. He took it as a personal criticism of his ability. Lately, he'd been jumpy as a hare, making it next to impossible for her to suggest anything to him.

She kept her expression steady, her voice calm. "I

know. But that was before Big Bertha, here." She motioned toward the pale green reflector now being hoisted by the crane onto its slate-colored pedestal. She watched Paddy and Jack secure the three-hundred-pound dish while Cyril installed the feeder. To Karin, the silvery antenna looked like a space-age thunderbolt.

"You've just added eight hundred pounds and you've gone up fifteen feet," she said evenly. "Do you know what that's going to mean in a gale-force wind?"

Geoff shrugged. "I ran the calculations. The structure'll stand up to anything Mother Nature can throw our way. Have a look if you don't believe me."

They walked back to the trailer, where Geoff pulled a sheaf of papers out of a coffee-stained brown folder.

"Here. See for yourself."

"I will," Karin murmured.

"Always the perfectionist," Geoff sneered.

"Geoff, you asked me to look over your work, remember?"

"All right, all right." He held up both hands in a gesture of defense. "But that was before. I'm okay now. Besides, if my design is good enough for Marsden, it should be good enough for you." He gave a short laugh, abruptly swept the set of blueprints into his arms, and stomped out of the office. The door slammed hard.

Karin stared after him. Dear God, first Rowan and now Geoff. How would she be able to get through this assignment? It was like being on an emotional roller coaster.

She sighed and laid out Geoff's figures in front of her again. She pulled her calculator from the upper drawer of the desk and checked the equations. Geoff she could handle with mathematics and logic, but Rowan?

The irony made her wince. Somehow, she hadn't figured he would matter so much to her. For years she had avoided involvement, easily sidestepping relationships the minute she sensed a man's interest in her. Now, she was the one who was interested, who was in fact seriously involved with someone.

Not someone, she amended. Him. Rowan Marsden. If it had been anyone else, she would be content to drop it, remain alone. Or even to have a casual affair. But not with Rowan.

Rowan was different. He drew her to him like a soul hungry for nourishment. She wanted to be with him, wanted to have and hold him for the rest of her life.

To play for such high stakes, for permanency, she could not afford to settle for Rowan's terms. An affair had a beginning, a middle and an inevitable end. That was not what she wanted with Rowan. An affair would never be enough.

By nightfall, her head and shoulders ached. She neatened her desk and walked wearily to the mess hall kitchen to see Thorny. Pleading fatigue, she excused herself from dinner and, after latching the connecting door between her room and Rowan's, settled her exhausted body into bed.

Hours later, she awakened to Rowan's impatient knock.

He tried the door, then rapped again. "Karin. Open the bloody door!"

She lay silent.

He swore softly, then knocked once more. "I need to talk to you, Karin."

"We don't have anything to talk about."

"Are you going to open the damn door, or do I have to break it down?" he thundered.

Karin recoiled at the dull thud against its surface and the sharper crack of splintering wood. Another blow and his fist would smash through the thin panels. She stumbled out of bed and tripped the latch.

Rowan filled the space. Steam from the shower swirled into the room. His dark hair was tousled, and his eyes burned. She saw the faint mottling of color splashed across his face and the stubborn set of his jaw. His black shirt was open to the waist; droplets of water glimmered on the slash of hair dappling his chest. A pulse leaped in his neck.

She stood very still beside the bed. She ran her tongue over suddenly dry lips, her gaze following the line of coarse, dark hair down to the fastening of his faded denims, then moving back to his face. Their eyes locked as the tension mounted.

"I make no apology for this morning," he said at last.

A wave of anger shook her at his blatantly unyielding stance. "None was expected."

Damn him. What was he doing in her room? Why didn't he leave her alone? Or—she groaned inwardly—drag her onto the comforter and make violent love to her. Her throat closed, and her knees turned to water.

"Get into bed," he snapped. "It's much too cold to be standing there without a robe." His gaze flicked over her flannel gown, lingered on the hard points of her nipples. His eyes flashed with dark light, but his strained face registered only fatigue.

Without retort, she did as he commanded. Let him

think she was cold. It would ease her struggle. She compressed her lips into a thin line.

He focused on a spot somewhere near the bed. "You said before you wanted to move to the village. Perhaps that would be a good idea, under the circumstances."

"That was before the test schedule was moved up. Now I have to stay near. The more time I can spend on finishing the project, the sooner I can go back to the States."

But she didn't want to leave. Couldn't he see that?

"As you wish. But keep that door locked at night." He gestured toward his bedroom. "You'll be safer."

Safer? It hadn't stopped him just now. "From what?" she asked, needing to hear him say it out loud.

"God, Karin. You are the most maddening—" He leaned suddenly over the bed, his eyes glittering. "From me. After all, I'm a man with . . . needs."

Her heart lurched, and she fought to keep her voice even. "Needs that come and go, depending on who's available. Needs that don't include marriage." She enjoyed seeing his grimace of pain.

"I've been married."

"And you had a bad experience. Do you think it would be like that with me? That I would make you unhappy, hurt you, as she did?" She blinked to hold back unexpected tears. "You said"—her voice caught—"you said I was nothing like her." She looked up. "When you hold me, do you still think of her?"

A muscle in his jaw quivered, but he said nothing.

She went on, deliberately going for the jugular. "When I'm with a man, I want to feel that I'm valued for myself, not because I'm some vague reminder of a long-past pain. Thank God I came to my senses before letting myself become emotionally involved."

She saw him wince.

It was a lie. She'd been involved from the first moment he touched her.

The next two weeks passed in a blur. The workmen welded the last horizontal cross member into place. Paddy and Jack pitched in to dismantle the old wooden walkway and bolted the new portable stairway to the platform. Using the hydraulic-powered hoist, they lifted each of the thick steel plates onto the deck and anchored them securely. Then they hoisted the heavy positioners into place on top of each mounting plate. The footprints matched perfectly.

Each day, Karin ticked off another completed task on her punch list and watched as Geoff did the same. Despite her concern, and Geoff's frequent absences from the site, they had finished within the deadline. A few days more for checkout and sign-off, and she would be going home.

She gazed across the fifty-foot expanse of metal plate reflecting sunlight in the crisp October afternoon, and smiled. Each section fit neatly in place. Her portion of the structure, spanning the two engineering trailers, had gone well. Even Rowan acknowledged this when he inspected the platform.

She felt less confident about Geoff's work. If only he weren't so cocksure. A strange uneasiness settled over her as she watched the large antenna dish rotating on its pedestal. Maybe I'm being paranoid, she thought with a frown.

Geoff's calculations appeared to be correct, but something wasn't right. Should she speak to Rowan?

No, she sighed. For the past two weeks, Rowan had

met her every word with stoic silence. He kept to himself, issuing his directives through Geoff. Even Thorny was puzzled.

Today, the workmen cleared away the last of the rubble, and Cyril suggested a party. Neville Pickering himself was coming from the home office to inspect. Why not celebrate? "After all," the bearded blond said, "with Mac and Paddy leaving on holiday Saturday, now's the perfect time for a thumping great feast."

Rowan looked thoughtfully at Thorny, then at the date calendar on his watch. "Can you arrange it for Friday? That's only two days notice."

A Cheshire cat grin spread over Thorny's lined face. "Leave it to me. I know just the ticket."

Friday afternoon, Neville Pickering, a grandfatherly figure with alert dark eyes and a shiny bald head, arrived at the head of a home-office entourage. The antennas, serviced and checked, gleamed on their gray pedestals, and the spare reflectors stood like sentries in a line along the equipment shed, awaiting inspection.

Rowan introduced Geoff and Karin. His comments brought a twinkle to the older man's eyes and an increasing sense of wonder to Karin. Rowan actually praised her engineering effort. Of course he must have spoken for Pickering's benefit. She doubted that five civil sentences had passed between them in as many days. Her heart thudded dully in her chest.

When the formalities concluded, Thorny uncorked bottles of champagne. The sun shot vibrant pink and orange color on the clouds along the horizon, and Mendelssohn poured from a CD player as the cook strode around the deck passing heaping trays of canapés. Rowan filled and refilled their glasses.

Neville Pickering waved away a third refill and settled in a chair next to Robin and Derrick, reminiscing on the early days of the company. Geoff downed three glasses of champagne in succession, then disappeared.

Karin watched various conversation groups, glancing occasionally at Rowan as he moved from cluster to cluster. He acted the gracious host, but his mood seemed somber.

He stopped to fill her glass, but she stepped back. "I've had enough. I think I'll see if Thorny needs help in the kitchen."

His eyes met hers. "You're not enjoying yourself."

"Not especially. Should I be?"

His mouth hardened, but beneath the tight expression a spark of pain flared in his eyes. "It could have been different."

He moved past her, then made a half-turn, his gaze flicking over her pale yellow sweater and slacks. "Try to see it from my point of view, can't you?" he said, his voice low. "I will not be hurt again, not ever!"

But he hurt now. She could see it in his eyes, in the lines between his nose and chin, in the slight droop of his shoulders. And it was his own damn fault.

She snatched up an empty glass and set it onto a tray. "That's because you've shut yourself up in a vacuum where no one can touch you. And all because of an experience that occurred fifteen years ago."

She took a deep breath. She had to get it out now while she had the courage. "Rowan, you've become sensitized about women, about what you think goes on inside us. You won't let yourself see anything but what you want to see. And you do it to protect yourself. You're afraid—not of women, but of yourself."

Rowan froze, brows slanting downward.

"I'm not at all like Claudia. I'm me, and I don't compromise my values. Not for you, not for anyone." She paused for breath, willing herself not to soften at his bleak expression. "You're too arrogant and stubborn and scared to even try to change." She turned at the stair and looked back at him. "I feel sorry for you, Rowan. You're missing out on life."

She balanced the tray of glasses and trudged down the stairs and through the grass to the mess trailer, fighting the sting of tears. Her face felt hot, and she drew a shuddering breath.

Thorny looked up from his dishpan when she entered the tiny kitchen. "Just drop them here," he said, gesturing to his left.

She picked up a cloth and began to dry the bowls and trays spilling over on the counter.

Thorny's expression clouded as he glanced at her face. "What's the matter, missy?"

"Nothing."

He plunged several glasses into the dishwater. "Strange it is how folks can fabricate stories to hide their true feelings. Our man Rowan says the same thing, when he says anything at all."

Thorny's pale blue eyes searched her face. "Is it him that's troubling you?"

She nodded, lowering her gaze to the glass in her hand. "He's only interested in me on a temporary basis." Tears spilled onto her cheeks, and she redried the glass.

"I wondered about that."

Karin looked Thorny squarely in the eye. "You've known Rowan a long time. Has he always been like this?"

Thorny carefully folded the dishcloth over the sink.

"Can't say he was when I stayed at the manor. But after his marriage broke up, he wasn't the same. He's a very private man, holds his emotions inside."

"Did . . . Was he very much in love with her?"

The bulky cook smiled sadly. "Her leaving devastated him. He's never forgiven her." He scooped up the plate of leftover canapés and fitted a sheet of plastic wrap over them. "I'd hoped you would find the key to unlock all his hurt."

"I'd hoped so, too, Thorny. But he's hidden the key away, as well."

Saturday dawned with lowering, steel gray clouds and a cold wind that ripped through Karin's layers of shirt, sweater and jacket. She hugged her arms against her chest and chatted with Paddy and Mac in the parking area as the two waited for Rowan to drive them down to the village. From Cairnbeck the men planned to travel by train to Brora for two weeks of Highlands salmon fishing along the river. She'd be gone when they got back.

Mac enfolded her in his large arms and gave her a whiskery peck on the cheek. "It's been grand workin' wi' you, lass. I'll miss your pretty face across the table from me of a morning."

"I'll miss you, too, Mac. Enjoy yourself. I hope you catch lots of fish." She gave him a squeeze and stepped away. "And you, Paddy." She held out her hand. "You've all been so nice to work with."

The Irishman hoisted her off her feet and whirled her around. "It's been grand having you here. All the lads'll miss you." He jerked his head toward the platform as Rowan descended the stair and strode toward them, a jacket slung over one broad shoulder. "Even him, though he's not likely to admit it. Don't give up on him, Karin," Paddy whispered as he gave her a final hug.

"Have you finished your good-byes? I haven't all day." Rowan's tone was coolly disapproving. He slid into the driver's seat and started the engine.

Paddy climbed into the rear seat behind Mac. "Remember what I said."

Karin watched until the Rover disappeared around the bend. Paddy's words echoed in her mind. It was too late; she *had* given up. Rowan would not—could not—change. And neither could she. Her job here was finished, and there was nothing to be gained by prolonging her stay. She turned toward her trailer.

At dusk, cold and weary from packing the folders and sorting through the stacks of items to be shipped or stored, Karin wandered over to the engineering trailer. Rowan sat beside Robin at a console, monitoring data. Bent over a screen, he didn't hear her come in. She cleared her throat, and he looked up sharply.

"I've decided to stay here tonight. I've some things to sort through before . . ." She took a breath. "I'll be leaving in the morning."

He said nothing.

"If you're going down to the village, I'll be glad to keep an eye on things," she added.

Rowan eased his lean length out of the chair and surveyed her, his gray eyes shadowed. "That won't be necessary. I'll be staying behind myself. We've picked up a transmission on Radio Four that a weather system is developing off Northern Ireland. The CAA have confirmed and asked us to stand by." He looked at Robin. "I'd like you, Derrick and Thorny to remain on-site as well in case anything comes of this." He glanced at Karin. "Where's Ellis?"

"I haven't seen him since this afternoon."

Rowan frowned. "Odd. Well, he'll have to stay behind, too. Tell Jack he and Cyril can take my car. One of the Rovers is down, and I'll need the other in case we need to clear off the mountain." He flipped a set of keys toward Robin.

"What do you mean 'clear off'?" Karin asked.

"Storm fronts can get pretty nasty this time of year. If this one goes large scale, as they anticipate, we could be in for a gale. I want to be sure we all can leave the mountain should we need to." He raked long fingers through his hair. "I hope we're adequately braced."

A sudden chill shot through her. Now she knew what had bothered her. Why hadn't she acknowledged it before? She spun and reached for the door handle.

Karin raced across the ground to the long span of the platform and peered upward, underneath, to inspect the bracing. Then she whirled around to the short span. They were the same. The horizontal members for the longer span were missing!

A wave of foreboding hit her. Oh, God, in a gale-force wind, the vibration on the heavier, unsupported section could bring the entire span down and the antennas along with it. How could Geoff have forgotten the horizontal bracing? She had to see him.

Karin raced across the grass to the room Geoff shared with Jack.

"Door's open." Geoff glanced up over an armload of bedding. He was moving his gear to the opposite end, where Mac had slept. He grinned sheepishly, stepping quickly toward the desk where an open bottle stood. "Tonight I can have a real bed."

"Geoff. How could you!"

"What's eating you now?" His voice was petulant, his words slurred.

"You forgot the horizontal braces on the long span," she shouted. "A storm's coming in. If that section collapses—"

"Hey. No need to go high order," he huffed. "I'll take care of it." He dropped the bedding in a pile on the floor and scratched his head. "You say the braces are missing? Funny, I was positive I'd put them on the drawings." He took a healthy cut from the bottle and sank onto the bed.

Karin lunged toward the bed, snatched the bottle from Geoff's fingers and flung it against the door. Glass tinkled to the floor, drenched in an amber pool.

"Damn you." She spit the word like a bullet.

Geoff sat mesmerized, staring at the broken bottle.

A sickening wave of fear washed over her. Geoff couldn't help. He was too far gone, and there wasn't time. She had to tell Rowan. Now.

By the time she raced back to the consoles, the wind was shrieking down the valley.

"Rowan," she panted. "The horizontal braces are missing. Geoff forgot them. He's been drinking and . . ."

Rowan waved her quiet. "Slow down. Repeat what you just said."

"The platform—some of the braces are—"

Fury darkened Rowan's features. "Later about the braces. What did you say about Ellis?"

Karin's shoulders slumped. "He has a drinking problem. I should have mentioned it before, but I thought he was working on it and—"

Rowan studied her with sudden alarm. "You knew Ellis had a drinking problem? In God's name, why didn't you tell me?"

"I . . . I thought he had come to his senses. He asked me to help him, to check his work," she finished lamely.

Rowan's face muscles tightened, he focused deliberate eyes on her. Very slowly, he asked, "Exactly what were you going to say about the braces?"

Steeling herself, Karin faced his scrutiny. "They're not there—the horizontal supports are missing."

Rowan swore. "Then for damn sure we'll have to keep a 'heads up.' If this storm is anything like they predict, we could be in for a night of it. CAA sent this just a few moments ago." He handed her a printout.

Her eye caught the first line. *The Meteorological Office issues the following gale warning at 1600 hours Greenwich Mean Time for the sea areas of Malin and the Irish Sea.* Puzzled, she handed it back. "What does it mean?"

He sighed. "Possible big trouble. The RAF is putting some device up there they want tested under severe wind conditions. They think this is the storm that will do it. It's going to get nasty, Karin. And I haven't enough crew here to install bracing. Or handle an emergency." His eyes met hers. "I want you to stay inside."

Her heart jumped. "How will you manage?"

"I don't know. I just will."

She glanced at the printer as it spat out another sheet of paper. "I can monitor for you. Why don't you go have something to eat."

"Later." He leveled his gaze at her before turning back to the screen.

The network hummed with the flow of data. The storm front moved with excruciating slowness over the Irish Sea to the Cumbrian coast where it struck the fishing town of Maryport before moving inland. Lash-

ing winds and record tides kept travel at a standstill.
For hours, Karin tracked the storm's progress and read
the reports as they filtered in. Outside, trees bent and
swayed, slapping against the trailers. The windows whistled with the gathering strength of the winds.

They waited.

Thorny scuttled in and out, bringing pots of coffee
and sandwiches. The lights flickered and dimmed.
Rowan paced the trailer restlessly, periodically focusing
his attention on the controller directing the large antenna. Geoff, subdued and apparently sober, moved
back and forth assisting Robin and Derrick with the
cables. Later, Thorny sat with Karin at the monitor. The
night stretched out into blocks of minutes that dragged
by.

Karin's eyes grew heavy as she handed the latest
transmission to Thorny.

"Winds increasing," he read. "Should top eighty
knots before dawn."

She glanced at her watch. Eleven fifty-five. Lord, she
was tired. Her shoulders ached, her head ached. She
ached all over.

"Why don't you try to get some sleep?" Thorny suggested. "I can sit in for you."

She glanced at Rowan. He nodded, his face haggard
as he shifted his attention from one control bay to another.

"No," she said. "I'll stay."

The weather system hit full force at 0100 hours—one
A.M. Rain and hail beat against the trailer, and the violent wind shook it until it reeled on its blocks like a
drunkard. The door flew open and water spewed in
and ran along the floor, spattering the console. The
lights flickered twice as the trailer groaned. Above

them they heard the vibration of the platform, and seconds later, they were plunged into blackness.

"Damn," Rowan muttered. "The generator's failed." A spate of blasphemies followed. He threw on a yellow slicker and bolted toward the exit, grabbing a flashlight from a clip on the wall. The door slammed.

After a moment of stunned silence, Thorny and the other men headed after him.

The noise outside was deafening. The trailer shook with such violence Karin was knocked from her chair. She heard a shout, then the sickening crunch of metal. Instantly the far corner of the trailer became visible as light stabbed through the sky. Karin's eyes focused on a gaping hole where the rain gushed inside. Then a man's scream tore through the air, dulled by another blast of wind-driven rain.

She had to get out. Rowan or Thorny or one of the others needed help.

She pulled a sou'wester from the hook and threw it over her head. The sleeves engulfed her hands as she ripped the remaining flashlight from its clip and pushed against the door.

The wind tore the flimsy panel from her grasp. It sagged on its hinges, then crashed against the siding.

The impenetrable blackness sent an icy chill through her. She could see nothing beyond the steps, could hear nothing but the roar of the wind and the cracking of nearby tree limbs as the wind buffeted everything in its path.

Suddenly, a blast of wind caught the trailer broadside. It lurched crazily.

Off-balance, Karin hurtled down the steps.

SIXTEEN

Karin landed on her knees amidst a tangle of branches. She groped for her flashlight in the muck, found it in a sodden clump of grass and switched it on.

Tree limbs littered the area. Derrick tore past her. She shouted at him, but the rampaging wind whipped her words away.

Clinging desperately to the trailer, she edged around to the platform. Dumbfounded, she viewed the destruction. The entire antenna section had collapsed, the decking swung crazily in the air.

The long span careened over the trailer. A groan of metal beneath the platform grated on her ear, and she edged closer to the trailer wall.

Without warning, the entire span buckled, and a section of the platform swayed to one side. Karin jerked away. A downed support beam caught her heel, and she toppled backward, landing squarely on her tailbone. She struggled to a sitting position and froze, horrified, as the section of grating directly above her hurtled downward.

As the beam struck, a stab of pain ripped through her and the world went black.

When she came to, her head exploded in colored

lights. Waves of nausea rolled over her. She drew a breath and moaned. Paralyzing pain tore through her chest.

She sucked in short, jerky gasps of air. She had no feeling in her right leg. She struggled to rise, but knives of fire radiated up her thigh. Her head lolled back.

"Rowan?" she called out. She groaned with the effort.

"Karin?" Rowan's voice sounded nearby. "Oh, God. Karin."

Her lids fluttered open. Rowan's face swam before her. She felt his hands grasp her face, felt his breath against her cheek. He trembled as he crouched beside her, supporting her head. "Karin, Karin."

"Rowan . . . what—"

"Hush," he soothed. "Don't try to talk."

Voices floated nearer.

"Over here," Rowan shouted.

Thorny appeared, his light slashing through the rain. He beamed it beside Rowan. "Karin? Good Lord!"

Rowan passed a hand over his face. "She's trapped under the grating," he shouted. "It's too risky to move her. Go for help."

"Where're Derrick and Robin?"

"At the generator."

"I'll get them," Thorny shouted, already trotting into the blackness.

"Have Robin ring up Keswick," Rowan shouted hoarsely. "Tell them we've an emergency, and to stand by. And bring that damned crane. Hurry!"

* * *

"Is there any change?"

A masculine voice drifted somewhere above her, vaguely familiar. Then another voice spoke, and a swirl of gray shadows settled over her. She listened to the sounds, unable to focus on the words.

Rowan sank into a vinyl chair in the small surgery. He winced at the sting of the needle as painkiller was injected into his forehead, but he was too tired to do more than slump against the ugly orange chair back while the doctor on duty sutured a three-inch cut above his left eye. Luckily, the tree branch hadn't struck an inch lower. He was fortunate.

But Karin lay unconscious in a room down the hall. A tremor shook his body. If anything happens to her— Oh, God, if she . . .

"Hold still, mon," the doctor spluttered in a heavy Glaswegian accent. "Ye'll be having yer eye sewn shut if you make another move like that." He frowned down upon his patient. "You should have said something about this cut to the duty nurse last night. Could've disinfected it hours ago."

Rowan forced his body into submission under the pull of the needle. "This was the least of my worries."

When the doctor finished, Rowan lurched to his feet. His denims chafed where they had dried in a mass of muddy creases. Rough stubble covered his jaw, and his head pounded as if being pummeled with a fist. Sweat collected at his armpits and down the middle of his back, and his mouth tasted of stale coffee. He pushed back the shock of hair over his eyes, swearing when he accidentally brushed against one of the stitches.

"May I see her now?"

The doctor rubbed his chin thoughtfully between his thumb and forefinger. "Yes, that'd be all right. But, mind you, just for a moment." He scooped up his instrument tray and handed it to the assisting nurse. "Miss Williams has had quite a shock and she must be kept quiet. Are you a relative?"

A leaden weight settled in Rowan's chest. "No. She works for me." He raised his eyes to the doctor's. "She *will* recover?"

The doctor's head tilted, and he ran freckled fingers through a mass of ginger hair. "One can never be sure about situations such as this, but I'd say her chances are good. She has a collapsed lung and a bad concussion, which, of itself, is serious. However, I'm also concerned about that leg. The femur has a spiral fracture, and the patella tendon is torn."

"Will she walk?"

"In time. And with God's help and good therapy."

Rowan took a deep breath. "She'll have the best."

The doctor's expression was guarded. "She's fortunate to have such a caring firm."

"Not caring enough, I'm afraid." He held the doctor's gaze a moment and looked away, clenching and unclenching his fists. Then he started down the hall.

"Oh, Marsden."

Rowan turned.

"Care for a sandwich? The duty nurse can get you one from the lunchroom."

"Thank you, no."

Karin's bed lay shrouded in white canvas curtains. A shade over the window dimmed the light.

She looked small and pale against the stark white of the hospital bed. Her hair fanned the pillow, a dark cloud against the coarse linen. A drip hung from a hook suspended above her, the clear solution feeding slowly into her left arm. Her chest rose and fell, the movement barely perceptible beneath the cotton blanket. A weal jutted above her brow, just below the hairline.

Rowan settled into the side chair next to the bed. Her right hand lay alongside her body, the fingers still. He reached over and cupped them with his own. They felt cold. Too cold. A lump swelled in his throat.

"Karin. Can you hear me?"

Silence. Only the sound of his breathing disturbed the quiet. He tried again.

"Karin, love. I have to talk to you. I know you can't hear me, but I must tell you how I feel. Listen to me, love, if you can. I want to say something."

Ten minutes later, he rose.

The doctor patted his shoulder. "You might try again tomorrow."

Rowan stumped down the hall. It wasn't the same as telling her when she was awake, but it was the best he could do at the moment. Relief washed over him that he'd got the words out. Now, if only she'd wake up.

He stopped at the bay of telephones near the admitting desk and placed a call. Then he strode outside. He'd stay at the hotel across the street where he could grab a wash and some sleep. If he could sleep.

Karin heard the murmur of voices, and her eyes flickered open. The room was unfamiliar, darkened. Just as well. Her head throbbed as if her brain would explode at any moment.

A white curtain hung from the ceiling. Odd. She was certain Rowan had been talking to her, telling her things . . . things about himself. She must have dreamed it because no one was there.

Voices filtered in from beyond the curtain. Rowan's, hard-edged and sandpapery . . . and another.

"You're back." The strange voice spoke in a soft, Scottish burr.

"I had to come, doctor."

"Yes, of course. By the look of you, you've managed a bit of sleep."

"Some." Rowan's voice was brusque. "May I see her now?"

She was in a hospital! And Rowan was just outside. The doctor's answer was lost as she attempted to call out. Her throat felt dry, and her nose itched. She struggled to raise her arm. Suddenly a hand halted her movement.

"No, miss. You mustn't do that."

The curtain parted, and Rowan's form loomed before her. "Thank God," he murmured. He looked at the nursing sister. "It's all right," he whispered. "I'll see she's not disturbed."

The nurse rose. "Very good, sir. But only for a few minutes."

Rowan bent over her. His gray eyes were shadowed, and his skin was stretched taut across his cheekbones. Karin opened her mouth, but sound wouldn't come.

"Don't try to talk. You're in hospital—in Keswick. We brought you down after the accident. Do you remember?"

She shook her head, but attempted a smile as he settled on a chair beside the white bed. He drew his finger gently along her cheek, stopping at her nose and lip. "You're going to have to live with tubes and such for a few days." He smiled unevenly. "You have two broken ribs and a collapsed lung. Your leg took the brunt from the section of platform when it fell. It's a miracle you weren't killed." His eyes blazed briefly, then he dropped his gaze to the coverlet. "But you're going to be all right, Karin. I promise." He cupped her free hand in his and, bending, drew it to his lips. He held it a moment, then rose.

Karin moved her fingers to the watch on his wrist.

"You want to know the time?"

She shook her head, wincing at the stab of pain.

"You want to know how long you've been here? Three days." His rich-timbred voice sounded unsteady.

The nurse's thin form appeared at the foot of Karin's bed. "I'm sorry, sir, but you'll have to leave now."

"Certainly, Sister. Thank you for letting me see her."

He touched his forefinger to the corner of Karin's mouth. "I'll be back tomorrow."

Rowan visited each afternoon, bringing a gift. As the days passed, her room overflowed with flowers from him and from the crew. A three-foot plush ocelot graced the single chair beside the bed, next to a burgundy leather volume of Wordsworth's poems. On her nightstand, two dozen red roses filled a large Waterford vase, a gift from the Marsdens.

On the fifth day, the nurses removed the tubes from her nose and mouth, and she was permitted a little juice and some broth. Later, they disconnected the IV from her arm. The next day she received a sponge bath. Annie, the thin nursing sister, worked carefully around Karin's bandaged torso and the plaster cast on her leg. She brushed Karin's hair, securing it in twin ponytails at her nape.

"May I see?" Karin asked.

Annie handed her a mirror.

Karin gazed at her reflection in horror. She was sickeningly pale and gaunt, her chest encased in tape, above which a fine network of bluish veins was visible just beneath the skin surface. She pulled the coverlet higher. Her eyes shone, enormous in her ashen face, huge and chocolaty, fringed with a sweep of thick black lashes. She looked like a death-camp victim. She stared, then turned away.

Annie brought her tray. Karin pushed the soggy pudding around on her plate, ate a few bites and set it aside to wait for Rowan.

At four o'clock he pushed his head into her room. "Sorry I'm a little late. I've had special workmen at the site all day. Here." He placed a brown paper bag in her hand.

Inside she found a newly released paperback novel. Another gift. She smiled. "Thank you."

She shifted to one side as he settled on a corner of the bed. "How is the job going?"

"Fine. We'll be back on-line in two weeks. I've had the crew on twelve-hour shifts getting everything put right."

Something flickered far back in his eyes. "I apologize for allowing Ellis to take over as much of the project as he did."

"It's understandable." She stirred uneasily under the cotton blanket. "How is Geoff?"

"Geoff," he said with a significant lifting of his dark brows, "checked himself into an alcohol-abuse clinic." He shot her an uncertain smile. "Geoff will make it just fine. But not on my project."

He shifted his weight on the bed and turned toward

her. "I understand you spoke with the doctor this morning."

"Yes. He said I should be able to travel within a week."

A lead weight settled in her chest as soon as she spoke the words, but she managed a weak smile. "I'm supposed to start physical therapy as soon as I get home. I'll have to work to regain full use of my leg."

She raised her eyes to find him watching her. It was easier to deal with Rowan's cynicism than with his concern. When he was like this, gentle and attentive, an almost uncontrollable longing swept over her. An image flashed into her mind of Rowan, bending over her bedside, pouring out his feelings, his need for her, in a torrent of husky murmurs. What foolishness. Still, it had seemed so real. She blinked back a mist of tears.

He peered thoughtfully at her, and the depth of his gaze awoke a gently flickering fire. An odd warning sounded in her brain. She felt her control slipping.

"There's no need to risk further injury to the leg, or to delay therapy, when the best therapist in the country is in Yorkshire," he said smoothly. "I want you to come to Knaresborough and be attended by Dr. Crosse in Harrogate."

Karin's mouth opened in surprise. "To Knaresborough? Oh, I can't—"

Rowan brushed away her protest. "Oh, but you can. It's all been arranged." He bent his head slightly forward, turning his smile up a notch.

"We leave tomorrow morning."

SEVENTEEN

Karin shifted her gaze from the stone-walled fields to Rowan's form, unmoving beside her in the Range Rover, his determination evident in the stiff set of his shoulders. A half-dozen times in the last hour she had tried to voice her thoughts. Each time she'd hesitated, at the last moment, caught up in her own uncertainty and put off by his grave, apparently angry countenance.

Another minute passed. She took a deep breath and forced out the words.

"Why are you doing this, taking me to your parents' home?"

His hands stilled on the steering wheel. "I thought I made that fairly clear." The bite came back into his voice.

"Rowan, you don't owe me anything. It was an accident. I just happened to be there at the wrong time."

For an instant his gaze left the road, the expression in his eyes dark, unfathomable. "Karin, I am doing this because . . . I want to." His words soothed her. His voice did not.

His hand moved to the radio dial. Punching in the BBC news effectively silenced further communication.

His hesitation niggled at her, his obviously controlled tension stirring the same unease in her mind he'd evoked earlier. What had he intended to say?

She turned away, stared at the window. She knew he wouldn't answer. By now she recognized the signs when he was retreating behind his barricade.

Karin settled uncomfortably under the woolen lap robe he had wrapped around her and wiggled her toes. Her right leg was splinted and taped, her foot resting on pillows on the floor of the car. No way could she have fit into the Jaguar seat trussed up the way she was. Even so, the Rover jolted her until her entire limb was one throbbing ache.

Billowy clouds skittered over a pale sun as they broached a narrow stone bridge. Rowan slowed and waited for a farmer and his herd of black-faced sheep to cross. Karin watched the animals, her thoughts tumbling.

She was seeing a new side of Rowan, one he rarely revealed. He must feel responsible for the accident, perhaps even guilty over what had happened to her. Otherwise, with the situation between them as awkward and painful as it was, why would he want her to come to Knaresborough? He had to know how difficult it was for her to be near him; his own tension was palpable, even though he hid it well.

From the day she'd regained consciousness in the hospital, he'd seemed different. His solicitous attention to her was the talk of the floor, her nurse had said. Once she had longed to see this softer side of Rowan; now she didn't know what it signified or—worse—how to deal with it. A concerned, attentive Rowan she found a greater danger than the man she'd

sparred with for the past three months. She wished
she knew how to deal with her feelings.

Knaresborough Castle loomed in the distance, gray
walls stark above a sandstone cliff. Was she mad to let
him persuade her to come? Wasn't it just going to twist
the knife? She clenched the fabric of the lap robe and
sneaked a glance at the man beside her.

As usual, he drove in silence. When a voice over the
airwaves lauded the latest Tory victory in Parliament,
Rowan muttered something and snapped off the radio.

She longed to touch him. They wanted each other,
loved each other. But Rowan didn't *want* to love her.
He wanted to be able to leave whenever he felt too
much. But, oh, how she wanted to reach out to him.

Could she withstand Rowan's charm while she was
thrown together with him at his parents' home? She'd
come for the physical therapy, nothing more. She'd
given up hope of Rowan's ever changing.

Given the impasse between herself and Rowan, she
felt extremely uneasy about visiting his parents. She
had no idea how she would be received. She wasn't a
family friend, and certainly she was not Rowan's fi-
ancée. She was no longer his employee, either, since
the accident. Where did she fit in?

Mr. and Mrs. Marsden met them in the circular
drive.

"My dear," Mrs. Marsden clucked, "We'd so hoped
to see you again, but under such different circumstances." She glanced at Karin's bandaged leg. "But,
Rowan's absolutely correct. If anyone can get you on
the mend, it's Dr. Crosse."

She clasped her husband's hand and turned a soft-
eyed look on him. "He did wonders for Arthur's
back."

Mr. Marsden beamed. "He did indeed. Now, young lady, let's get you inside and settled. Later we'll have a chat."

"Mary's put you in the Blue Room," Mrs. Marsden said. "We thought you might be more comfortable being downstairs. The room opens onto a lovely patio. Rowan, will you see to Karin's bags?"

Rowan deposited Karin's duffel and carryall on the bed inside her room. True to its name, the Blue Room was done entirely in shades of muted blue, from the textured paper on the walls to the carpet and damask drapes. Even the four-poster bed was swagged with pale blue damask hangings. The room had its own marble bath and a private sitting area. French doors led to a bricked patio and walled garden, festive in the late autumn sun with huge gold chrysanthemums and crimson dahlias.

"You'll stay to tea, of course?" Mrs. Marsden asked her son.

Rowan strode toward the entry door. "Sorry, Mother. I have to get back to the site." He turned to Karin. "I'll return at the weekend to check on you."

Karin caught her breath. No way did she want to see more of him. It was hard enough just to know she was a guest in his parents' home, that he'd arranged for her care.

"Thank you, but that's not necessary. I'll be fine, really."

His dark brows lowered in a frown. "Probably true. Just the same, I'll be here." He turned once more and made his way out the front door.

Karin stared at the door. Always the manager. His presence at the manor would only intensify her long-

ing for him. Still, some part of her was warmed by the
idea that he'd be back to see her.

Despite her apprehension, Karin settled in with ease
at the Marsdens. Mary brought her morning and noon
meals on a covered tray, and, at Mr. Marsden's insis-
tence, trotted in a variety of books he'd selected from
his library. Mrs. Davies, their longtime cook, outdid
herself concocting tasty English dishes. The week had
been divided between visits by the youthful Dr. Crosse
and periods of rest and relaxation.

Yesterday, she had ventured upstairs for the first
time. At the top of the stairs, almost directly above her
room she came to an open door. Each room she'd
seen projected a clearer image of the Marsdens and
Mrs. Marsden's flair for decorating. Curious, she
peeked inside to look. Rowan's travel bag sat on a luggage rack. This was his room.

She glanced up and down the corridor. Empty.

She'd just take a moment to look. She stepped inside.

The room was exactly as she had pictured—a massive, carved oak bed with snowy linen sheets under a
down-filled comforter. Bookcases lined one wall, and
a large rectangular desk of rosewood sat in one corner
of the large room. Walls of pale green and tall windows
draped in a matching green complemented the dark
armoire and wing chairs that flanked a fireplace. It
was a sumptuous, masculine room. Understated and
eloquent. Like him.

She closed the door quietly behind her and made
her way downstairs again. The rest of the afternoon,
visions of that room where he'd spent his youth and

the contrasting caravan at the site crept into her thoughts. He'd given up much for his dream. But, so had she.

Now she sat in the garden, awaiting Dr. Crosse's arrival. To her right, an arm of the main hall extended from the garden, its gray wall ablaze with a splash of crimson Virginia creeper. She drank in the sunlight and watched finches plunder the red-fruited yew trees in the mowed grounds beyond. Despite her desire to have a career, she could think of no greater pleasure than life here at Marsden Manor. With Rowan.

A dull ache settled behind her breastbone. She had to return to the States soon. She had to! Each day she stayed made it that much harder to leave him.

Rowan had returned late yesterday to spend two days with his parents. She hadn't seen him yet this morning. She wanted to, and yet the thought of a freshly showered and shaved Rowan made her stomach flip-flop.

She glanced at the gold watch on her wrist. Ten o'clock. Dr. Crosse would be here at any moment. Saturday visits by doctors were unheard of back home. Evidently, the physician was an old family friend, or perhaps he owed Rowan a favor.

The doorbell jangled. Moments later, the doctor knocked, then poked his shaggy blond head through the open French doors.

"Ah, here you are." Flashing her a toothy grin, he swung his wiry frame over the threshold and dropped his medical bag on a chair.

Karin's gaze traveled over the doctor's unorthodox uniform. A canvas vest with a half-dozen hand-tied flies attached to a pocket flap partially covered a plaid shirt;

worn moleskin trousers covered his long legs. He was obviously setting out for a fishing trip after his stop.

He whipped off a cloth cap with a narrow brim and shoved it through the handles of his bag. "Doing better today?"

She flicked a glance at the brace. "Even better when I can get rid of this thing."

"In due time. Now, if you're ready, I think we'll start with the stretching exercises."

For forty-five minutes, as Dr. Crosse kneaded and massaged, twisted and pulled the damaged tissue, Karin's leg muscles screamed in protest. Every muscle was pummeled until it ached from exertion.

She rested on the edge of her bed while he again secured the brace on her leg. "Another two weeks for this contraption, I think."

She groaned.

Dr. Crosse's gaze snapped to her face. "Leg's not completely healed," he said. "I don't want to take chances."

"How long before I can leave?" Karin blurted out.

A curious expression flashed into his eyes. "Hard to say right now. Depends on how well you take care of yourself. I don't want to hear any talk about getting up on it too soon."

"She won't, Roy."

As if by magic, Rowan materialized at the patio door, balancing a tray with teapot, cups and saucers in one hand. He gave her a lingering gaze that took in not only her appearance, but seemed to see inside her as well. His eyes registered something else, too, which she found disturbingly provocative. She jerked her mind away from dangerous thoughts, dropping her gaze to the edge of the bed.

"Mary was headed this way," he said at last. "I thought I'd save her a trip. We'll have tea on the patio." Without waiting for a reply, he strode to the glass-topped table and set the tray down.

"I trust you're finding Karin a good patient?" He poured out a cup and handed it to the doctor.

"Wish they all might be like her," Dr. Crosse answered. He slanted her a quick grin, then took the cup. "Thanks, old boy."

Rowan turned to Karin. "A little milk, no sugar." He handed her a cup.

"I should be rid of the brace in another week or so, Dr. Crosse says."

"Two weeks." Rowan's even tone belied the challenge in his eyes.

"I have to go home, Rowan, get on with my life."

He went still. "Do you?" Pinpoints of light glittered in his eyes.

She turned to her teacup. What did he want from her?

Her cup rattled on its saucer. Her hand shook as she set it on the table. "I—I'm much improved. Only quick movements bother me. By the time I leave, I'll just need a cane and—" She stopped, aware she was rambling.

"Is she ready to travel, Roy?"

Dr. Crosse coughed. "I'd prefer to see her quiet for another week or two. After that, it's up to her."

Rowan said nothing. With deliberate motions, he gathered up the dishes. Once again, he seemed remote, unreadable.

"Father and Mother hope you'll join us for dinner tonight. He flicked a glance toward Dr. Crosse, gathering instruments into his black bag. "Sevenish, Roy. Profiteroles for dessert—Mrs. Davies' special recipe."

Dr. Crosse closed his case with a snap. "Now you tell me!" He glanced at his watch. "At seven, as you know, I should be camping well up the Nith with a creel of salmon."

"Next time, perhaps," Rowan murmured without a trace of regret. His gaze slid to Karin. The expression in the smoky depths telegraphed a heated message. "Wear something . . . feminine."

Karin searched her wardrobe, but the only suitable item she found that masked the clumsy brace was an ankle-length crinkle-rayon skirt in deep jewel tones on a black background. She topped it with a black silk shirt and gold, hoop earrings. Six-thirty chimed as she examined her reflection in the full-length mirror. Not bad. She'd lost weight since the accident, but the draped blouse hid any changes. She dragged a comb through her thick russet hair, coaxed the ends to turn under, then added a dash of lipstick in a rosy tone.

She made one last check and started down the corridor toward the dining room.

A huge, tiered chandelier sparkled over the enormous rectangular table. Rowan faced the tall window, his back to her. His father, shorter by several inches, stood beside him, and Mrs. Marsden reclined gracefully in a side chair. She glanced up when Karin stepped into the dining room.

"Karin, how stunning you look."

Rowan snapped around. A slow smile of approval illuminated his features.

A thread of joy coiled around her heart. "Thank you, Mrs. Marsden."

Mr. Marsden offered an arm. "My dear. Let me seat you."

Four places were set at one end of the rich mahogany table. Silver and crystal gleamed at each setting, alongside plates of translucent bone china with fluted edges.

"Care for a sherry?" Rowan asked. His eyes twinkled with some secret amusement.

Karin nodded.

His fingers brushed hers. Warm. Intimate.

She took the glass, inching her hand away from his. When she was seated, she set the glass down on the table, untasted.

"Amontillado," Rowan murmured. "Though we've no cask down in the cellar."

Karin bit back a smile. Somehow he'd spied the volume of Poe on her nightstand earlier.

He eased his large form into the chair beside her, his leg grazing her thigh.

She edged away, then wished she hadn't. With a jolt, she realized she wanted to feel much more than his thigh next to hers.

She swallowed and tried to shift her thoughts to the snatches of conversation between Rowan's parents, seated across from her.

Mary brought a tureen of delicately spiced, curried cream of carrot soup which Mrs. Marsden ladled into shallow bowls.

Rowan handed her a basket of baguette slices. Again their fingers brushed. She jerked away, but not before a hot current stabbed deep in the pit of her stomach.

He smiled, and spooned up a mouthful of the fragrant soup. Mischief danced in his eyes.

What was he thinking? Karin dragged her thoughts

from Rowan and answered a question Mrs. Marsden had asked.

Suddenly, Rowan raised his glass. "A toast. To family and friends." Still watching her, he took a sip.

Karin stiffened, the glass in her hand. "Friends." Rowan had told her they could never be friends. What did he mean by his words?

Rowan continued to stare at her, a curious, questioning light in his eyes. The silence lengthened.

Karin's throat closed.

Mr. Marsden glanced first at her, then at Rowan. He raised his glass again. "To family and friends—most certainly." He gave Karin a hearty smile. "And to new beginnings. To Karin, the maid with laughing brown eyes."

"Hear, hear," said Mrs. Marsden, glass raised.

"To Karin," Rowan added.

Tears stung her eyes. She held them in check and swallowed a mouthful of the fruity white wine. She glanced at Mr. Marsden. "You're very kind."

The older man smiled.

"Not at all," Rowan murmured. His roguish grin rippled through her, affecting her more than the wine.

"Another roll?" Rowan's tone concealed a hint of laughter, his eyes sparked with hidden fire.

She took one, avoiding his fingers.

"I think we'll see a cold winter," Mrs. Marsden remarked. "Already, there's frost in the air."

"I feel it might be warmer than is predicted," Rowan answered, keeping his eyes on Karin.

She finished her meal with difficulty as she struggled to keep her mind on the conversation. When Mary cleared away the plates, her dinner lay barely touched.

"Rowan never came to see us this often before," Mr. Marsden remarked over coffee, in a voice meant for her ears. "I think you're good for him, Karin. For Mrs. Marsden and myself, too."

Karin smiled. "You've made my days very pleasant."

Mr. Marsden harrumphed. "Only that? I rather thought you fancied the old house, as well."

Karin caught her lower lip between her teeth. "I do. I really love the manor with its secret nooks and staircases. But the walled garden is my favorite."

"I thought so. I've seen you reading there on many a morning. Didn't want to disturb you." He reached over and patted her hand.

After the meal, Mr. Marsden drew Karin along with him to the library. Rowan followed with his mother.

"Yes, my dear. Your being here has made a big difference." He cast a wistful gaze across the room. "In a way, you've brought us back our son."

Her throat closed. Had she really done that? Had her presence touched them as much as Rowan's had touched—changed—her?

"I've always managed to spend time with you," Rowan answered.

"Time, yes," his mother remonstrated, "but we want to see you when you can give us more than just your presence. Half the time you were wanting to be someplace else."

Rowan paused. "Did I really do that? Well, I'll have to pay more attention to details—make sure you have my undivided attention."

"That would be lovely, dear. And make sure you invite Karin to join you."

Suddenly, it was all too much. Rowan's parents hadn't the remotest idea of how she felt about their son, of how impossible the situation between them was. She felt pulled between joy and agony, like a rabbit caught in a snare.

She extricated her arm from Mr. Marsden's. "I think I'd better call it an evening. I'm feeling rather tired."

Instantly, Rowan was beside her. "I promised Roy you wouldn't overextend yourself. Are you ready to walk to your room?"

She stifled an impulse to refuse, said her good nights. Too tired to argue, she allowed him to escort her to her room.

At her door he turned, looked down at her. "Mother and Father enjoyed your company tonight, Karin. And so did I."

Before she knew what happened, his fingers gripped her shoulder and his lips brushed her forehead. "And so did I," he repeated, his eyes dark with desire. He stared a moment longer.

Her shoulder burned where his hand remained. Trembling, she dropped her gaze.

"Karin, I—"

She stiffened.

He expelled an audible breath. "Nothing. Enjoy your sleep. I'll see you in the morning."

Late into the night, she heard him pacing the floor above her room. She lay awake for hours listening to the sound of his footsteps.

Did he think of her? He'd wanted to say something else at her door, but had cut short his reply. What did he want to say?

The next morning she found a note under her door. Rowan had returned to the site.

A lump settled in her chest. She'd seen the look in his eyes, knew what he'd wanted. He'd retreated again.

Mary brought in a tray, and she carried it to the patio. Even though she wasn't hungry, she forced herself to finish the plate of scrambled eggs, letting her gaze follow the line of trees in the distance. Again she pondered her decision to leave. A dovecote rose beyond her garden, and she watched the gentle birds drift onto the lawn in search of early morning worms. Rooks roosted in the beech trees, their cries raucous in the crisp autumn air. If she stayed . . .

She imagined herself strolling these grounds with Rowan, imagined him making love to her on his massive oak bed.

Ah, sweet heaven, she thought as she peered toward the house from her patio seat. She had to stop letting her imagination wander. Rowan's hot-one-minute-cold-the-next manner invited, then rejected. He promised, hinted, then withdrew. They'd been over that road before. It led nowhere.

She would leave in ten days. Her future lay in the States. Rowan's future lay within the wall he'd erected around his heart.

EIGHTEEN

The following weekend Rowan again drove up from the site.

"How are you progressing with your exercises?" he asked when he had climbed out of the Jaguar and greeted his parents. "Dr. Crosse tells me the torn cartilage has begun to repair."

Karin hesitated. Lately, Rowan had seemed different, less withdrawn. But today she sensed something deeper, an intensity that drove him as though he was approaching some crossroads in his life.

"I'm doing better. My brace will come off in a week."

"Good. We'll get his report, then discuss your plans. How about a bit of a walk later?"

After tea, with rain washing the grounds, she walked with him along the upper gallery, where portraits of Marsden ancestors hung in a long line along one hallway.

"Each heir was painted in his thirty-fifth year," Rowan explained. "That one is Great-grandfather Harry." He gestured to the portrait hanging beside it. "His wife, Caroline. She bore eight of his thirteen children."

"Thirteen?" Karin gasped.

"Those accounted for in the birth registry," Rowan said with a lopsided grin. He moved to the next portrait. "My Grandfather Nathan. Though not the first-born, he had the good fortune to be on the proper side of the blanket." He turned devilish eyes on her, his mouth twitching.

Karin looked away, unable to hold back a laugh. Yes, he had changed in some way. Softened.

She looked at the tall man beside her as if she'd never seen him before.

His eyes held a secret amusement, the fires of passion carefully—but not completely—banked. Absent was the arrogance, the defensive mechanism he threw up whenever she trod on private ground. This part of him was different, but all of the sensuality remained. This Rowan, she acknowledged, was an even greater threat.

And she? She had changed, too. No surprise that, after almost four months of Rowan lessons. She might never get over him, but she was not sorry it had happened. She realized now what the whole experience had taught her about herself. She was an engineer, true. A career woman. But more than that, she was a woman in and of herself, a woman with a lot to give. A woman with a hunger in her heart that—until Rowan—had never been filled. Rowan had forced her to look at her real self—complete with vulnerabilities which she acknowledged and assets which she valued. What greater gift could a man give a woman?

"It is a bit of a humorous thing to look at now—the question of illegitimacy," Rowan went on, "but it was quite commonplace then if you were a peer of the realm. Grandfather never had an opportunity to sow any wild oats. He married on his seventeenth birthday, and for the remainder of his life my grandmother kept him in tow."

Karin shot a glance at Rowan, stifling a smile. Independence and single-mindedness marked him. No woman alive could keep Rowan Marsden in tow.

"Look"—she pointed—"there's your father. And your mother." Arthur Marsden at thirty-five could have been Rowan's twin. His wife, then blond, exhibited classic Nordic beauty. A striking couple.

If their lifestyle wasn't what Rowan wished for himself, apparently their marriage was. She'd spent enough time with the Marsdens to know they were deeply in love.

She drew a shaky breath. Would to God she had that with Rowan.

But she *did* have that with Rowan, she thought suddenly. The heart of their relationship was rich and solid. She believed in its special, unique bond between them, and she knew Rowan did also. That, of course, was what frightened him away from commitment— that emotional resonance between them.

At the end of the gallery hung a single painting— Rowan, resplendent in a gray morning coat and cravat, ivory breeches and black riding boots. Karin's pulse pounded at the look in his eyes. She recognized that peculiar combination of beauty and presence. The artist had captured it perfectly. The brush strokes clearly revealed his muscular thighs and powerful shoulders. He was striking. And no wonder. In the flesh, he was breathtakingly handsome.

She took a step back, flinching as the metal brace dug into her leg. She bit back a sound. She loved Rowan more that she had thought it possible to love any man. No one would ever take his place in her heart.

She turned away from the portrait.

"What is Dr. Crosse's prognosis?" Rowan asked suddenly.

Karin squared her shoulders. "If I keep up with regular treatments, I can have the brace off in December."

"You'll continue with your treatments until then? Roy will be pleased. I think he rather fancies you."

Karin shook her head. "I plan to go home to the States next week."

Rowan sucked in a lungful of air and focused on her. Something unexpected flickered into his eyes. Something new.

She worked to control a shortness of breath. "I mean that I'll have treatments at home until December."

"December. That should fit in perfectly with my plans," he announced, guiding her to a claret velvet settee. "Sit down."

Plans? What plans? Couldn't he see what was right under his nose? She was leaving.

Gratefully, she eased the weight from her throbbing leg. She had to distance herself from him. She had to get on with her life. She had to say good-bye to Rowan.

He slid alongside her, his thigh firm against hers. Electricity leaped through her body, and she edged toward the end of the settee, away from his heated flesh. Unable to move farther, she smoothed her corduroy skirt.

He stared at her with a curious intensity. Then his eyes clouded. Finally his gaze lowered. "You want to leave, then?"

"Yes, I—" Her voice trembled.

"I expect you'll have plans to make for the holidays."

She met his gaze squarely. "I'll spend Christmas with Mother and Leonard, most likely."

"Then you haven't made definite plans?"

She turned her head away. "I must leave. I need . . ." She dragged her gaze back to Rowan's. "I have to go, Rowan. For both our sakes."

His eyes darkened. "Karin," he said huskily, "don't go. Stay with me."

She turned away. "I can't, Rowan. You know I can't."

"I—um, well I thought. . . ." He drew in a noisy breath, coughed. His shoulders tightened. "You don't make this easy."

He raked a hand through his dark hair and started over.

"When I thought you might die, I felt my entire reason for being alive start to die, too. I . . . I struggled not to admit this to myself. Or to you." He stared at his fingers, then looked up. Naked hunger shone in his eyes. "But the truth is, Karin, I"—his voice broke— "I don't think I want to live without you."

She stared, unseeing, at the parquet floor, her hands knotted in her lap. She sensed his inner turmoil, longed to comfort him, yet something held her back. She wanted to stay. How she wanted to, but . . . if she stayed, she knew what would happen. It was only a matter of time. She and Rowan would become lovers. And then she would have traded her independence for the backstage of Rowan's existence.

It wasn't enough.

Or was it?

She still wanted him. She would give anything to be with him. Could she settle for a small part of Rowan's life?

She looked up, noted the pain in his voice.

Her heart squeezed. More than anything in the world, she wanted to feel the connection between them, wanted him to feel it, to know it would be there for him always. Rowan was a man who needed to be loved, needed to be assured that life did not end with the pain of betrayal. Life, and love, generated hope in the future and belief in the goodness of mankind.

She kissed the shadow of beard along his jaw, fastened her arms around him to press close to his hard-muscled chest. She felt him tremble, sensed his surprise and then his enjoyment.

He kissed her jaw, her neck, the skin of her chest, down to the vee of her blouse. Then he carefully set her upright.

She leaned back, supported by the upholstered cushion, and gazed into his eyes. They were darkest gray, expectant yet hesitant. Waiting.

She couldn't let him go, couldn't bear the thought of never seeing him again without giving him the only gift she had left to give.

"Rowan," she heard herself breathe out, "make love to me."

NINETEEN

"Oh, God, Karin." He drew her to him, crushing her against his chest, while he pressed his mouth against her lips. "Are you sure? Cassidy drove my parents to York this morning," he said after a long moment. "We've the house to ourselves. My room is—"

"Just above mine. I've heard you pacing the floor at night."

He flashed her a tortured look. "I haven't slept five minutes in this house since you came. Now I can't even seem to manage an empty caravan. Or an empty bed." He closed the space between them, nipped her lip with his teeth, settled his mouth over hers.

He rose and held out his hand. "Come."

She stood, slipped her hand in his and walked with him to the room at the top of the stairs. She leaned against him as he pushed the door open and guided her inside.

His woodsy scent swirled around her, tumbling her thoughts. Heat stabbed her belly, and she clung to his arm.

He closed the door with his foot, lifted her in his arms and deposited her on his bed. As he settled beside her, he began undoing the buttons of her blouse. "I've wanted to do this all week. I never thought—

Oh, Karin, I . . ." His voice trailed off, muffled as his lips brushed her temple.

Her heart thrummed to the motion of his shaking hands, the feel of his mouth on her skin. In her wildest dreams, she would never have guessed she'd be here in the bedroom of the man she loved, the man who, in less than two days, she would be leaving. She drew in an unsteady breath. She must live for the moment. Today was all that counted. She would carry the memory of it with her for the rest of her life.

She gently pushed away his hands and undid the last button, then flung the blouse toward the chair. Slowly, she unsnapped the waistband of her skirt, stood and let the garment fall. She sank onto the bed and began undoing the leather straps of the brace.

"I don't want to hurt you, Karin."

She stilled her fingers. The hurt would come later. "It will be all right." She looked into his eyes. "Don't worry. Please."

The brace dropped onto the floor.

Rowan groaned, then eased out of his shoes, socks, trousers. A spray of buttons hit the floor as he tugged the shirt from his body.

He was rock hard and desperate. And scared. It took every bit of restraint he could muster not to haul her onto the bed and ravish her.

His hands shook as he slipped the scraps of lace from her breasts and down her thighs. His entire body trembled when he stepped back to look at her. A band tightened around his chest. He'd never felt so full of need, or so frightened, in his life.

She had a crescent-shaped red mark on her left thigh he'd never seen before. God in heaven, how beautifully shaped her breasts were. He took a step nearer, gently smoothed them from underneath. They fit perfectly into each hand. He worked his thumbs in circular motions over the crested nipples.

Heat exploded in his loins, and his hands stilled. If he didn't take it easy, he'd lose control.

She moaned, and he pulled her into his embrace, tumbling her back onto the down comforter.

Lord, she was soft. She smelled of jasmine and her own female scent, so enticing it made his groin ache.

"Karin, I want you," he gasped, then stopped. His voice sounded gravelly to his ears. He struggled for a lungful of air. He choked back his fear, straining for control. "But first I want to give something to you."

He pressed hot, slow kisses down her neck, across one breast, down her midriff to her navel.

Moving lower, he felt her tense. "It's all right. I want to make it good for you. Do you want this, Karin?" He heard her indrawn sigh and deepened his kiss into the velvety skin of her belly. "I won't do anything you don't want," he murmured.

"I do want . . ." Her voice was half-whisper, half-sigh. "Rowan, I want you to love me. Oh, God! Now."

His heart lurched.

He sucked in a breath, steeling himself against an unbearable tightness of his aroused sex, and inched his lips lower still, over the fine down of her abdomen and into the curls between her thighs.

Heaven. She was in heaven. Flicking his tongue over the tiny bud, he circled slowly, felt her still, then open to him. He probed the slick flesh.

She moaned and began to move her hips in slow half-circles.

Rowan heard his own ragged breaths echo harshly in the room. Steady, he ordered his body. He directed his thoughts to the rhythmic slap of rain against the window pane.

A moment later, he felt her hands in his hair, urging his mouth deeper into her scented thighs.

"Don't stop. Please don't stop," she cried. "I want you inside me."

A fierce need for possession whirled inside him. He moved higher. With his knee, he spread her thighs wide to accommodate him, all the while moving his mouth over her lips, his hands stroking her breasts, shoulders. Then he raised up, balancing his weight on his hands, and looked down at her.

Her tousled hair spread over the pillow like a fan. Her eyes were half-closed, a dusky fringe of lashes sweeping the pale skin below. Her cheeks bore the flush of passion, and her scent— God, her scent drove him wild.

He knelt, poised himself above her. . . . And then he could wait no longer.

He plunged quickly, deeply. An instant later he was sheathed in her silken warmth. She gasped, moved, molded her body into his. He held back as much as he was able, but his fierce desire overcame his need for restraint. He thrust faster, faster, felt an excruciating tightness grip his entire body. His thoughts began to unravel, then he was consumed by his explosive release. With a shout, he spilled himself into her.

She jerked, wound her legs around his body and cried out. Her body contracted, her hot sheath closing around him. Such pleasure rippled through his body, he thought he'd die.

Moments passed, and he lay on top of her, his eyes closed. Supporting some of his weight on his forearms, he waited for his breathing to ease. If he never saw

Karin again, he would never forget the frightening intensity of making love with her.

Why was it so different for him? Was there some connection of souls that made him question everything about himself, his life? Something unleashed, unlocked within him? Something primal?

Heat pumped into his limbs, and he felt himself harden.

He pressed his lips to her forehead, kissed her eyelids, tasting the salt of tears. His heart constricted. He had to do it now. He steeled himself for the act that took more courage than he thought he had.

Karin felt Rowan shift his body and draw away from her. She turned to see him staring down at her, an odd light in his eyes. She eased into a sitting position as he reached for his trousers.

"I have something to say to you, Karin. I think it's best said dressed."

"You can tell me whatever it is like this, Rowan. What does clothing have to do with it?"

"Just do it, Karin," he replied, his tone brooking no argument.

She swallowed. Rowan was a complex man, she'd known that all along. What could he possibly want to say that couldn't be said with her naked beside him? She began the ritual of putting on her things.

Moments later, she sat on the bed beside him.

He gave her the ghost of a smile, but his eyes looked grave. The skin was stretched taut over his jaw, and she caught the slight jerking of a tic.

"I thought I could remain uninvolved," he began in a low tone. "I'd been hurt before, you see, and—I told you all this at the hospital. Do you remember any of it?"

"No," she lied. "Tell me now."

He took both her hands in his, ran his fingers over the backs as he looked into her eyes. "I need to explain some things, Karin. For weeks now, I wanted to get this out, but I didn't know how."

His gaze dropped to her hands. "I know you think I've carried a torch for my ex-wife. I haven't. I was deeply hurt, yes. But it was my pride that suffered, not my heart. Before, with Claudia, I was too young to know what love was."

His eyes blazed. "I've learned a lot since then. I've learned that the only woman I'll ever truly love is a dark-haired American minx who captured my heart in a Manchester airport."

Karin's own heart lurched. "I captured your heart? In Manchester? But we'd just met. You *hated* me, Rowan. Didn't you?"

"Apparently not," he said.

Rowan drew away and focused on her eyes. His words were barely audible. "I find I cannot give you up, so I decided I had to risk a"—he drew in a deep breath—"a commitment."

He turned her around slowly on the bed, tilted her chin to within inches of his. "Marry me, Karin."

Karin gasped. Had she heard him right? "What?"

"Marry me, my love." He pulled her hand into his, gently stroking the inside of her wrist.

"But I thought you didn't want—"

Rowan stopped her flow of words with his finger on her lips. "You're right," he said slowly. "I didn't. I tried not to love you. I didn't want to get involved. But I *am* involved, dammit."

He pulled her into his arms. "And I need you."

Karin's heart seemed to explode. Could this be happening? Rowan wanted not just a part of her but all of her? For the rest of their lives? *He wanted to marry her?*

"I never thought— I've got plane res— Oh, Rowan, are you serious?"

"I've never been more serious in my life."

There was nothing more to be said. In a way he had not revealed to her, he had learned trust. To trust her. She closed her eyes and murmured a silent prayer. "I love you," she said simply.

He reached into his pocket, pulled out a blue velvet box.

The ring was a massive ruby in an ornate setting, heavy on her hand. "Oh, Rowan, it's exquisite!"

"Great-grandmother Caroline thought so, too. Now," he announced briskly, "can you change your travel plans to the States and arrange your gown and trousseau by December twelfth?"

Karin gasped. "December twelfth?"

"My birthday. I always get presents on my birthday. This year, you're the only present I want." He kissed her nose. "Besides," he added matter-of-factly, "I've engaged Monsignor Doyle for the chapel."

"For the chapel? You mean you *planned* this? Asking me?"

His lips curved into a brief smile. "I did." His eyes questioned hers. "Karin, you haven't said you accept. Will you marry me?"

"Oh, Rowan, for heaven's sake. Just try to talk me out of it! Yes, I'll marry you."

She tented her hands behind his neck and drew his mouth to hers. "Yes." She dipped her tongue enticingly into his mouth, and when he turned her, urging her back against the headboard, she pressed her aroused body into his. "Yes. *Yes.*"

December's pale dusk cast shadows over the arched stained-glass windows in the chapel. Voices rose and fell. A bank of shimmering votive candles turned their cups a rich red hue, warming the wintry light. Tall white tapers, surrounded by red-berried holly wreaths, flamed on each side of the altar.

Rowan and Thorny strode to the left of the aisle. A cough echoed among the assembled guests.

Karin gazed at the man who in a few moments would be her husband. He stood tall and trim in a midnight blue suit and silver-gray tie, its marble hue reflecting the exact colors in his eyes. He had pinned a single red rose to his lapel. He shifted nervously as the room grew quiet.

Monsignor Doyle, a white surplice and silk cope over his dark cassock, walked solemnly toward the altar. The organ began Mendelssohn's Wedding March, and Karin felt Leonard nudge her gently.

She flashed her stepfather a tremulous smile, slipped her arm into the crook of his, and took a determined, steady step forward. Maggie gave a last-minute tug to straighten the yards of ivory silk in the train of her square-necked Tudor-style gown, then beamed a smile and preceded her toward the altar.

She started forward. All eyes turned toward her as she glided down the aisle toward Rowan. Athena, in the first pew, toyed with a handkerchief, her eyes luminous. On the opposite side, behind the Marsdens, sat Derrick, Paddy, Mac, Robin and Jack, decked out in suits and ties. The pungent perfume of scarlet and

white carnations drifted around her. She moved inexorably nearer to Rowan, shaking with emotion, passion and joy combined.

Leonard stopped before the priest, then handed
her to Rowan and joined Athena.

Rowan gazed down at her, his eyes suspiciously
shiny. She watched a muscle jump along his firm jaw.
A lump formed in her throat. He was scared to death.

She shifted the ivory roses in her hand, then
reached out to him. She tried to smile.

Monsignor Doyle cleared his throat. ". . . you have
come together in this chapel . . ."

Together—she and Rowan were sharing the most
important moment of their lives with each other and
with those who were dearest to each of them. She envisioned the familiar faces behind her.

". . . the Lord may seal and strengthen your love,"
the priest intoned.

Yes, she prayed. Strengthen Rowan's trust in me.
And, oh, God, give me the ability to love him no matter
what.

She raised her eyes to meet his. She could scarcely
believe she now stood here in the Marsden chapel,
her mother and Leonard seated nearby, witnesses to
her pledge to this man. She was whole, in heart, soul
and body.

". . . and so, in the presence of Christ and the
Church, I ask you now to state your intentions. . . ."

"I, Rowan Christian Frederick Arthur Marsden do
plight thee my troth"—his voice shook—"I pledge
thee my love, my worldly possessions, and my body . . .
for better or worse . . . for richer or poorer, in sickness
and in health, till death us do part."

Karin looked into his eyes and declared in a firm

voice, "I, Karin Marie Williams, do plight thee my troth. I pledge thee my love, my worldly possessions . . . and my body . . ." The last words came out in a throaty whisper. She stared at the man before her, the man she would love until the end of her days.

Her blurry gaze rested on the heavy gold band Rowan slipped onto her finger; then she moved into his arms. His beautiful mouth brushed hers, hesitated momentarily, then deepened, promising more. At last, he stepped back and offered his arm, turning her toward their families and friends, to face their life together.

BOOK YOUR PLACE ON OUR WEBSITE AND MAKE THE READING CONNECTION!

We've created a customized website just for our very special readers, where you can get the inside scoop on everything that's going on with Zebra, Pinnacle and Kensington books.

When you come online, you'll have the exciting opportunity to:

- View covers of upcoming books
- Read sample chapters
- Learn about our future publishing schedule (listed by publication month *and author*)
- Find out when your favorite authors will be visiting a city near you
- Search for and order backlist books from our online catalog
- Check out author bios and background information
- Send e-mail to your favorite authors
- Meet the Kensington staff online
- Join us in weekly chats with authors, readers and other guests
- Get writing guidelines
- AND MUCH MORE!

**Visit our website at
http://www.zebrabooks.com**